HUNT THE NIGHT

SUPERNATURAL LEGACY 1

EVERLY FROST

Find your fire.

CHAPTER ONE

My black wings drag across the damp stone floor, scraping back and forth as I prowl inside my cell. With every step I take, the chain shackled to my left ankle clatters, and my lank, black hair falls farther across my face.

I can smell the Serene Commander even before her footsteps sound on the staircase opposite my cage. Her scent is as pure as a crisp winter's day when the air is unburdened by the perfume of flowers. As her name implies, she is faultless. She possesses the kind of purity I certainly don't have.

Because of the way the ceiling slopes and the staircase is hewn within the rock walls around me, her feet appear first as she descends, then the hem of her white dress. She's carrying a beige leather satchel that dips as far as her knees, and my anticipation increases.

It's the satchel she uses to carry my hunting clothes.

Finally! She might let me out to do what I do best.

She halts before she descends farther, one foot poised above the step below, her golden slippers forming two bright spots in the dim light.

"Cover your eyes!" she snaps.

I allow myself to smile, taking a small delight in this moment of rebellion.

I'm supposed to wear a blindfold when she visits.

The band of dense material hangs from a nail on the wall inside my cell door. The moment I hear an angel descending the stairs, I'm expected to scurry like a little mouse to put it on.

I rarely scurry, but I always put it on.

Despite my delight in pushing the boundaries today, I understand why I must cover my face.

I am wicked. An angel born with a corrupted heart. A hunter to my core.

The Serene Commander told me that for another angel to look into my eyes is to see only darkness. Apparently, it physically hurts them. She once told me that she would rather stab herself repeatedly with a knife.

Her voice grows in strength when I hesitate. "Lana Harlowe!"

She addresses me by the name she's given me, not the name I was born with.

"I will not suffer your gaze," she says. "It's hard enough standing in your presence. You will cover your face immediately."

I let out a sigh, take a knee on the stone floor, bow my head, and press my palms to my eyes. It's not what she wants—not what I normally do. She wants the blindfold secured around my entire face, and normally, I would comply, but today…

She hasn't let me out of my cell for the last three months and, well, I'm angry about it.

After all, anger is a sin, and a sin is what I am.

As soon as I place my hands over my eyes, she resumes her descent. "Better," she says, her tone light again.

Apparently, the depth of my corruption is so palpable to her that she can sense whether or not my eyes are covered even from a distance. Although she doesn't seem to have realized that I'm not using the blindfold.

Her footfalls resume and my other senses—hearing, smell, even touch—discern the eagerness in her steps, her slightly elevated breathing, and the faint rasp of the satchel she carries as it brushes against her silken dress.

I've learned to hone all of my other senses so that I can operate without eyesight. Despite my hatred of the blindfold, sometimes I choose to put it on, teaching myself to listen to every trickle of water down the damp stone walls, the small vibrations through the floor, the slight changes in the air that wafts from the distant stairwell—the only entry or exit from my cage.

I may hate the blindfold, but it's made me a better hunter.

The Serene Commander's final footfall lands on the bottom step, where she stops again. Her scent shifts from a pure winter's day to the thick haze of a fog that covers a meadow—the kind of mist that a wolf could be hiding in.

"Where is your blindfold?" she snaps.

"Careful, Serene Commander," I reply, allowing my voice to vibrate with a growl, since *I* am the wolf hiding in the mist. "Anger is a sin."

I prepare myself for a verbal lashing, but, to my surprise, it doesn't happen.

Her footfalls resume. There's a swish of material. I'm familiar enough with our routine to know that she's reaching into her pocket for the key to my cage. Then metal clanks as my cell door opens.

"Stay where you are," she orders me, her scent becoming stronger as she wafts past me to the bed that sits in the far corner.

I tuck my wings in to let her pass.

My cell meets my basic needs: a sink attached to the wall, a toilet with a seat but no lid, and a shower in the far-left corner that's not much more than a section of tiles—all open to the front of the cage and without privacy. The bed is a simple mattress on a wooden frame. I have one blanket. Beside the bed is a small desk with a chair, and above the desk is the only part of my cell I like: a shelf of books that keep me sane.

The bed creaks a little as the Serene Commander takes her time placing things onto it. I listen carefully for the sounds of material and more—multiple objects being positioned across the mattress. It must be my hunting clothes.

I also take note of what I don't hear: the Serene Commander's wings don't scrape against the ground, which means she has fully retracted them. It's not unusual. She would never sully her white wings with the grime of my cell.

She swishes past me again, her footfalls carrying her to the door. "Turn to face your bed," she orders me. "You may look at what I've brought you. Do not look back to me."

Keeping my hands over my eyes, I swing toward the bed, expecting to see my black leggings, fitted bodice, hunting dagger, and boots laid out on it.

I stare at a sage-green evening gown. It appears to be made nearly entirely of delicate tulle gathered over a structured bodice with a fine tulle strap on each shoulder. The skirt falls gracefully in a neat A-line shape. Butterfly appliques adorn the waist and bodice at intervals. *Butterflies.*

A pair of matching sage-green heels sits beside it, along with underwear, a handheld mirror, a small purse, and a large pouch of what appears to be makeup.

"What is *this*?" I ask. "I'm not a fairy."

The Serene Commander's voice is as soft as windchimes. "This dress," she says, "is your way in."

"Way in where?"

Her voice thrums with excitement. "To a special performance of the Philadelphia Orchestra tonight. You'll find your ticket under the dress."

I take a breath as I consider the implications. My hunting expeditions usually take place in dark alleys, warehouses, and even in sewers. After all, that's where the vermin of the world are found.

There's only one reason the Serene Commander would risk pulling me out of the shadows and putting me somewhere I can be seen.

I rein in my anger, attempt to control my hope, and exhale my question. "You found him?"

Her footsteps are quiet as she approaches, stopping between my wings at my back. "I found him."

My breathing is suddenly erratic, my whisper sharp. "Callan Steele."

"The source of your redemption," she says.

For the last five years, I've been hunting dragon shifters, although I hesitate to call them that because none of them are pure. They're heinous imposters, only able to manifest dragon wings and to harden their skin, but none of them can take dragon form, and none can breathe fire.

They certainly don't operate with the bravery or honor of the original dragons. Because their power isn't pure, they also don't have the sort of identifiable traits that other supernaturals have. They can't partially shift, which means they don't have changing irises or sharpening claws that might give them away like wolf shifters do.

Unless they manifest their dragon wings and skin, they are so human in appearance that they can assimilate completely into human society—and yet they use their strength to prey on humans and supernaturals alike.

They are predators with dark hearts.

The city of Philadelphia used to be overrun with them.

That is, until the Serene Commander made me a promise and gave me a purpose: If I hunt the dragon shifters to extinction, she will help me regain my purity and set me free.

I've been getting closer to achieving my goal ever since.

There used to be three clans: the Scorn, the Grudge, and the Dread. It took me several years to wipe out the Grudge, who lived in the sewers and in warehouses and would come out to attack humans in the dark of night. They were all grown men and the stench of darkness in their souls made it easy for me to annihilate them without remorse.

The Scorn dragons were tougher to target since they had assimilated into the supernatural underground of thieves and murderers. But again, the ones I killed were all grown men, all reeking of malice. I'm still working on wiping them out, although there aren't many of them left now.

But the Dread... *the fucking Dread*... They have integrated themselves into the highest echelons of human society. They have accumulated money, built businesses, and forged alliances with wealthy humans. They live in sparkling penthouses and surround themselves with human bodyguards. They have learned from the most corrupt of the human population how to hide behind shell corporations and make deals behind closed doors.

All the while, they have been quietly and systematically annihilating other supernaturals who could challenge them. Four months ago, an entire pack of wolf shifters went missing and I have no doubt the Dread are responsible—given that the wolf pack was sitting on prime real estate that the Dread would have coveted.

Because of the way the Dread blend into human society, it's nearly impossible to track them down and distinguish them from the humans they mix with.

Their leader is Callan Steele, a shifter who has no digital footprint, no photos anywhere. He's the epitome of a billionaire recluse who rules from the shadows.

Until I take him out, the Dread will continue to flourish.

But now... finally... the Serene Commander says she's found him.

If it means ending Callan Steele, I will wear any dress she puts in front of me.

"How will I identify him?" I ask.

She sounds a little less certain. "You'll have to use your senses."

I grit my teeth. "You're telling me he's going to be there, but I'll have to pick him out of a crowd of hundreds?"

I nearly spin to her, but she plants one hand on my back. I'm wearing a loose tank top cut at the back to allow my wings to extend and retract easily, along with old black jeans, both items of clothing faded and torn.

She sighs, a patient sound, as she presses her palm against my spine, her thumb pressing against one of the ropey scars that criss-crosses my back. "Tell me: What am I feeling now?"

I blink, fighting the point she's trying to make, but finally close my eyes. Her scent has changed from the heavier fragrance of mist back to a clear winter's day.

"You're calm again," I say.

"That's right," she whispers. "Now, imagine you're standing in the alley where you last killed a dragon shifter. Tell me how you knew he was a dragon shifter and not a human?"

I shudder so hard that I nearly shake off her hand. My shoulders hunch and my muscles tense, but not from fear or regret. If I allow myself to think about it too much, the rage rises beyond my control.

It's difficult for me because any person who has committed a violent crime will trigger my senses—whether or not they're human or supernatural. Only other angels don't trigger me.

I was born with a corrupted soul that can identify other corrupted souls. Murderers, thieves, predators. Even the lesser sins of lies, envy, greed, and deceit. But worse, I'm hellbent on retribution.

It's a relentless compulsion.

I see evil, and I *need* justice—in the form of death.

My snarl breaks the heavy silence. "He smelled like copper, the evidence of blood on his hands. When he spoke, his voice was sharp like the blade he used to kill an innocent. His mouth was twisted, his eyes were angry, and his heartbeat was heavy with guilt."

She presses harder against my spine. "And?"

"When I lured him into the moonlight, his dragon was misshapen and dark."

Unless a dragon shifter chooses to reveal their wings and skin—and it's always both at the same time because they aren't strong enough to choose one or the other—the only way to distinguish them from a human is to draw them into moonlight.

Then, the silhouette of a dragon forms around them. It's as if the dragon they were meant to be projects itself beyond their body, a glimmering image drawn out by the light of the moon.

But they have to be exposed to direct moonlight. A difficult achievement in a city that sparkles with artificial light, which dragon shifters have learned to use as a shield.

"Lana," the Serene Commander says. "You were born for this."

My shoulders hunch even further, but this time, it's with resignation.

Her hand falls away from me. "Wash up. Get dressed. Make yourself beautiful. You have an hour to get ready. I'll leave your cell unlocked. Remember to wear your blindfold on your way out. You know how much you can hurt our souls."

The Serene Commander bends to unlock the shackle that sits around my left ankle, and I savor the moment the chain falls away from my body.

Her golden slippers swish on the floor as she turns, her footsteps light as she hurries away, leaving me to reach for the pretty dress. The material is softer than anything I've ever worn against my skin. Even the cotton tank top I'm wearing is scratchy in comparison.

Carefully checking out the contents of the pouch, I discover scented shampoo, perfume that smells like roses, along with makeup, which I'm not really sure how to apply.

Never mind. I'll figure it out.

Rolling my shoulders, I retract my wings fully, their heavy weight disappearing, their power settling back into my body. Stripping off my shirt and pants, I wash myself thoroughly in the shower before towel-drying my hair and parting the long, black strands, finding a gold clip in the pouch to tie my hair back on one side while the straight strands otherwise fall freely around me.

Pulling on the dress, I check myself in the little mirror. The sage-green makes my blue eyes *pop* and the dress is a perfect fit to my slight curves. It's high enough at the back that it covers the worst of my scars, and my hair covers the rest of them.

I shun the perfume because I don't want it to mess with my senses, but with a touch of powder on my face and a little lip gloss—two pieces of makeup that I can't mess up—I look positively innocent. Maybe even pretty.

When I sigh at my reflection, my breath fogs up the mirror, concealing my bright eyes, my high cheekbones, and the unhappy press of my lips.

Pretty was never a descriptor I dreamed I'd apply to myself.

Savage. Angry. Determined.

I feel more comfortable in my old clothing.

It's a damn good thing that looking into my eyes doesn't seem to bother other supernaturals. Well, not unless I'm crashing down on them with a dagger in my hand. Then I'm pretty sure it's not my eyes they're worried about.

Given that I'm wearing an evening dress tonight and don't have my usual blade, I'll need to fight with my hands, but it doesn't worry me.

Blades can be messy.

I kill more efficiently with my hands.

I wobble in the heels but stride around my cell, determined to conquer these shoes before I reach for the small purse—also sage-green—and my ticket to the concert.

Then I retrieve the blindfold. I won't tie it around my face until I get to the end of the corridor that sits at the top of the steps.

The evening dress swishes gently around my ankles as I leave my cage and ascend the staircase. Pushing on the door at the top, I brace for the impact of the light around me.

The corridor is empty but well lit. It's a safe space between my cell and the rest of the Cathedral. Its walls are paneled with ivory stone and decorated with gold filigree. I can only imagine how beautiful the rest of the Cathedral is, because I've never seen it.

I sense the angels waiting at the end of the corridor to escort me from the building, their presence like glimmers of light even through the walls.

Quickly, I pull on the blindfold and take a moment to center myself, 'seeing' my surroundings without using my eyes. The air moves around me when I take a step, allowing me to sense the distance to the walls and the far door, and I stride along it confidently, my head held high.

The door swings open when I reach it. I don't miss the sudden hush when I appear. Each of the five angels is a warrior—the pure kind who help humans and supernaturals who are in need. I may be a hunter, but I'm not immune to the way the air changes when they shiver at my presence. There's a heaviness around them that speaks of discomfort, bordering on fear.

I remind myself that I wasn't put on this Earth to make people comfortable. Not the angels. Not anyone.

The angel closest to me speaks first. "This way, Lana."

I recognize her from her voice and her scent. Her name is Aria, and she smells like spring. *Too many* flowers.

"I know the way," I snap when her fingertips brush my arm, as if she were about to lead me across the room. It's a daring move on her part, considering what I'm capable of.

She quickly steps away from me. "Of course. Follow me."

As I stride after her through the many rooms and corridors, I sense the tension as the other angels surround and follow me. Until I exit the building, they won't let me out of their sight. On my return, they will be waiting to escort me back to my cell. Under no circumstances am I to wander within the angels' stronghold.

But… once I'm outside the Cathedral…

"A car is waiting for you," Aria says when we finally reach the exit—a concealed door leading to a side alley.

When the door closes behind me, I swiftly remove my blindfold, shaking off the soft shackle that may as well be a chain around my face. I've used this exit so many times over the past five years that the Serene Commander had a hook positioned on the wall beside it—ready for me to hang my blindfold.

Tipping my head back, I seek the location of the moon. It's a cloudy night, the moon's silhouette is a vague outline, and the air smells like rain. It's not a good night for chasing any Dread dragon, let alone their leader.

I guess he's smart. If he's going to make a public appearance, then tonight is as safe a night as any. After all, it would be reckless to come out when the moon is crisp and full.

The quiet hum of a running engine draws my attention to the vehicle waiting for me a few paces away. I swallow my disappointment. Despite still having to learn how to manage in high heels, I was looking forward to the walk through the city.

Unafraid of making the driver wait, I take deep breaths and fill my chest with fresh air, relaxing my shoulders and taking a moment to enjoy a little slice of freedom.

Even if it only lasts for the five steps to the car.

The trip takes less than ten minutes and, when we finally pull into the line of vehicles approaching the concert hall, I jump out of the car without waiting to be driven to the front entrance. My driver—whoever he is—is shrouded in a heavy fog of guilt that fills the enclosed space, and I need to get away from him as soon as possible.

I step out into worse.

Damn the Serene Commander for keeping me in my cell for the last three months.

The isolation has made me even more sensitive to my surroundings. It's an advantage when I'm hunting alone in a sewer, but not when I'm standing in a stream of humans, all of them riddled with guilt of some sort or another.

I close my eyes and try to steady myself, turning toward the entrance, focusing on my movements. One foot in front of the other, the impact of my weight down each heel, the sharp cut of my fingernails into my palms, the deliberately controlled inhalations and exhalations of air from my chest.

I have no illusions that my responses are going to settle down once I'm inside and sitting in a packed theater. It will only get worse.

I'd better get a fucking hold of myself.

Striding toward the entrance, I continue to focus on my breathing, momentarily distracted by the posters along the sidewalk. The theme of the performance is fairy tales and folklore, so my dress makes sense. The women around me are also wearing delicate evening gowns, some with glittering fairy wings, while the men are mostly in tailored suits.

The Serene Commander described this as a special performance and I'm seeing a lot of expensive jewelry that makes me think it's reserved for those who can afford a ticket. Separating myself from the stream of people as much as I can, I enter the building and focus on finding the way to my seat.

A quick glance at my ticket and the signs above the various staircases within the theater indicate that my seat is located upstairs within one of the private balconies. I choose the staircase corresponding to my seat number. One of the ushers at the top of the stairs greets me before glancing at my ticket.

"Right this way, please, Ms. Harlowe. You have your own booth tonight."

I respond with a nod since my voice would only come out as an angry growl right now.

Fuck, it's taking everything I've got not to tear this place apart.

He leads me along the gently-lit corridor onto a small, private balcony with an ornate railing at the front. It has two plush seats positioned on the left and two on the right with a walkway between the pairs.

I stride onto it, praying for a moment of peace.

I don't get it.

The palpable pall of guilt within the theater hits me like a sledgehammer. It's filled with people who have something to hide, and the heavy haze is slowly choking me like fingers reaching around my throat and squeezing.

Sharp jabs of judgement ram into me like daggers.

Liar. Thief. Abuser. Liar...

I tell myself I just need to find the guilt of a *killer* among the crowd—assuming Callan Steele has already arrived—and the most likely place to find him is on one of the other private balconies located on the same level as mine. The sooner I identify him and memorize what he looks like, the sooner I can get the hell out of this packed theater and wait for him to emerge.

Remaining on my feet while I scan the other balconies, I'm hit with the extreme levels of greed and envy radiating from their occupants. Despite the patrons' expensive attire and the champagne glasses glittering in their hands, my senses tell me they aren't satisfied with what they already have.

But no killer. Not yet…

The choking sensation tightens around my throat. My breathing is ragged, a cold panic rising inside me as my mind crowds with the layers of guilt around me.

Trying to shield myself, I slip behind the chair on my far left and sink to the floor, pulling my legs up to my chest and dropping my head to my knees, curling up into a tight ball.

I tell myself I just need a moment.

A moment to isolate myself from everything around me, to gather my thoughts and refocus on my task. Just a moment to get it together so I don't give in to my rage and do something stupid like turning this theater into a bloodbath.

Liar, thief, liar, thief…

Fuck! I let out a moan against my knees.

Liar, thief, killer, liar—

Killer?

"Miss?" A quiet male voice cuts through the wash of my rage. "Are you okay?"

My breath catches as I lift my head to meet the eyes of a man whose presence washes everything else away.

CHAPTER TWO

He crouches beside me, close enough for me to reach out and touch him.

I'm startled that I didn't sense him approach and even more startled by his size. Even bending, he towers over me in a tailored suit with a jacket that pulls over his large biceps, and pants that cling to his thigh muscles, but it's the clash of his gaze with mine that really freezes me.

His eyes are a surprising combination of cinnamon brown and juniper green, the colors blending in such a way that I'm not sure if he has green eyes with brown flecks or the other way around. His dark hair is swept back, slightly damp, and again I can't quite tell the color—the darkest chocolate brown or maybe charcoal black. He's clean shaven with the slightest hint of a cleft in his strong jaw, his appearance immaculate.

He's quiet and I'm acutely aware of how unusually calm the space around me has become. When I allow my senses to expand, it feels like I'm surrounded by warm sunlight, and I'm immediately struck with a protective essence.

He repeats himself gently. "Are you okay?"

I find my voice, even though it's scratchy. "I'm fine."

He doesn't reach for me or try to touch me, but his voice seems to fill the gap between us. "Can I help you?" he asks. "Get you a glass of water?"

Again, I'm hit with the warmth of the sun, rays so soothing that they break through the cold mist around me, clearing my head.

It strikes me hard: *This man has no guilt.*

It's rare but not impossible. Children often have no guilt. I used to hope I'd meet an adult who didn't carry any guilt because I needed to believe that there are good people out there. Somewhere.

I quickly gauge his supernatural status—no aura, no telltale signs of shifting, no magical essence.

My cheeks flush with embarrassment as I consider how tightly I'm curled up behind the chair, clearly not okay, but I say it again anyway. "No, thank you. I'm fine. I was just a little dizzy."

I rise to my feet and he does the same, taking a step back to maintain the non-threatening distance between us, confirming my estimation of his height and build: over six feet tall, and if it weren't for how perfectly fitted his suit is, his broad chest would bust out of it.

"If you're sure?" he asks.

I give him a short nod, smoothing down my dress, suddenly realizing that he's not meant to be here since I was told I had this booth to myself.

"Wait, who are you—?"

He's already turning to the door. "All clear, sir."

As he turns, I note the white earpiece he's wearing and the gun holster partially concealed beneath his jacket.

He takes up position on the other side of the booth, behind the other set of chairs, a moment before another man strides onto the balcony. The newcomer isn't as tall as the first man. His blond hair is slicked back and an expensive-looking gold watch gleams at his wrist. Despite his slightly shorter stature, he's no less bulky than the first man, and he's also wearing a tailored suit that conforms to a broad chest and lean waist. His sculpted biceps and thigh muscles are evident when the material pulls around him as he moves.

"Thanks, Chris," he says, addressing the first man.

A third man enters behind him, also wearing an earpiece, and I catch a glimpse of his concealed weapon, too. He raises his wrist to his mouth and murmurs into it, "Tyler is in the booth."

I quickly sum up the situation: a rich, blond patron—supposedly named *Tyler*—and his two bodyguards, the biggest of whom is named Chris, who is a trained protector and doesn't carry any guilt.

I'm immediately on my guard. It's typical of a Dread dragon to have human bodyguards and after all, before I opened my eyes, I briefly sensed a *killer*. It doesn't matter what name they call the blond man. Callan Steele is unlikely to use his real name in public.

Focusing on Tyler while he steps onto the private balcony, I release the hold on my senses, searching for the essence of a murderer that I detected before.

All I feel is the sun. It may as well be summer inside this booth; the human bodyguard's presence is too strong. *Dammit, why is goodness so much stronger than evil?*

Tyler pulls up sharply when he sees me, his relaxed posture disappearing, his jaw tightening. His eyes are a pale blue bordering on gray, a steely glint in them as he squares his shoulders. A twist appears on his lips as he draws a quick breath to speak.

I jump in first, my voice a firm snap. "I was told I had this balcony to myself."

"As was I," he says, looking me up and down. It's a grating appraisal that doesn't lessen his contemptuous snarl. "Clearly, we're both disappointed."

I grit my teeth at the insinuation that if I were sexier, it might ease his annoyance.

"I have more reason for disappointment," I retort. "Given that there are three of you."

Tyler leans across the distance while the bodyguards stand clear. "Well, you should have brought some friends."

With the decreasing gap between us, a sliver of his scent filters through. It's heavy. Dangerous. Like the shadows in an alley.

The bodyguard, Chris, speaks up from his position guarding the other side of the balcony. "May I suggest you take your seat, sir?"

Tyler gives me a last derisive glance before he huffs. "Sure. I can share."

I wait for him to sit down in the seat on the far right. Chris remains behind him against the wall, positioned to scan the audience more generally for threats, while the second body-guard stands behind Tyler's seat and will no doubt be prepared to pull him away at a second's notice if needed.

Within moments, a server brings champagne and food, and I seem to be forgotten.

I slip into my seat.

I still can't get a complete handle on Tyler, but the clearing of the air around me due to Chris's presence means I'm no longer overcome by the pall of guilt from the rest of the audi-ence. I can focus again. I didn't identify a killer in the crowd before Tyler arrived, so chances are high that Tyler is the elusive Callan Steele.

The theater lights dim, the curtain rises, and I plot my exit from the balcony. I can't confront Tyler until I confirm he's a dragon shifter and that means following him from the theater—hopefully catching sight of him in the moonlight.

Just as I'm about to rise, the orchestra starts playing and I'm struck still.

I've never heard anything like it.

No matter what the people around me are guilty of, this music is pure beauty. I find myself leaning forward in my seat, drawing the sound into my heart, filling my senses with it.

Sometimes, in my cell under the Cathedral, I catch strains of music floating down through the ceiling, and of course, while on hunting missions, I sometimes hear the thump of music from nightclubs, but the acoustics in this place… and the ethereal combination of violins, cellos, flutes…

It feels like floating.

I close my eyes and sink into the sound, not even trying to fight the burn of tears.

Is this what joy feels like?

To experience it is painful. Especially because I know it will end soon. Still, I soak it up because even a monster like me can appreciate beauty.

Even if my next task is ugly.

I open my eyes to find Tyler staring at me across the distance, a champagne glass held lightly in his big hand. His gray-blue eyes glint and the smile on his lips is dangerously relaxed as he takes a long look at my legs—my partially exposed calf where my dress parts—and then up at my chest.

I recognize his thoughts even without sensing them.

Fucking predator.

He thinks I'm vulnerable right now. Will probably offer me a drink laced with something.

Inwardly, I sigh. I'm not afraid for my safety—this man should be afraid of *me*—but it's time to leave this balcony, find a place to hide in the shadows, and plan my attack. That means closing my heart to the beautiful music, but I promise myself that one day, I will be free to hear music like it again.

Before I can pull my purse closer to my chest, Chris appears, placing himself between Tyler and me. He crouches down, again maintaining a non-threatening space between us, but close enough that I can hear his quiet speech, muted by the swelling music. "May I suggest that you find a safer place to sit?"

His gaze flicks briefly, but meaningfully, back at his boss.

Holy damn. It would explain why he has no guilt if he steps in to stop situations like this.

"My thoughts exactly," I murmur, noting the way Chris backs up into the walkway and turns his body into a visual barrier between me and Tyler as I stand and step around the seats.

I pause, wanting to acknowledge the rare act of kindness and the moment of peace that his clear conscience brought me. So unexpected for me to receive this from a human.

I meet his eyes, feeling possibly more open to another person than I have ever felt. "Thank you."

His lips part and his head tilts, as if he's surprised I thanked him.

Quickly, I slip out of the booth without giving him a chance to respond.

The minute I leave the space, I feel less safe than I did inside it. While the warmth of the sun fades the farther I step from the balcony, the danger of my compulsions returns. The rage that drives me to vengeance.

I find a corner down the corridor where I can wait and watch, digging my fingernails into my palms and counting my breaths to keep myself grounded.

By the time patrons spill from the private balconies, I've composed myself, prepared this time for the onslaught of their emotions. If Tyler's bodyguards are any good, they'll wait for the corridors to clear before they escort him from the building, which will make it easier for me to follow them.

Finally, the crowd disperses, and I hear Tyler's voice, slightly slurred—not surprising if he consumed a whole bottle of champagne on his own.

I hold my breath as the group of men passes me and then I

steal after them, silently following their path to the right—away from the main doors. Chris strides ahead, leading the way across a side room, where patrons can have a glass of wine before the performance, and through a service door beside the bar on the far side. He tips his chin at the waitstaff, who wave him through.

I pause as the door closes behind the men, wait a moment for the staff to turn back to their work, and then slip past, hurrying to follow Tyler as his group disappears around the corner ahead of me.

Finally, they exit a side door and I steal up to it, easing it open to peer into the dark service alley beyond it.

An SUV waits for them. Another man, also dressed in a suit like the other bodyguards, exits the vehicle to stand beside it while Tyler saunters toward the back passenger side. I'm suddenly not sure where Chris is and I'm filled with a moment of hesitation since I don't want him to get hurt. Worst case, I hope I'll only need to knock him out.

My only real target is the dragon.

The sky above the alley is clouded. A single dim light sits above the door on the outside wall, but I estimate that the radius of its light doesn't reach far enough to interfere with the moonlight that will shine near the vehicle—that is, provided the clouds clear.

Staring up through the strands of my black hair, I pray for the clouds to open, pray for confirmation of Tyler's identity.

Please, let the moonlight shine.

Just as Tyler steps toward the vehicle's open door, the clouds part.

Moonlight fills the alley.

A silhouette forms around Tyler's body—the shape of a large, black dragon.

I gasp when it appears perfectly formed, its strong neck and tail curving to the side, its wings lifting slightly before settling back to its glistening body. It's unlike any dragon projection I've seen before. Not misshapen or twisted. It has powerful legs and sharp claws, and even sharper teeth when its lips draw back.

When the clouds move across the moon again and Tyler's dragon disappears, I struggle with the decision ahead of me.

He has to be the leader of the Dread. I can't imagine anyone else having a dragon so perfect.

I could follow him to a place where there are fewer human bodyguards, but there are no guarantees that I'll get another chance like this.

I need my redemption. My freedom. I don't want to return to my cage tonight.

I *won't* return to my cage.

I glide through the door, my feet flying as I run straight for him, my speed increased with my strength. The bodyguard standing by the open vehicle door doesn't have the chance to utter a cry of warning before I veer to him, grab hold of his shoulders, swing, and hurl him into the wall behind me.

Tyler's shout of alarm washes over me as I whirl back to him where he has jolted away from the vehicle. His cry ends abruptly when I use my momentum to ram my fist into his face, knocking the side of his head against the doorframe and splitting the skin across his cheekbone.

I'm aware of the other bodyguard running toward me now—the one who was inside the theater with Chris—but he won't reach me in time to help Tyler. I briefly catalog that I still can't see Chris, but I can't worry about his absence right now.

Grabbing Tyler's shoulders while he's dazed, I release my wings with a *thump* and prepare to end him as efficiently as I can. With a sweep of my wings, I wrench Tyler into the air and allow his shoulders to slip from my grasp so that he drops, and gravity brings his head into my hands.

I prepare to twist and break his neck.

He's shouting and I suddenly hear what he's saying.

"Clip her fucking wings!"

Thwack! A cold object hits my back, what feels like freezing wires wrap across my shoulder blades, and pain explodes down my spine. My wings suddenly fail, retracting against my will so that I tumble to the ground, dropping Tyler at the same time.

As we fall, he shoves my arms wide and away from his head.

I swallow my scream as we hit the ground at an awkward angle. Somehow, my heels have remained on my feet despite my ascent into the air, and now they slip against the pavement and I'm lucky I don't break both ankles.

Before I can leap back to my feet, Tyler spins and his fist collides with my chin. My lip splits, and I'm sure my jaw would have shattered if I were any other supernatural. Not only is his dragon perfectly formed, but his strength is far greater than any dragon shifter I've encountered.

I hit back, but the two bodyguards have reached us—including the one I threw across the alley, who recovered far more quickly than I was expecting.

With astounding efficiency, they grab my arms and legs, slapping chains around my wrists and ankles.

I scream as the chains adhere to my skin as if they're glued to me. Within seconds, I'm shackled and being driven to my knees, each man pressing one of my shoulders while Tyler takes a step back.

I scream with frustration, trying to free myself without success.

The efficiency with which they chained me... It feels like they were waiting for me, as if they were prepared for my attack.

These chains... The wire across my back...

Tyler leans down to me, stroking a finger across my jaw. His voice is no longer slurred. "Finally. We got you."

"We should give her the death she gave the Grudge dragons,"

one of the men says. He was the one who was in the theater. "Merciless."

As he speaks, the moon comes out again, and the dragon silhouettes around all three of them as they crowd around me are undeniable.

They're all dragon shifters. They must all be Dread.

The man I threw across the alley shakes his head at the suggestion that they should kill me quickly. "She deserves a slow death. We should—"

A shout cracks across the alley. "Nobody fucks with her!"

My heart lurches when Chris steps out of the shadows. He isn't wearing his jacket now, or his tie. Not even his gun holster. The buttons at the top of his collared shirt are undone and his sleeves are rolled up, revealing his muscular forearms.

"Tyler," he says. "Step the fuck away from her."

Tyler snarls, a low growl, before he shoves me back against the vehicle. Pain shoots through my head and neck, spearing down my upper back, where my wings are constrained.

The other two men also step clear, releasing my shoulders.

I gasp for breath, refusing to slump against the vehicle, struggling to free myself, while Chris takes steady steps toward us.

Tyler rises to his full height, staring the bodyguard down, another snarl on his lips. "Whatever you say, Callan."

The world suddenly spins around me.

Callan?

The man I knew as Chris takes another step into the moonlight, where he stops and stares down at me. The warm rays of sun are gone and in their place is a deep rage, the scent of a storm, the electricity in the air making my skin tingle.

I can't breathe when a silhouette forms around him: a golden dragon more beautiful than any I've ever seen, its enormous body filling the space within the alley, its wings held at its sides, its tail curling along the far wall. It's covered in scales that glisten like jewels and its eyes burn down on me from above.

"You're the angel who has been slaughtering my people." Callan crouches in front of me, a towering form, his cinnamon irises blending to juniper green like a field of burned grass as his gaze clashes with mine.

He glances at his men. "As I was saying. Nobody fucks with her." His voice lowers as he makes me a dangerous promise. "Except me."

CHAPTER THREE

I stare up at Callan Steele, taking in the hard lines of his jaw and the anger in his eyes. My hair clip hangs halfway down the straight, black strands that fall beside my face, my rapid breaths blowing across them. Every puff of air stings my split lip.

How could I have missed his real identity?

A part of my heart breaks at the realization that the warmth of his presence was a lie. Yet even now that I sense his rage, he doesn't carry any guilt that triggers my anger. Nothing that allows me to hate and loathe him. After all, I'm the one who hunted his people.

He didn't hunt *me*.

Until now.

Because clearly, he was ready for me. Ready for the attack tonight. He possibly even orchestrated it so the Serene Commander would take the bait and send me after him.

Yet he gave me hope that a good person exists, and now my hope fades. The warmth in my heart vanishes.

I remind myself: There aren't any good people.

What is *good* anyway? A fucking illusion.

My heart hardens.

He told me he would fuck with me.

Well...

"Go on, then," I whisper. "Nothing you can do to me hasn't already been done."

He can chain me, starve me, threaten me, even beat me—although the Serene Commander thinks twice before trying to beat me these days. I'm not sure if it's because I've grown stronger or because she's given up on striking the corruption out of me.

Callan tips his head to the side, his brow furrowing, the darkness in his eyes intensifying. He probably wouldn't guess that the angels treat their hunter like the dangerous creature that I am. He must imagine that I live in luxury, adored by others, pampered in the halls of the Cathedral.

He regains his balance and leans forward, his face only an inch away from the strands of my hair that billow with my rapid breaths. "Trust me, angel, nothing I do to you will have *ever* been done to you before."

Despite my resolve, a shiver of apprehension rides my spine.

I want to tell him to get the fuck on with it, but he raises his hand. It's a fast enough movement that I brace for impact, surprised and confused when he slows down, reaching carefully forward instead of striking me.

What really surprises me is the reaction of his men. Each of them tenses behind Callan. Tyler takes an active step back, holding his hands out and encouraging the others to back off, too. Within seconds, they've retreated to the far side of the alley, as if they want to be as far away from us as possible.

I have no freaking idea why.

Warily watching Callan's approaching hand, I lean back in increments to evade his touch until my head presses against the side of the SUV and I have nowhere else to go.

"Stay very still," he says. A soft command.

My heart pounds with a new rush of adrenaline. Contrary to his order, I tell myself to struggle, but my rage hasn't returned, and my instincts override my reason, screaming at me to obey him. Fuck knows why.

At the last moment, before he would brush my cheek, his thumb and forefinger veer to the side, closing around the end of the golden hair clip.

With great care, he opens the clasp and slides it away from my hair, managing to capture it without touching any part of me, not even brushing the errant strands of hair that rest against my cheek.

He closes his fist around the piece, as if he's claiming it, and it's a mystery to me why he took it.

Behind him, the other dragons relax.

His focus on me remaining intense, Callan asks, "Who else knows you're here?"

"All of the angels," I say, a confident response as I return his gaze.

Technically, it's not true. There are at least a hundred angels living at the Cathedral, and not all of them would be aware of the missions the Serene Commander sends me on. The five warrior angels who showed me to the door certainly knew where I was going. I tell myself I don't know the answer for sure, so my response isn't a direct lie.

"Will they come for you?" Callan asks, his eyes seeming to change color as he tilts his head. Juniper green. Cinnamon brown. Intriguing shifts of color in the encroaching shadows as the clouds above us move to partially cover the moon and the outline of his golden dragon fades.

As the moonlight wanes, the dragon arches its neck, its giant head lowering to me, a fathomless stare before its face disappears into the darkness.

Callan asked me if the angels would come for me, but it's harder to mislead him this time. I should reply with an emphatic *yes*, but the truth is a certain *no*. I'm dispensable. The Serene Commander once told me that if I were captured on the hunt, nobody would come to rescue me.

If I'm killed, they won't try to retrieve my body.

Cruel? Probably. But dragons are vicious. Before I started hunting them, the Serene Commander tried sending other angels to find and eradicate them. None of those angels ever returned alive. For some, their bodies were so badly beaten, they were unrecognizable. For others, their remains were never recovered. When her favorite warrior, an angel named Melisma, asked to be sent and then never returned, the Serene Commander mourned for weeks. After that, she made it clear she wouldn't risk the death of another angel. And, in this instance, she would be entitled to believe that the Dread would kill me quickly. There would be no point in sending a rescue party.

When I remain silent, Callan rubs his jaw. "Hmm," he says. "You might think they won't come for you. But eventually, they will. After all, you're their greatest asset. As you will be mine."

His claim triggers the barest sliver of rage. Snarling at him, I wrench as hard as I can against the chains around my arms, but with every tug, it feels as if I'm tearing my own skin. As for my wings, I can't sense them at all now. It's as if whatever metal contraption he used on me has not only caged them but is interfering with my ability to sense them.

"What have you done to my wings?"

"I clipped them," he says. "Don't worry. It's not permanent."

"*Don't worry?*" I snarl, my voice dripping with sarcasm.

I risk taking my eyes off Callan to try to see the bindings—hoping to find a weakness in them. In the second that I have to look at them, I see thick, golden bands wrapped around my lower calves and feet, which are pulling my ankles tight. The same kinds of bands are entwined around my wrists, snaking and looping between them. I don't see a join where they could be stretched apart. There are also no loose ends, as if the bands have conformed exactly to my size.

Damn. These chains must be magical. "What have you bound me with?"

Swinging back to Callan as I speak, I'm suddenly aware that by thrashing against my bindings, I've brought myself closer to him. My left shoulder swings right by his chest, barely missing him.

I inhale his scent, an intoxicating mix of sun-warmed grass and a log fire.

He said that nobody would fuck with me except him and—by heaven—he's fucking with me purely by leaning toward me.

As I inhale his scent, his lips curve into a disarming smile that lights up his eyes. His gaze shifts to my lips. "You smell like a clear night sky after the rain falls," he says.

I'm surprised. Not so much about how he described my scent—although I never imagined I'd smell like a night sky, more like the dank cell I came from—but the fact that he's using his sense of smell in the same way I do. I know that wolf shifters use their olfactory senses all the time and it only reinforced my view of my own predatory nature, but now that Callan's doing it too... I might have to reevaluate my knowledge of the Dread...

As I lean closer, I'm aware of the commotion behind him, although Callan's presence—nearer even than when he captured my hair clip—is dominating my senses.

Behind him, Tyler and the two other dragons have jumped back again. Not so quietly this time.

"Tell her to keep her fucking distance!" Tyler snaps at us, his blue eyes wild with what I can only interpret as genuine fear. His biceps and thigh muscles are tensed, as if he's preparing to tackle me if he has to.

But... why?

It puzzles me that his rebuke seems directed more at Callan than at me.

In response, Callan's expression hardens. Remaining crouched exactly where he is, he turns slowly to cast a shadowed stare at Tyler, who swallows visibly and presses his lips together into an unhappy line.

"Relax, Tyler," Callan says, although Tyler doesn't appear to relax one bit.

As Callan turns back to me, his eyes glint with a hint of gold within his cinnamon irises. The smile returns to his lips, and it almost looks like a dare he's casting my way.

I have no idea what he's daring me to do.

"You're bound with chains made from dragon's gold," he says.

I blink at him for a second since the tension between Callan and Tyler made me forget I asked Callan what he chained me with. As for dragon's gold, I know it exists, but I don't know much about it. I've certainly never seen it, or been subjected to it, before. I imagine it's reserved for the richest dragons. It's not as if the Grudge dragons I encountered were flush with wealth.

"Only the dragon who owns the gold can control it," Callan says. "This gold is mine. I commanded it to bind you. You won't escape it."

Slowly, I bare my teeth at him. "Watch me try."

His eyes crinkle with what I can only interpret as delight before he rises to his feet and inclines his head at Tyler. "Get her into the vehicle."

With every step that Callan takes away from me, Tyler's muscles relax, but a hint of anger in his expression remains. He strides toward me, as if he wants nothing more than to get this over with.

He throws a question back at Callan. "In the trunk or the back seat?"

Callan takes a moment, his focus shifting to the golden clip, which he continues to hold. "Back seat. We can't chance taking our eyes off her. Watch her carefully."

It seems odd to me that Callan isn't going to put me in the vehicle himself. I'm not clear on the inner workings of dragon hierarchy, but he's their leader. I would have thought he'd enjoy the control he has over me right now.

"Understood." Tyler gestures to the other two men, first the man who was waiting with the vehicle and then the man who was posing as the other bodyguard within the theater. "Byron. Davison. Help me with her."

They crowd in behind Tyler as he approaches me. Callan doesn't go far, positioning himself halfway across the alley and watching us carefully.

One good thing about him keeping his distance is that the calming sensation of the sun lessens. It isn't gone completely, but enough that my rage returns.

I welcome my anger like oxygen.

If I'm to have any chance of escape, it's right now, before Tyler and the other men move me into the SUV.

When Tyler reaches for me first, his arms about to close around me, I mentally scream at myself to free my wings, willing myself to dislodge whatever contraption is attached to my back. The cold metal bites my skin, shooting pain down my spine when I wrench forward, but I ignore the agony.

"Stop struggling," Tyler snaps at me. His face is bleeding from the split across his cheekbone, but his eyes are as steely as the first moment I saw him.

As if I'm going to listen to him.

Giving up on freeing my wings, I wrench at my wrists as he reaches for me. I groan as my biceps bunch and... for the briefest moment... I'm sure the golden bands are about to stretch. I just need a little more time.

"Fuck you," I snarl back at him, headbutting him before his arms can close around me.

Thwack!

Tyler's head snaps back.

"Fucking bitch!" He lets out a series of curses, but I let them wash over me, using the moment of distraction to heave at my restraints and try not to overbalance.

The bands stretch again. I'm sure they're about to loosen around my wrists—

Tyler's fist flies toward my face so fast that I can't avoid it, not while I'm leaning forward. His knuckles smack into my cheekbone, the skin splits, and I'm knocked back into the vehicle again.

Oh... fuck... Agony spirals through me, both from the impact on my face and the knock against the back of my head, which ricochets down my spine.

Byron and Davison are already at Tyler's side.

I don't know which of them hits me next.

Pain explodes across my face and my blood splatters the pavement. My cheekbone would have shattered if I wasn't built the way I am.

Gasping for breath, not wasting my energy on screams, I desperately try to regain control of my spiraling senses, trying to pivot away from their punches, trying to hunch and protect my torso, tearing the tulle skirt on the coarse pavement, where it's pinned beneath my knees. Another blow lands on my side, and then my shoulder, and this time, I can't stop my scream. The pain is hot, a burning sensation that tears through my muscles.

Choking back a sob, I look up in time to see Tyler's other fist flying toward my face and I'm sure I won't remain conscious.

Goodnight, world.

Right before the punch would land, a long, golden chain wraps around Tyler's arm, wrenching him backward so fast that he shouts, grabs his shoulder, and sprawls on his chest on the pavement.

"What did I fucking tell you?" Callan's voice is filled with rage as he looms over Tyler, pulling the chain tight, yanking the cable upward, and forcing Tyler to look at him.

At the sight of their alpha's anger, the other two men jump away from me, both of them crouching several paces on either side of me.

"Hit her again, and I will burn all of your fucking hearts out." With a deep, disgusted rumble in his chest, Callan drops the chain onto Tyler's chest, steps around him, and strides toward me.

In a single fluid movement, he drops to his knees in front of me and his own fist swings toward me.

There's a glint of metal.

A blade!

I don't have time to inhale, let alone scream as the metal object rams into the side of my neck.

My blood is about to spill.

Closing my eyes, I prepare myself for death.

CHAPTER FOUR

There's a sharp prick in my neck and that's all.

My eyes flash open. I stare at Callan, confused. "What...?"

He leans back, holding up the object he used so that I can see it. It's the golden barrel of a syringe and it blurs as my vision starts to sparkle and swim.

"There's something you should know about Dread dragons," Callan says, his voice low, a warning, as if he's trying to teach me. "Hit them and they'll hit back. Without exception. Without mercy. You should remember that."

I attempt to speak, but my voice sounds distant to my ears. "What have you... done to me?"

"You won't be able to fight back for a while. I didn't want to go to these lengths, but you've given me no choice."

My arms and legs no longer obey me, and my head starts to loll, blood catching in my hair as I slide ever-so-slowly down the side of the vehicle to form a crumpled heap on the pavement.

Callan doesn't try to pull me upright, rising and swinging to Tyler instead. "Get her in the truck! Now!"

Tyler jumps to his feet. The chain that had wrapped around his arm falls to the ground with a clatter before he skirts around Callan and heads toward me.

Tyler's face is pale and his teeth are clenched. "Davison, get her up for me."

Davison launches himself at me. I brace for another attack, but he bends and wrenches me over his shoulder while Byron opens the vehicle door.

Whatever substance Callan injected into me, it's messing with my vision and my senses in a big way. I expect to pass out, but I remain lucid as Davison dumps me into the middle seat in the back of the SUV. I collapse against the leather covering, slowly slipping to the side, unable to keep myself upright.

Davison's hand whips out. He grabs my neck to stop me from falling onto my side. His grip is hard and uncomfortable, but I'm aware that the pain is somewhat numbed, sparkles across my vision distracting me from it.

Byron opens the other back passenger side door to slip in on the other side of me. Tyler slams the door shut as soon as Davison is safely inside, and within seconds, I'm squished between Davison and Byron in the back seat.

Outside the vehicle, Callan appears about to stride toward the driver side door, but Tyler steps into his path. Callan pulls up sharply. Their voices are low and with my dulled senses, I have trouble making out what they're saying. Judging from Tyler's rapid hand gesturing and the hard lines of Callan's jaw, they're arguing.

I can't focus on them for long because it's incredibly awkward sitting with my hands tied behind my back. My fists form a lump against my lower back that forces me to lean forward, and in my drugged state, my shoulders sink until I'm doubled over.

With a huff, Davison wrenches me upright again, yanking the seatbelt over me to keep me in place, but it's not the discomfort of my hands pressing to my lower spine that makes me gasp.

A sharp pain bites my left side closest to where Byron sits.

I'm unable to do more than swivel my gaze to the blade that glints at the edge of my vision—or, more accurately, what appears to be four blades, since my vision is creating all sorts of weird visual phenomena right now.

"We should have killed this bitch already," Byron says to Davison. His gaze darts toward Callan outside the vehicle before he continues. "We still could."

Byron presses the knife between my ribs and the level of pain is concerning. He's breaking skin.

Unlike the other men, who are clean-shaven, Byron has a short but slightly scruffy beard. His skin is fair, his eyes are a sharp brown and sit beneath thick eyebrows, and his lips are thin. He has a tattoo on his left arm, although it's barely visible from beneath the cuff of his sleeve and I can't make out what it is—certainly not now that my vision is swirling. I didn't see tattoos on the other men. Their ink could be hidden underneath their shirts, but I'm sure they won't be dragon-related images. They're too smart to wear dragon tattoos to betray their species to an angel.

"Callan made it clear we can't hurt her again," Davison replies. His hair is also dark brown, but his eyes are olive green and his skin is light brown.

"He said not to *hit* her." Byron bares his teeth in a smile that makes me run cold. "He never said anything about cutting her up. A quick knife between her ribs is all it would take. She's completely helpless right now."

Davison glares at him. I'm not sure if he can see the dagger until his focus drops. His eyes widen. "Not here, you fucking idiot!"

Davison's hand whips out as quickly as a dragon's tail might flick. I half-expect him to wrap his fist around my mouth in case

I scream, but he grabs Byron's hand before the other man can ram the knife deeper into my side.

"Do you want to end up a charred corpse dumped outside the city somewhere?" Davison snarls. "I fucking don't."

Byron leans closer, his breath warm on my cheek. "I'm not afraid of Callan—"

"You fucking should be," Davison snaps.

"He won't burn us. There are too few of us now to deplete our numbers. We should kill her while we still can and get it over with." Byron's voice grates within my ears like steel against my skin. Inhaling deeply, I taste copper on the tip of my tongue, salty and tangy, like biting down on a coin. It's a sign that he has blood on his hands, his past guilt manifesting as a metallic taste in my mouth.

Davison's hold on Byron's wrist tightens as he leans closer, both men angled across me now. When I inhale Davison's scent, I taste copper, too, but it's far more subtle and doesn't carry the heaviness that Byron's guilt does. I interpret this to mean Davison has been complicit in murder, but probably hasn't committed it.

Davison's olive green eyes flicker briefly over me before his voice lowers. "Callan has a plan. We agreed to follow it."

Byron shakes his head, his lips twisting with derision. "Callan's plan is flawed. We all know it."

Before Byron can say another word, I whisper to him, "You killed someone close to you."

Byron's thin lips part in surprise, his focus snapping to me. Right now, he has four sets of eyes and two sets of lips, and his beard is a dark wash in my vision, but my drugged state only serves to enhance what I know. The heaviness of his heartbeat confirms that he carries deep remorse as well as guilt.

"You regret what you did," I say.

Byron jolts away from me, dragging the blade against my

ribs as he pulls away. I moan at the sharp pain, and he doesn't stop staring at me. "The fuck?"

Davison clicks his tongue at the patch of blood blossoming across my dress. "Clean your blade. Tyler's coming. You'd better fucking hope he covers for us."

Byron hurriedly wipes his knife on a handkerchief he pulls from his pocket before he conceals the blade again.

The two men are very quiet when Tyler slides into the front passenger side of the vehicle. He glances my way, narrowing his eyes at the spreading patch of blood at my side, but he doesn't look too closely before he turns to face the front.

Sucking in my breaths, I refuse to moan again with pain, even though the cut hurts like hell, my split cheek is killing me, and my lip is swelling up.

I may be stronger than other angels, but sadly for me, I don't heal as quickly as they do. The Serene Commander once told me it was punishment for my corruption. I'm destined to feel pain longer than others. Taking a pragmatic approach to this affliction, I gave up wishing things were different and worked hard at avoiding injuries, perfecting my evasive maneuvers. Until tonight, I haven't suffered a grievous wound in a fight for years.

Outside the vehicle, Callan is sauntering across the alley away from the SUV and over to the door that leads into the building—right where I dropped my sage-green purse when I first attacked Tyler.

He picks it up, scans our surroundings, and carries it deeper into the alley, where he reaches up to the windowsill of a small exterior window that's situated above his head. There's a glint of gold as he carefully places my hair clip and purse side by side on the windowsill. They won't be obvious to anyone walking in and out of the service door, and because of the height, it's unlikely they'll be noticed by anyone taking out the trash. But someone who might come looking for me will find them.

It's the sort of thing I would do if I wanted someone to know I'd taken their loved one: leave some little mementos behind. A purse can be dropped, but the hair clip is more personal. It says: *I've got her.*

I guess he didn't believe me when I indicated the angels won't come for me.

Returning to the vehicle, he slides into the driver's seat and once again, his calm presence blocks my senses. I exhale my tension. If my rage has to be blocked, at least I can take something from the peace it brings. Right now, I need as much breathing space as I can get. Sitting between two killers makes me want to fucking scream.

Callan glances in the rearview mirror and then swivels sharply, focused on the growing patch of blood on my side. "What the fuck happened?"

While Byron and Davison remain silent, Tyler casually follows Callan's line of sight. His focus flicks briefly to Byron, but he doesn't otherwise show any alarm. "I guess she was hurt in the fight outside the car. I must have scratched her."

Some scratch.

Byron leans nonchalantly toward his door as if it's nothing to do with him, and Davison is the only one who meets Callan's eyes. "We need to move, Callan. We've already stayed too long."

Callan grits his teeth. "Davison, blindfold her. The serum will scramble her senses and ensure we get home safely, but I don't want to take any chances."

Davison immediately reaches into the pocket on the back of the front seat and retrieves a blindfold, which he ties around my eyes. Normally, it wouldn't faze me one bit, but Callan wasn't joking about my senses being scrambled.

Combined with Callan's presence, the drug and the blindfold make it difficult for me maintain any certainty about which way we're traveling and how far we've gone. I'm aware of the vehicle moving and the shifting lights outside, the left and right turns, stretches of road, more turns, but I'm turned around before I know it.

On top of that, Callan drives fast. His operation of the vehicle is smooth, in control. I don't sense that he's speeding, but he somehow avoids stopping—not even at traffic lights, which I was sure we'd come across at some point.

By the time the vehicle descends down a slope, and I hear the metallic clanking and whirring of what I presume is a garage door, all I'm sure about is that we're not as far from the concert hall as I thought we would be. Definitely no farther than two miles from it.

The vehicle purrs to a stop, Davison pulls the blindfold off my eyes, and I blink in the bright light that confirms we've stopped within an underground parking garage. There are no windows to confirm our location, but swiveling my gaze left and right allows me to ascertain that the space is unusually large and contains multiple vehicles—some of which make my eyebrows rise. Several ridiculously sleek two-door sports cars sit side by side within parking bays on my right, along with several equally shiny sports motorcycles.

When Tyler turns to me, I can see that his face is completely healed—no sign of the cut on his cheekbone now—and neither Byron nor Davison appear bruised from our altercation earlier. Damn dragons seem to heal faster than warrior angels do.

In contrast, my lip is more swollen, my cheekbone is burning with pain, and the bleeding wound in my side is going to cause me major issues if I don't tend to it soon. Blood loss is the immediate problem. Infection is the second.

I grit my teeth and promise myself I'll escape before that happens.

CHAPTER FIVE

Callan barks orders at the other men before he rapidly exits the vehicle. "Tyler, bring the angel upstairs. Davison, Byron, go home. I'll summon the Cohort when it's time."

Davison opens his door, leaves me right where I am, and saunters away without a backward glance. Byron is slower, casting glances back at me as he exits the SUV, as if he's still considering stabbing me, before he, too, strides away. He quickly gets on one of the sports motorcycles while Davison takes one of the cars, and within moments, the parking garage fills with revving engines that fade as they drive away toward the garage door.

I don't have time to watch them leave. Appearing at the door through which Byron exited, Tyler reaches in and hauls me across the back seat, yanking me out, nearly dropping me on the hard concrete floor before dragging me up and over his shoulder. I swallow my whimper when the pressure on my stomach pulls at the cut across my side, but I'm momentarily distracted from the pain by a small but important detail that I missed earlier.

Tyler is wearing a wedding ring on his left ring finger. I see it clearly when he shoves my hair away from his face. Assuming dragon shifters follow human customs, I guess he's married.

It's not what I expected from a man who managed to look me up and down so convincingly at the theater. He also convinced me that he was drunk, slurring his speech when they were exiting the building.

Byron may be a murderer, but Tyler is a trickster.

Dammit. If it weren't for Callan's strong presence, I would have detected it sooner.

Now that I'm slung across Tyler's shoulder, I have a good view of his back and not much else, but I'm aware of Callan striding past us, his overwhelming presence shuttering everything else around me, even though he keeps his distance from Tyler.

"As soon as we get the angel upstairs, go home to your wife," Callan says gruffly. "Sophia will be worried."

My brow furrows at the fact that Callan seems anxious to send everyone home, yet Tyler continues to carry me around. It's definitely strange.

I still can't move my limbs, but my fingers and toes are starting to tingle in a promising way. While Tyler strides across the garage with me, I test my toes, twitching them in my heels.

I'm relieved to discover that the serum is wearing off when I manage to wiggle my foot. Not so pleased when my wriggling causes one of my heels to slip off.

The sage-green shoe clatters to the pavement and Tyler jumps like a startled cat at the sound, my body gaining the slightest amount of air before his grip resumes, and he grunts. "Just her shoe."

As much as I want to test my other limbs, I force myself to remain limp, determined not to alert Tyler or Callan to the fact that I'm recovering my mobility. Not until I see an opportunity to escape.

There's a slight scraping sound and, when Tyler resumes

walking, Callan falls back a little so that I can see my shoe gripped in his big hand.

I listen carefully for clues about my whereabouts. There's the whir of an elevator, and then Tyler carries me inside. He takes up position at the front while Callan stands in the back corner.

The elevator rises for long enough that I know I'm high up by the time we arrive at a cold hallway. It's air-conditioned and chilly enough that goosebumps rise on my skin. This new environment is certainly not the dark cell I'm used to, although it has similarities. There's no natural light, no windows as far as I can see. Not that I can see much beyond Tyler's back, and I don't want to lift my head too far in case I alert him that I'm able to move again.

Now, my main problem is breaking the restraints around my wrists and ankles that currently make running impossible.

A door opens and we step into an even colder environment. So cold that I shiver violently—which only makes Tyler grip me harder.

As we pass through the doorway, I have a sense that the space around us is large. Tyler's and Callan's footfalls echo in a way that indicates the room doesn't have a lot of furniture to dampen sounds. It smells clean. Overly so.

A black marble floor appears beneath us, and then multiple female voices reach me, along with various floral scents that waft through the air around me.

Callan's presence may have dulled my ability to sense someone's true nature, but the swishing movements within the room indicate there are two... no, *three* women... rising to their feet on the other side of the room.

Tyler pulls up short. "Sophia! What are you doing here?"

A soft, feminine voice floats toward me while light footfalls bring her closer. "I was worried. I couldn't sleep. I needed to know you were safe."

Within my field of view, Callan has frozen, the muscles of

his forearm bunching and his hand tightening around my shoe so hard that he's crushing its leather upper. I can't see his face, but his posture tells me he isn't happy.

"This isn't a safe place for any of you," Callan says, a near snap. "My instructions were clear."

Another female voice sounds, this one heavy with remorse. "I'm sorry, Callan," the new speaker says. "We were all worried. And Sophia wouldn't stay at home—"

"You need to leave. Now." Callan's command is sharp as he takes a step toward them and out of my field of view.

Seeming to ignore him, the first woman—Sophia—gives a dramatic gasp. "You captured the angel!"

It took her fucking long enough to notice my tulle-clad butt elevated over Tyler's shoulder.

The anger in Callan's voice is harder than the tension in Tyler's shoulder beneath my torso. "Tyler, take the angel to the cage in my room. Then get Sophia and Zahra to safety." He pauses as if he's giving someone a pointed look. "Martha, too. None of them should be here a second longer than necessary. It's too dangerous."

So far, only two of the women have spoken. One is Sophia, but I'm not sure if the remorseful one was Zahra or Martha. I try to break through the different perfumes to glean something about the nature of their wearers, but it's impossible. They're all flowery, artfully vulnerable.

Damn artificial scents.

Damn Callan's warm sunshine presence.

Even so, I shouldn't feel this wooly in my head. Now that the effects of the serum are wearing off, I hoped I'd feel a little better. The fact that I don't tells me I'm losing more blood from the cut in my side than I thought I was.

At Callan's command, Tyler swings to his left and starts to move, presumably in the direction of the cage Callan mentioned.

Finally, I can see the room and its female occupants.

Sophia hovers close by—close enough that I could raise my bound feet and kick her with both of them. She has fair skin and large, green eyes. Her face is framed with long, tousled brown hair that falls over her shoulders and gleams with golden highlights—not natural ones, judging by the slight regrowth at her scalp. She's wearing a loose, off-the-shoulder T-shirt that's cropped below her breasts to show off a perfectly flat stomach before tight jeans cling to her long legs. If we were standing side by side, she'd be about the same height as me at five and a half feet tall.

A second woman is poised halfway across the room, and I take a guess that she was the second speaker, given the flush of remorse across her cheeks. Her skin is light brown, her eyes cinnamon—a very similar shade to Callan's. Her dark brown hair is tied up into a topknot, a few loose strands telling me it has a wave in it, and she's also wearing jeans and a T-shirt.

Behind her, an older woman stands within a rectangular-shaped sunken lounge that appears to be cut into the floor and is made only of marble with no cushions or anything soft around it. She has emerald eyes like Sophia's and pale skin, her dark brown hair streaked with silvery strands. She stands taller than the other two women and she's swathed in an elegant silk shirt that flows past her hips to her pants-clad legs. Multiple golden necklaces hang around her neck and her wrists clatter with bracelets.

The room around us is large and rectangular with an extremely high ceiling. The wall opposite the door is a single pane of glass that reveals the sparkling cityscape beyond it—or at least I think it does, until the image transitions into a tranquil green forest, and I realize that I'm actually looking at some sort of screen.

My first impression was correct. There are no windows in

this place, no furniture, and the air-conditioning is set to freezing.

I take it all in within the blink of an eye before my focus swings back to Sophia. A golden bracelet with an emerald charm dangling from it slips down her arm when her hand flies to her mouth to stifle another dramatic gasp.

At first, I think she's somehow aghast at my disheveled appearance, although I'm not sure what could have offended her so much. I washed my hair, after all.

"Tyler!" she all but shrieks. "You're bleeding!"

Oh. That.

The damp pool of blood seeping from my side must be working its way down his shirt front—or maybe his sleeve, I can't see for sure.

"What?" The surprise in Tyler's voice tells me he didn't notice the blood, or maybe he just didn't care until his wife pointed it out. He relaxes. "It's not my blood. I'm fine."

His arm loosens around me as he adjusts his hold, and I take my chance, possibly the only one I'll get.

Harnessing all of my strength, I use every muscle in my stomach and torso to wrench myself up against his arm, launching myself out of his hold. Fighting the pain in my side.

At the same time, I heave at my restraints, screaming with effort. The metal stretches—

It separates!

So much for Callan's claim that the gold will only obey him.

My arms and feet are free by the time I land on my feet. I expect the chains to drop away from me, but to my frustration, the bands re-form around my wrists and ankles, the cold metal conforming to my skin again—but at least it's like bracelets and anklets this time.

I don't have time to second-guess my freedom.

Kicking my foot up, I snatch my remaining shoe into my hand and swing the stiletto heel at Tyler's surprised face. As soon as I move, I sense the bands around my limbs trying to reconnect, to pull my wrists together and constrain me again. It throws me off-balance just enough that Tyler avoids having his forehead impaled, but only by the scantest inch.

He roars as he leaps backward, and behind me, the women are now screaming.

I ignore them, focused only on Tyler, who is standing between me and the exit.

Snapping the heel off the shoe, I grip it like a dagger and stab at Tyler again. My moves are quick. Sharp. He narrowly avoids each one of them.

Sophia's reflexes are slower. I've already taken three shots at Tyler when she finally jumps away from us.

On my next swing at Tyler, I kick back at Sophia at the same time—a high kick with the flat of my foot that lands on her shoulder, purely intended to get her out of my way. The last thing I need is for her to trip me.

It's not the hardest kick I've ever delivered, but she screams as if I've dislocated her shoulder.

"Sophia!" Tyler launches himself at me with new vengeance in defense of his wife.

Behind him, Callan paces back and forth—somehow managing to look more caged than I feel. He didn't fight me in the alley and it looks like he's determined to stay out of the fight here, too.

Why, why, why?

His continued evasion is messing with my head.

The sharp heel I'm holding whooshes past Tyler's cheek, and on my next thrust, it narrowly misses his neck.

The damn thing isn't getting me anywhere.

I trust my fists more than any weapon.

Ignoring Sophia and the other two women, who are now dragging Sophia out of harm's way, I hurl the heel at Callan, trying to provoke him. Unless combatants are trained at fighting together, they're more likely to get in each other's way, and I'd rather draw Callan away from the door than have him remain near it.

Callan dodges the projectile but still doesn't rush at me or try to join the fight, taking a step back toward the front door instead.

Now he's blocking my only escape.

My gamble with throwing the heel definitely didn't pay off.

Tyler's fist flies toward me, but I retaliate with a series of strikes that knock his shoulder and his stomach and then reopen the wound on his cheek. *Thump-thump-thump.* They're all hard hits that force him onto his back foot but don't knock him out. He doesn't know how lucky he is. If I had access to my wings, he'd be dead already.

The hits give me the space I need to get past him.

Darting forward, preparing to fight Callan, I gasp when I'm grabbed from behind and swung back.

Expecting to find Tyler at my throat, I come face to face with the woman with the light brown skin who has eyes like Callan's.

"No, Zahra!" Callan's shout fades into the background as I focus on this new assailant.

So this one is Zahra. And she means something to Callan, judging from the sharpness of his cry.

She uses my momentum against me, pulling me farther away from the door as skillfully as if I weighed nothing, her movements smooth and fluid.

I recognize immediately that she's far more skilled than Tyler, her training much more sophisticated, as she delivers a combination of martial arts moves that are as forceful as a gale-force wind while as graceful as stalks of tall grass bending within that wind.

Beautiful to watch. Not so much to be the target of.

Luckily, I have a whole shelf of books about combat and I've had a lot of time to study and practice.

I switch gears, responding to her next attack with a fluid evasion and then a series of attacks that nearly unbalance her. I watch the way her eyes widen. I guess she thought I'd only know how to attack with brute force, not with elegance.

I can't help the smile forming on my lips.

A true opponent.

I will hate to kill her.

Of course, I'm ignoring the fact that every move I make tears open the cut in my side and I'm more likely to collapse than to defeat her.

She strikes again, her balance perfect as she attempts to grab my wrist and twist me around on myself—a move I evade before I strike back hard, trying to force her to make a mistake.

She doesn't, her focus remaining strong.

With each of her attempted strikes, it dawns on me that her moves have a particular purpose. They don't appear intended to hurt me. Each time she attacks, she tries to drag my wrists closer together—and each time, I sense the metal wanting to rejoin.

"No!" I shout, barreling into her with sudden brute force. I risk worsening the state of my wound by switching tactics, but I need to take her off guard.

She doesn't defend herself fast enough and my palm closes over her shoulder, pushing down at the same time as I sweep her right foot out from under her.

She collapses to the floor with a cry.

I don't have a moment to spare as Tyler launches himself at me again. Narrowly darting around him, I run straight for the door.

Straight for Callan.

Zahra screams behind me and the sudden fear in her voice

manifests like hot waves within my senses, a burning anxiety. "No, Callan! Don't touch her!"

He braces ahead of me.

I don't know why he's so reluctant to grab me, but if he doesn't want me to leave, he'll have to stop me somehow.

I judge his position relative to the wall on my right, certain that I can launch myself toward it at the last minute, hit the surface, spin, and land behind him, evading him that way.

He'll be forced to turn, and the delay will give me the split second I need to bash through the door. It's another ten paces behind him, and I'm sure I have the strength to break it down. I've shattered wooden doors before. It's cages that worry me.

That is, assuming the door is made of wood. As I draw closer to it, the gleaming surface indicates it might not be.

Callan's startling size is intimidating. His height, the breadth of his shoulders, the way his shirt pulls over his biceps and his suit pants tighten across his thigh muscles as he braces. In the soft lighting, his hair appears less black and more brown, his eyes more cinnamon than juniper green now.

I'm only four steps away from him, but he continues to stand his ground, which gives me confidence that he won't anticipate my jump to the right.

Behind me, I sense Zahra's light footsteps, but she's too far back to catch me.

She screams. Pure fear. *"Callan! No!"*

His chest rises and falls as if he's inhaling his last breath.

I hit the ground a step in front of him, propel myself to the right, and prepare to bounce off the wall when I realize that he jumped with me.

My lips part, I try to evade him, but the air moves around me, his arms slip neatly around my chest, and then his body collides with mine.

Hard muscles and warm skin. The full force of sunlight. A sense of weightlessness and then—

I can't breathe.
Can't think.
Can't scream.
Suddenly, my entire body is on fire.

CHAPTER SIX

A wave of flames washes around me, the heat billowing across my face, torso, arms, legs—every inch of me burning beyond my endurance.

My feet are no longer on the floor, my legs wrapped around Callan's waist, the force of his movement lifting me into the air, where we remain suspended in the heat. Fire billows through my hair, the long, black strands whipping out at the edges of my vision and cutting through the flames like brilliant knives.

I meet his eyes, which are now pure golden, all hints of cinnamon gone. If the breath weren't already stopped in my chest, I would cease breathing now.

His face shimmers with waves of heat.

His skin has transformed. Fine, golden scales glisten across his cheeks, down his neck, and across his torso, fitting perfectly to the shape of his human form. His torn shirt floats away at our sides, shriveling within the raging fire burning around us.

Immense golden wings rise on either side of him, spreading outward... and outward... beating the air to keep us aloft. His wing bones and the membrane between them look like sculpted gold.

I stare in shock at the streams of fire that swirl with every exhalation Callan makes.

He's breathing fire. He's actually… breathing… *fire*.

The Serene Commander told me that dragon shifters don't control fire anymore. She told me this means they aren't real dragons. Yet every breath Callan takes, he exhales a torrent of flames that are so brilliant, so alluring that I'm drawn to him.

Instead of trying to escape, I lean forward, acutely aware of the pressure of his hand over my heart, the inward press of my thighs against his waist, and the deepest ache within my chest.

I should be dead. Burning right now. Screaming in pain. Not edging closer to the source of my destruction.

Inching my fingertips upward, I brush the underside of his jaw. The hard scales are smooth but also iridescent and translucent in a way that leaves his human skin partially visible. It's almost like he's put on a suit of armor fitted exactly to every inch of him. Well, except that he's also bigger now than he was in his human form—his shoulders broader, chest wider, thighs larger. It's impossible to tell pressed up against him, but I imagine the waistband of his suit pants hasn't fared well.

My fingertips seem to glow within his flames, the fire he's exhaling *whooshing* across my hand in a way that should terrify me. I'm peripherally aware that every beat of his wings spreads the flames farther through the room, swirling them like ribbons.

I'm suddenly acutely aware that Sophia is screaming and the older woman—Martha—cowers beside her within the sunken lounge area.

Tyler has thrown himself across both of them like a shield, launching his body between them and the flames in the nick of time, and now he transforms like Callan.

Enormous black wings tear through his shirt, and ebony scales shimmer across his face, neck, and back—the ones on his back only visible where his shirt is torn—before he closes his wings around the two women.

Zahra is curled up in a ball on the floor closer to us, her skin transforming and glistening with bronze scales as her wings shoot out, also gleaming bronze, and wrap around her so that from above, she appears to be enclosed in a cocoon.

All around us, the room glistens, the bare walls a shining metallic hue that doesn't seem to have caught fire.

Suddenly, the lack of flammable objects in the room makes sense.

My heart pounds so hard that it's going to burst out of my chest. My arms are pressed to Callan's hard chest, right up against his scales, and the texture continues to feel strange within my senses.

Smooth. Rough. *Both.*

I hold my breath, trying to clear my head while the straight strands of my hair blow around me without harm.

Somehow, I'm not on fire.

My focus returning to Callan, I find his eyes widening, his grip tightening on me, a deeply wild expression forming on his face. I don't have to be a mind reader to know that he expected me to burn to death in his arms.

The fact that I haven't seems to have shocked him.

Well, I may be surviving the fire, but if I don't get oxygen soon, I'll asphyxiate. I can't hold my breath forever.

I'm on the verge of blacking out when the ceiling erupts with countless small metallic devices that spray a white substance and, suddenly, a snowstorm erupts within the room.

Freezing, ivory crystals rush around us, sizzling against Callan's skin, and the fire dies down, although trickles of flames still emit from his lips, softer now, as the room becomes colder than it was when I first arrived.

The crystals tingle against my skin. I'm not overly familiar with human fire extinguishers, but this substance feels very different, calming and magical. It doesn't pile up when it lands on the floor, disappearing on contact instead.

Slowly, Callan's wings beat, and he lowers us to the floor, but I can't seem to unfurl from around him. I tell myself it must be because I'm now freezing and in shock.

When he drops to a kneeling position on the floor with me in his lap, my legs still wrapped around him, I lean closer to him, trying to take as much body heat as I can from him.

He may be my enemy, but I'll be damned if I freeze to death after surviving his flames.

Tiny wisps of fire continue to swirl from his mouth. He remains shifted, the bottom of his enormous wings draped across the floor, his skin shimmering.

I can barely speak through my now-chattering teeth, but I force sound from my mouth. "What… happened…?"

He sounds strained, his focus on me intense. "Touching another supernatural triggers my dragon. Only the strongest dragons can survive my flames and even then, if I want to, I can kill them." His jaw is tight. "You should be dead."

Across the room, Zahra lifts her head, peering through the gap between her wings, drawn out from her safe cocoon, I guess, by the sounds of our voices.

After taking a quick look around, she pulls her wings back completely and rises to her feet. The final snow crystals fall across her shoulders as she gapes at me. "How is the angel still alive?"

Before Zahra can take a step forward, Martha overtakes her, brushing past her in a rush. "Do we care?" she asks, striding toward us. "She survived. The plan is intact. That's all that matters."

Tyler is slower to rise, lifting Sophia into his arms. She nestles against him, her cheeks ashen. The scent of burning hair wafts from their position. Her brown tresses are singed in a patch on the left side of her head. She and Martha didn't protect themselves, which could mean they aren't strong enough. Perhaps there's something wrong with their wings.

I can't spend any more time focusing on them. Now that the fire is subdued, my wound is in even worse condition. I struggle against Callan, trying to see past my arms to the cut on my side, only to realize that the bands around my wrists have adhered to each other again.

Quickly testing my legs, I discover that my ankles must be secured to each other as well, my legs basically locked around his hips.

Damn.

In a final attempt to free myself, I desperately draw on the last of my energy to thrash against him, thumping my connected fists against his chest. "Release me!"

He barely moves. I may as well be a dragonfly flitting against him.

Martha, on the other hand, jumps back with an alarmed shout. "By the ancient dragons, she's like a wild animal!"

Ignoring Martha, Callan grabs my hands, immobilizing me so fast that it's indicative of my failing health—or perhaps his increased strength now that he's shifted.

I tell myself to fight back, but... I'm so tired... and far too wounded...

My hair falls across my face again, damp with new sweat that is quickly crystalizing in the cold environment.

I can't fight him anymore. I need to conserve the little strength I have left. Despite wanting to snarl at him, promise him I'll kill him soon, I can't keep holding his relentlessly fiery gaze.

My defiance fails me.

The unwanted whimper that escapes my lips is an awful sound of surrender as my head sinks to his chest, the only place it can go.

He exhales slowly. His grip on my hands remains firm but softens as he wraps one hand around my wrists, pressing them between us while his other arm slips across my back, holding me close. Once again, I sense a protective essence that is completely at odds with his promise to mess with me.

My breathing is ragged, but now that my ear rests close to his heart, I can hear how hard his heart is beating. A loud, thumping sound.

Martha's silhouette blocks the light as she steps back up to Callan's side, seeming satisfied that I can't attack her now.

Her derisive tone is impossible to miss. "You need to tame her, Callan, or all of this will be for nothing."

He tenses but doesn't look up at her, his focus remaining on me. A deep rumble sounds in his chest right beside my ear and a final wisp of fire escapes his lips as he says, "*Get out.*"

Martha blinks at him, suddenly frozen, as if he never speaks to her like that.

I'm surprised by the vehemence in his voice. His ever-calm presence hid the storming anger I now glimpse in his expression as I peer up between the strands of my hair.

His golden eyes flash at me, a dangerous glint of power, before he casts Martha and the others a searing glance. "All of you. Get the fuck out. Or I'll remind you why I'm still the leader of this clan."

The blood drains instantly from Martha's face. She backs away.

Tyler misses a step. He was already carrying Sophia toward the door. Her head is tucked into his shoulder, and she doesn't look up as they pass by, but when Tyler casts Callan a quick, tense glance, Callan's jaw clenches. I'm not sure how to interpret that silent moment between them, but Tyler hurries past.

Within seconds, Martha, Tyler, and Sophia have exited through the far door—the door I desperately want to escape through—and it clicks shut behind them.

Only Zahra remains. Appearing unafraid, she approaches quietly before kneeling parallel to me, facing Callan.

"What can I do to help you?"

He exhales as if he's controlling his temper. "I need you to ask Jada to lock down the building. Make sure only she and the other human guards remain. I don't want to see a single dragon until I summon the Cohort. No matter how long it takes. Days. A week. A month." He pins her with his golden eyes. "No visitors. Can you do that for me?"

"Y-Yes," she says. "But the clan will want to see—"

"She isn't a fucking freak show!" Callan's harsh rebuke echoes around the empty room. "She's mine to control. *Mine.* They'll see her at a time of my choosing."

Zahra's response is strained. "Callan, she survived your fire. I know that makes her unique, but—"

"It changes everything, Zahra."

She takes a quick, sharp breath. "No," she whispers. "You can't let it change anything. Don't let your emotions get in the way of what's best for our clan." Her voice grows in strength and conviction, each syllable pronounced. "You can't feel anything for this angel except hatred."

"I will do what's best for this clan," Callan growls through gritted teeth, shifting his position slightly, and I imagine his golden glare on her. "I want you to make sure Jada locks down this building. Nobody gets in, Zahra. And I mean fucking *nobody.* Can you do that for me?"

I can't see much of Zahra, but I don't miss the press of her lips as she considers my face.

"If you think that's best," she says, her expression closed off. "I'll make sure of it."

Some of the tension leaves Callan's body. "You're my sister and my beta. You're the only one I trust. Obviously, the *nobody* rule doesn't apply to you. If you need me, I'm here."

"I know," she says, as if she never doubted it. She gives him a small, cautious smile before she rises and strides away.

The far door closes behind her.

"Fuck," Callan whispers into the silence.

His arms close tightly around me before he rises to his feet, keeping me pressed against him. Not that I could go anywhere. My head continues to rest on his shoulder, my bound hands against his chest, and my constrained feet are secured behind his lower back.

"You may have survived my shift, but you won't live long if you continue to bleed out," he says.

"We can't have that," I murmur against his chest. "What would happen to your plan, then?"

Whatever fucking plan it is anyway.

He doesn't miss a beat, striding to the side of the room, where he shifts his weight so he can press his palm against a panel on the wall.

A concealed door slides open.

We enter a room that's similar to the one we left behind. Black, marble floor and gleaming, gray walls. Colors that I now realize will more easily hide burn marks. It's massive with a high ceiling, too.

Positioned against the far wall toward the left hand-side of the room is a four-poster bed with posts that appear to be made from steel and rise all the way up to the ceiling, where they're attached. The bed frame also appears to be made from steel, although a thin mattress rests on top of it that's covered in silken, white material—the only flammable substance in the room. There's nothing else on the bed. No pillows, no fluffy blankets.

A wide-open bathroom area sits on the far right of the room with a large, white bath at the front of the space and an open shower in the back corner where the floor gently slopes to catch the water.

There are two doors on the opposite wall—one on each side of the bed.

The structure closest to me on the right-hand side makes me tense up. A silver cage takes up a good portion of the front right corner. It's made of metal bars that reach up to the ceiling like the bed posts do.

There's nothing inside the cage. Not even a pillow.

Callan pauses, hovering for a beat between the cage and the bed before he curses again. Softly.

With a frustrated rumbling sound in his throat and his wings scraping across the ground behind us, he strides toward the side of the bed, where he pauses again. Curses once more. Not so softly this time.

"Fuck it," he says. "You'll fight me either way."

I'm not sure what choices he's trying to decide between, but I don't have time to guess.

His body weight suddenly pushes down on me and, at the same time, he grabs both of my hands. Without his arm supporting my back, gravity drags me backward. Before I know it, he shoves me onto the bed and wrenches my arms up above my head.

His movements are so quick, so strong, that a scream of fury has barely made it to my lips before he yanks my wrists apart, separating the metal chains so that they form instant bracelets again, before snapping them back together.

This time, my arms are tied around the post at the end of the bed.

While my arms are now extended above my head and my back is pressed to the bed, my legs remain clamped around his waist. In the process of leaning over me, his pelvis has pressed to mine and there's not much of a barrier between us except for my underwear and his torn suit pants.

It hasn't escaped me that I'm in an incredibly vulnerable position right now. I understand lust and what it can make humans and supernaturals do. But I've never experienced it. I don't think I'm capable of physical pleasure. Even now, I'm aware of his body—his hard length—between my legs, but the knowledge is clinical and detached.

At least… I think it is.

Every rapid breath he takes as he grips my hips serves to press his pelvis to mine and I'm not sure what to make of the sensations tightening my lower stomach, making my toes curl…

I tell myself that I was born for one purpose and only one purpose: killing.

It's time to remind him of that.

CHAPTER SEVEN

I glare up at Callan, fighting against the conflicting sensations running through my body.

"If you try to bed me, I will kill you," I promise him. "Even if I have to do it with a sheet." My gaze swivels across the sparse options at my disposal as I speak. "Or with a water faucet." *Which I'm sure I can wrench out of the wall. Maybe not right now, but eventually.* "Or with my bare hands."

"Killing is the reason we're here," he says, more softly than I was expecting. "You already have too much blood on your hands. My people's blood."

I snarl up at him. "Not enough. I will have yours, too."

Maybe.

I give my head a little shake because the longer he looms over me, the calmer I feel, and the more my anger fades again. When he was surrounded by fire, I felt his rage and I could finally feel my own, but now that he's quiet and in control…

His presence is like unicorns and fucking rainbows.

I reiterate, "Try anything and I *will* have my revenge." Somehow. *Eventually.* Even if I'm not in a position to kill him right now, I will find a way.

He draws back a little, his wings held tightly to his sides, his biceps bunched, his jaw tight, but other than a sense of frustration, I can't read his thoughts at all.

"I'm keeping you here because it's my home," he says. "And because it's my responsibility to keep my clan safe. My goal, first and foremost, is to take you out of action. If that means killing you, so be it. If I choose to keep you alive, then it's my responsibility to keep you caged."

His gaze flashes across my face. "I have to keep you with me at all times. The risk is mine to bear."

He drops down onto me again, as if to punctuate his point. This time, his wings curve downward too, the edges of them settling against the bed and blocking my view of the room on either side. His downward movement only grinds his hips against mine and my breath stops as heat grows between my legs. I fight the urge to close my eyes and relax into the sensations. Maybe even explore them…

He continues. "As for the fact that this is my *bedroom*, know this: I would rather plunge my cock into an ant's nest than fuck a killer like you."

My eyes snap open. I stare up at him, scrutinizing his features across the mere inches between us. His vehemence indicates that he *believes* he's telling the truth, even if his physical reactions tell a different story. His golden irises are iridescent, the faintest wave of heat slipping across his lips as he exhales.

He's so close to me that I inhale the warmth.

"Your body is making you a liar," I whisper.

He grits his teeth. "My body can feel whatever it feels. It's my will that determines what I do about it."

The longer I peer into his eyes, the wider my own become.

He said that touching any supernatural triggers his dragon and his shift was instant and clearly uncontrollable when it happened, but now I sense his iron will, his control clamped so tightly around his animal that the wild creature I glimpsed earlier is shut down.

"If you're in control, why haven't you shifted back?" I ask.

"My dragon has settled. Once I return to my human form, I won't be able to touch you again without triggering him all over again."

Somehow, the word *touch* is emphasized in my hearing. I tell myself I should be fighting this dragon for my freedom right now. In fact, if I heave my torso and hips far enough to the right, I have a chance to unbalance him. But any movement will grind my pelvis against his, and I'm far too distracted by the contact between our bodies as it is.

Fuck it. I have to try.

Engaging my stomach muscles, I wrench to the right, shoving my hips forward and yanking at the bands around my wrists at the same time.

He stands firm, his feet planted on the ground, his weight bearing down on me and forcing me to stop—but not before his hard length presses perfectly between my legs and I gasp at the pure pleasure that plays through me. My back was already arched, but it tugs up a little and my thighs clamp more tightly around him, wanting to draw him closer.

What. The Fuck. Is this feeling?

It has to be lust. The first time I've felt it.

Callan presses his hands down onto my shoulders. "Be still," he says, his voice throaty. "You're hurting yourself."

The damp across my side tells me that every move I make draws new blood from my wound, but, hell, I don't care. The need to explore this new sensation is overwhelming me.

"Let me go, and I'll stop," I whisper, a raspy response.

He gives me a rough smile. "You won't ever stop. Not unless I give you a reason to want to."

Martha called me a wild animal, and I'm not afraid to act like one. I bare my teeth at him. "Nothing you can say or do will entice me to stop fighting you."

"Then I'll *make* you obey me," he says, giving me reason to pause.

I still myself and watch carefully as he eases himself upright and reaches behind his back. His hands are warm as he wraps them around my ankles, gripping both firmly. His touch is soothing, making me realize just how hard I'm straining against the chains—and just how many bruises I'm developing.

Holding my breath, I prepare myself in case he releases my legs in a bid to free himself. After all, he's as tied to me as I am to him in this position, and he won't be able to stay like this forever. The moment he releases me, I picture myself kicking his perfect chest, somehow pulling myself free...

Instead of separating my ankles behind himself and stepping out of the circle of my legs like I hope he will, he shoves both of my legs toward me, bending my knees to my chest and pushing my ankles together in front of himself so that I'm bound again before I can blink.

"There," he says, his hands pressing down on my bent knees, his thumbs brushing against my inner thighs.

He looks pleased with himself—and I guess he should be— but I'm not without options.

I heave to the right again, angling toward the edge of the bed and pivoting around the post, but he's ready for me.

I release a cry of dismay when the golden chain around my ankles instantly stretches within his fingers, extending and snaking around his own wrist, where it seals up.

Now I'm chained to him.

I kick out, both feet together, hard enough to knock him off-balance, but he jumps out of the way, hefts his arm upward, pulls my legs back onto the bed, and, a second later, beats his wings so that he lifts my lower half back into the air.

Within seconds, he's shot right across the bed to the post

diagonally opposite the one that my wrists are tied around. The chain lengthens as he flies—all the way across the bed—before it tightens when he wraps it around the post, pulling it taut.

I'm secured again, this time with my legs tied together, demurely crossed at the ankles, the chain stretched out to the opposite bed post. Not so demurely, my skirt is hitched all the way up over my hips and my legs are completely exposed.

Callan touches down on the floor on the other side of the bed, his back to me. He exhales a long breath, but he remains shifted, so I guess he isn't done touching me for now.

His shoulders hunch a little before he turns back to me. His gaze follows the curve of my face to my chin, over what must be some hideous bruising, before his focus lowers to my torso and flickers briefly to my feet.

His brow furrows as he fixates on the bloody wound that continues to seep at my waist. "Why haven't you healed already?"

I glare back at him.

"You need to talk to me," he says, "or you aren't going to survive another day, let alone another hour, judging by the state of that wound."

I snarl. "Release me and I'll talk."

He snorts. "Release you, and you'll never talk."

True.

He launches himself toward me, a single beat of his wings elevating him above me before he drops onto the bed. Straddling me, he drops so that his hands rest on either side of my head, his knees on either side of my thighs.

He leans forward again and reaches for my face, brushing the hair from my face, seeming to take care to avoid the worst of the cut across my cheek. His voice lowers, a deep demand for truth as he asks me again, "Why haven't you healed yourself?"

My jaw is locked with anger, but I grind out. "Because I can't. I don't control my healing. This is as fast as it gets."

His golden eyes widen. "But I thought—" He stops. Then he narrows his eyes at me, as if he thinks I'm lying. "How did you kill so many Grudge dragons if you can't heal yourself quickly?"

"Because I didn't let them hurt me," I say. "Unlike your friends who took a knife to me when I couldn't fight back. Fucking cowards."

Callan's lips thin and his eyes turn cold. I expect him to react to the way I've insulted his people, but instead, he seems agitated. "If I'd known you couldn't heal yourself—"

"What?" I ask. "You'd have helped me? Stopped them, perhaps?"

Bitter despair begins to build inside me. I'm bleeding slowly, but too fast for the blood to clot. It's making a big mess of the white sheets I'm lying on. I'm not sure how long I have before I pass out, and after that, I'll die. I can't even free my hands to put pressure on the wound.

For a second, his golden eyes brighten, but it's a dangerous flicker, a sign of the wild animal inside. With another beat of his wings, he lifts off the bed, lands lightly on the left-hand side, and hurries through the door to the left of the bed.

While his back is turned, my focus returns to freeing myself. The relentless need to escape pushes me on despite the numbness creeping through my body.

Gritting my teeth, I yank the golden band around my wrists against the post above my head and strain against it, hoping the metal pole might not be so securely attached to the ceiling as it appears. I discover that it's very well attached when I succeed only in bruising my wrists further.

Not giving up, I pull again, groaning and using all of my muscles in an attempt to stretch the power of the chain and break it like I did before.

It doesn't work.

I stop trying when Callan reappears a moment later carrying a small case.

"You're lucky I have this box of first aid supplies here for my human guards." He doesn't seem surprised that I'm still trying to free myself, but the frustrated press of his lips increases when his focus flicks back to my wound.

Every effort I make opens it. He wasn't wrong when he said I was hurting myself.

But to die here…

Or worse, to be kept captive…

"This won't be pleasant, but it will have to do until I can get proper medical attention for you." He climbs back onto the bed, places the box beside me, and flips open the lid. He pulls out a small glass bottle, a tube that doesn't have a label on it, some gauze, and finally bandages.

My skirt is in the way, so he tears it apart—seemingly without a second thought. I wince when he leverages up the torn material around the wound, ripping the sage-green bodice right up to the base of my bra and all the way down to my hip.

My underwear is fully exposed, but his attention remains on the cut across my side.

I, too, am seeing it fully for the first time.

It's positioned neatly below my lowest left rib, a longer wound than I thought it was, although I've clearly torn it farther in the fight, judging by the ragged ends. It's deeper than I hoped it was. A fresh wash of blood runs from it now that the pressure of my bodice is gone, and I quickly turn my face away from the sight.

My focus snaps back to Callan when he pours a substance over the wound that stings like fiery hell. Then he squeezes a clear liquid out of the tube along the cut, pressing the two sides together as he goes.

"Medical glue," is all he says before he begins taping the wound, his movements slowing, as if he's thinking it through. "This happened in the SUV, not during the fight in the alley."

"You told them not to fuck with me, but they did anyway," I snap. "Some control you have over them."

"Dragon hierarchy is more complicated than you could imagine."

"It seems simple to me," I say. "Your people act out while your back is turned and play nicely when you're watching. All the while, you're losing control of them. There's nothing complicated about that."

He draws back a little, his wings held firmly at his sides, but now there's a gleam in his eyes that wasn't there before. "What else?"

I scowl. "What do you mean… what else?"

He studies my face, as if he's watching for little clues as to my thoughts. "What else have you figured out about my clan?"

I give a shake of my head, feeling uncertain about why he's asking me, since it sounds like he genuinely wants to know. It makes me even warier. I answer his question with a question. "What is this plan your people keep talking about?"

His golden eyes are like small suns as he finishes taping the wound. "You're already part of it."

My brow furrows. I knew that much already.

"What I find curious is that you haven't asked where you are," he says. "The angels have been looking for my home for a long time."

I don't bother mentioning that my senses are honed enough that I've narrowed it down to within a two-mile radius of the concert hall. Not that that really helps in a crowded city.

"A cage is a cage," I say. "I've merely swapped one for another." I'm matter-of-fact, although as I speak, despair pushes at me again. My gaze drifts past him to the ceiling. "I was told I'd die in a cage."

He narrows his eyes at me. "What do you mean, you've swapped one cage for another?"

A slow smile creeps onto my lips. "The angels are afraid of

me. They keep me in a cell." I watch his response carefully, trying to glean information from his reaction, but he's a blank slate now. "Does that surprise you?"

He shakes his head. "The angels don't like anything that doesn't fit their idea of perfection and purity. I'm more surprised you were allowed to live beyond childhood." He purses his lips, seems to think for a moment, and then changes the subject again, "You were panicking at the theater when I arrived at the booth. Why?"

I blink at the abrupt question. If I were in better shape, I might even flush with embarrassment at the memory, but my body is growing colder.

I've lost too much blood and I'm worried that his help came too late.

Like a dream, I remember the way I'd curled up behind the chair at the theater, trying to subdue my growing rage, rocking back and forth, my head pressed to my knees. Overwhelmed. A retort rests on the tip of my tongue, telling him to get fucked, but I halt myself. My vulnerability in that moment is only evidence of my nature. I shouldn't be ashamed of it.

I look him right in his golden eyes. "Because I wanted to kill them all."

His forehead creases. "Who?"

"The people in the audience."

He seems surprised. "Even the humans?"

My snarl increases. "Every last one of them."

"But you don't kill humans." His jaw tightens. "Only dragons. Why do you target my people?"

I narrow my eyes at him. I'm certainly not going to tell him about the Serene Commander's promise of freedom. "You ask a lot of questions."

He leans over me to grip my shoulders. "You don't ask enough." He searches my eyes. "Instead, you make evaluations. You're obviously observant. But this doesn't explain to me why the angels chose you to come after my people. Of all the warriors they've bred over the years, why you? What makes you special?" His grip hardens. "Why are they afraid of you?"

His questions drive home to me that he knows nothing about me. Not my upbringing, not my life, who I am, or what I can do.

I don't know why I was born with a corrupted soul, but I've always known what I am.

I throw him a bone, although the cold in my voice covers the pain I bury deep inside. "I was born impure. I'm a hunter—"

"*How* do you hunt?"

I arch up toward him, my nearly naked chest pressing to his and sending confusing signals to my core. "I sense guilt. It drives me to act. I *need* retribution, so I deliver it."

He doesn't flinch. His expression is hard. As cold as mine. "Then tell me: What am *I* guilty of?"

I give a little shake of my head, my determination receding, my body sinking away from him. "You... I can't sense."

Even now, his presence douses my anger and calms it.

I whisper, "You're fucking faultless."

His lips part as if in surprise. He scrutinizes me for a long moment. "You don't want to kill me. Do you?" he asks, a low, shocked murmur.

I don't confirm his statement, but I don't deny it, either.

His grip on my shoulders softens. "You need to rest now."

My breathing is shallow, and darkness encroaches on my vision. Despite the creeping fear within my heart, I'm warm where he touches me, his thumbs brushing my upper arms in soothing strokes. I allow myself to relax under his touch, telling myself it isn't wrong to take this pleasure. The bed is soft beneath me, the sheets smoother than any I've ever lain on. If I ignore the chains, it's not the worst place I could end up dying.

"You're not done yet," he murmurs, as if he reads my thoughts, his gaze passing across my cheeks, down to my lips, back up to my eyes. "You survived my fire without the protection of dragon wings. You won't die easily."

"Ha." I let out a short laugh that hurts my side. "*Now* you claim to understand me. You don't even know my name."

He leans forward again. "Then tell me it."

A smile tugs at my lips. "I'm sure you can guess the title I was given at birth."

His forehead creases with apparent puzzlement, but he gives himself a shake and his expression slowly hardens.

"You're a means to an end," he says, an out-of-the-blue statement.

I sigh, losing the fight against the cold invading my chest and his constant changes of subject. "I was born to be a means to somebody's end. The Serene Commander's... Now yours..."

My eyes finally close. "If you don't want me to die, I need a blanket. Your home is freezing. I need warmth to have any chance of healing..." My thoughts become jumbled as I fight to stay conscious. "I need... fire..."

"I don't have any blankets in this room," he says softly.

A moment later, something warm wraps around me.

"Liar," I whisper before I pass out.

CHAPTER EIGHT

I wake to gentle hands and a firm female voice. At first, I'm disoriented, wondering if I'm back in my cell at the Cathedral, but the angels have never touched me so gently.

I'm lying on my right side, my upper arm curled in front of my chest and my other arm beneath what feels like a pillow. I'm aware of a soft sheet that covers my front but leaves my back exposed. There's a heavier weight across my lower legs, which could be a blanket now, but I'm not sure.

The memory of Callan's wing closing over me before I blacked out is far more intimate than I'm prepared to think about. Especially as I'm quickly aware that, other than my underpants, I'm naked beneath the sheet and I'm not sure how I got this way.

More importantly, and even more suddenly, I realize that I'm not chained.

If only my reflexes weren't so sluggish, I would leap up right away and get myself the hell out of here. But my limbs are heavy as I finally force myself to open my eyes.

Callan is the first thing I see.

He's sitting opposite me on a metal chair that's positioned in front of the bathing area on that side of the room. He leans forward slightly, his elbows on his knees, studying me quietly and carefully. He's shifted back into his human form and is wearing a gray T-shirt and gray sweats, both slightly too large. His hair is tousled, a sharp contrast to the slick outfit he wore when I thought he was a bodyguard.

Whoever's touching me is standing behind me, and it's obvious that she hasn't realized I'm awake. Of course, I've only opened my eyes a crack and I certainly haven't jolted or inhaled deeply.

I'm trained to lie still and wait for my prey and that's what I do now. Waiting and wondering about the risk Callan's taking by unchaining me and bringing a stranger into my midst, especially since it seems that he's also removed the wire contraption that was securing my wings.

He gives no sign of alarm, although his gaze is intense.

"I know you pay me not to ask questions, Callan," the woman standing behind me says, her hands resting lightly against my upper shoulder, "but this woman has clearly been beaten." She pauses and I picture her pinning him with a stare. "By *multiple* assailants. And this isn't the first time."

Her fingers feather my back as she trails them down my spine. Callan's eyes narrow, piercing me, as if he expects me to react at any second and he's preparing for when I do.

I don't move a muscle. Not until I understand who this woman is. Her light touch isn't threatening, and her voice reminds me of the wind through the leaves of a strong tree—resilient and certain.

"Have you seen these scars?" she asks.

Callan gives her the barest nod of his head. *Yes.*

My eyes narrow. If he saw the scars on my back, then he might have undressed me.

"If I didn't know better, I'd say she was whipped with some

sort of medieval instrument," the woman continues. "Possibly a cat-o'-nine tails. As crazy as that sounds."

I remember the beating well. It was the last one the Serene Commander gave me. I was fourteen and I tried to leave the Cathedral because I wanted to see the outside world. She told me that hitting me hurt *her* more than it hurt *me*. That was the first time I wondered if the Serene Commander was capable of lying. Even so, I never tried to leave the Cathedral without her permission again.

Callan's reaction is bigger than before, his eyebrows drawing down, a question forming in his eyes. "I thought those were scars from some kind of knife."

I guess he imagined I got them in a fight. I'm sure, given my lifestyle, that would be more predictable. Despite the pain, I should have healed completely, but the whip was imbued with a magical substance that means I will wear the scars forever. They're a brand that warns other angels to stay away from me.

"A knife would cut cleanly," the woman says. "These scars are ragged, as if her flesh and skin were flayed. The end points are deeper, like the metal tips at the end of each lash."

Her hands leave my back, and her voice sounds agitated. "Again, I know you pay me not to ask questions, but why the hell would you assume she was cut with a knife?"

"She's an assassin," Callan says, watching me so carefully that I still feel chained.

Without pause, the woman snaps back. "Fine. You don't have to tell me the truth, but don't minimize what this woman has been through with some bullshit—"

"It's the truth."

She lets out a laugh. "You're seriously telling me that this woman is—"

"A killer like you've never seen before. An extremely dangerous one."

There's a longer pause this time. "You're not joking. Are you?"

For the first time since I woke up, Callan's focus switches to a point above me. "Jada, would I joke about a serious threat?"

Jada. I roll the woman's name around in my mind. He mentioned her when he was speaking with his sister. It was in the context of ensuring that the human guards secured the building.

She's *human*. I mentally kick myself for not realizing it right away, but then, it's impossible to tell a dragon shifter from a human without moonlight, so she could have been either.

It might explain why Callan removed the chains, if he didn't want her to see that I'm his prisoner, but he's taking a massive risk that I won't kill her.

Then I remember. He asked me why I was panicking at the theater and I all but confirmed I don't kill humans. Of course, that doesn't mean I won't start now…

"Should I be worried?" Jada asks.

"Very."

Her hand tightens around my shoulder. "Then why the fuck is she in your bedroom?"

He looks directly at me. "It's very important that I keep her alive."

Jada sounds wary. "What for?"

He gives her a smile that plays around the corners of his mouth in mysterious ways. "I pay you not to ask questions."

"Dammit, Callan." Jada sighs. "I guess I should be satisfied with the few answers you've given me."

Callan finally rises to his feet and folds his arms across his chest. "She's in bad shape. Tell me you can help her."

Jada sounds affronted. "Of course I can help her. If you had any doubt about that, you wouldn't have called me. Now, get the fuck out so I can get on with it."

He grimaces. "I don't think I should leave."

"Why not?"

"Because she's awake."

I'm impressed with how fast the woman reacts. I hear her quick step back—a single footfall—before there's a metallic click and the barrel of what is unmistakably a gun presses to the back of my head.

"Easy now, lady," Jada says, and this time, I know she's speaking to me. "I'm here to help you."

"Then point the gun elsewhere," I say, gratified by how strong my voice sounds. I'm not sure why Callan even brought her here. I'm fine. I don't need any help.

I give her a moment to remove the weapon, but Jada holds the barrel against me a second too long.

Callan told me that dragons hit back. Well, so do I.

I swing, snatch the gun with one hand, and shove the woman with my other hand, my palm flat. She slides along the floor and nudges the wall—by which time, I've turned the gun on her.

I've ended up sitting on the edge of the bed and somehow, I've managed to keep hold of the sheet covering my breasts, although it's remained open at the back, which I assume means Callan's getting an eyeful of my backside.

Jada holds both of her hands out, her expression falling like any sensible person's would if their weapon were turned on them that fast. She was quick, but her human reflexes will never match mine.

She's dressed in military-style pants and a collared shirt—a heavy beige material that's clean and pressed. Her skin is light olive, her hair is dark brown and shoulder-length, and her eyes are deep brown with the blackest lashes.

A second gun rests at her hip, but she doesn't go for it. Maybe she realizes she won't be quick enough or maybe—less likely—she's taking a leap of faith that I won't kill her on the spot.

Keeping her within my sights and tucking the sheet across

my chest, I remove the gun's clip, along with the final bullet from the chamber, and drop the dismantled pieces onto the bed. Confident that Callan won't try to stop me leaving—since grabbing me would trigger his dragon and kill the human—I see my chance to leave.

Rising to my feet, I say to her, "Thanks for my freedom," right before my legs give out.

I stumble against the bed post and nearly drop the sheet. My right hand shoots out, gripping the pole, trying to stop myself from sliding down it.

What the...?

My legs are as weak as jelly and the floor is starting to look really good.

Jada peels herself off the wall. "You've lost a lot of blood and you have a concussion," she says. "You need to lie down."

"Nope," I say, clinging hard to the post, finally losing the sheet as my head swims and vertigo drags the floor up at me. "I'm fine."

The tension leaves her shoulders, and she lowers her hands with a scoff. "You're paler than the lilies at my grandmother's funeral."

Clinging hard, I scowl at her. "It's my natural coloring."

"Sure," she says. "A nice shade of about-to-pass-out. It'll look really good on you when you hit the floor."

I can't stay upright, and it's only because I'm angled toward the bed that I don't hurt myself on impact when I collapse against it.

"Shit." Jada bends to me before glancing up at Callan. She must be satisfied that I'm no longer a danger to her because she takes her eyes off me to speak with him.

"Well, my haphephobic friend," she says to him. "I guess you're not going to help me get her up, are you?"

Callan shakes his head. "That's why you'll be getting a bonus this month."

I squint up at Jada. "Haphe-what?"

"Fear of touch," she says matter-of-factly.

Huh. That must be how he explains to his staff why he never touches anyone. It grates on me a little that he would use a real fear for his own purposes. "So that's why he hasn't come to your rescue."

Jada shrugs. "He's rich. He can pay others to do the touching for him." She pauses. Seems to rethink. Flushes, but shakes it off.

She pulls my arm over her shoulder, ignoring my nakedness as she heaves me upward. She's strong for a human, although I'm not the heaviest supernatural. Angels are built light so that we can fly higher than other magical beings.

Once I'm lying down, she immediately covers me up with the blanket that remained on the bed. She retrieves a large, black bag from the corner of the room, and sets to work.

Within minutes, she's attached multiple surgical lines to my arms and injected me with painkillers and antibiotics. I'm not convinced they'll work—until the painkillers kick in and I breathe a sigh of relief. Funny how I don't realize how much pain I'm coping with until it's gone.

She's gentle. Hers is the kindest touch I've ever experienced, and every time she speaks, her voice is like fresh air. It's completely unexpected and catches me off guard. I wish Callan's presence wasn't filling my senses because I really want to know about this woman's true nature.

She explains what she's doing each step of the way, telling me which drugs she's administering and why. Talking to me as she refreshes the bandaging on my wound, telling me it's looking good for now, but my head wound is the one she needs to monitor.

"You need to rest now," she finally says. "Will you have any trouble sleeping? I can give you something if you like?"

If I like? It's such a startling request. What would I *like?*

I'd like to be living another life. Maybe as a pure angel who brings light to people who need it. Maybe even as a Sentinel who guards the angels' greatest treasures. I'd *like* to be someone else, somewhere else.

She waits patiently while I stare at her. Despite Callan's warning that I'm dangerous, she hasn't treated me like I'm her enemy. Well, other than initially pointing a gun at my head, but she hasn't attempted anything like that again. It astounds me that she hasn't. The dragons I met would have taken advantage of my weakness and ended me already, but this human—whose life I could usually take in two seconds flat—is trying to help me.

The backs of my eyes burn with tears I didn't know I had in me.

Fuck.

Part of me wants to take her up on her offer of sleep because I won't be able to fully defend myself until I'm stronger. The other half of me is anxious about what could happen while I rest.

I make a decision. "Knock me out."

Callan didn't have to bring the human to help me. He's gone to great lengths to keep me alive. Whatever he's planning, he wants me well and whole. I have to take advantage of that while it lasts.

"Okay." She measures out a dose and injects it into the canula. "That should kick in quickly." She adjusts the blanket before she brushes the hair from my forehead. "I'll come back to check on you again soon. You might not be awake for that, though, because I'll keep you sedated until I'm happy that your concussion is under control. Okay?"

I give her a nod to show I understand before I roll back onto my side, watching her pack up and head toward Callan. She stops a good two steps away from him, and it's not until she's standing close to him that I fully appreciate how massive he is.

He towers over her.

She doesn't seem to care as she glares up at him. "I'll come back every few hours, but call me if her condition worsens. And for fuck's sake, she needs some new clothes. The bloody dress I cut off her is only good for the trash."

"I plan on taking care of that," he says, striding ahead of her to the door that leads into the lounge room. He presses his palm to the wall beside it to let her out.

My heart sinks to see that the same security mechanism is required to open the door from this side. It will make it harder for me to escape, but given how much effort he put into chaining me when I first arrived, he must believe that I have some hope of breaking the door down by sheer brute force alone.

As Jada exits the room, I catch sight of four men, all of them dressed in the same beige military-style clothing, all heavily muscled and armed with multiple guns each. They must be a second layer of defense and once again, Callan would be counting on me not harming a human.

One of the men with dark skin and a crewcut turns to Callan and Jada. "Everything okay, Callan?"

Callan gives him a quick nod. "All good. Thanks, Brock."

Jada pauses in the doorway. "Are you sure I shouldn't stay for now?"

Again, Callan nods. "I'll be fine. She'll be fine. I promise I'll call you if I need you."

Jada hesitates another moment. "One day, you'll let me put surveillance in here."

"In my bedroom?" He laughs. "Fuck no."

I find it curious that he seems so much more at ease with these humans than he is with his own people, laughing with them, talking with them as if they're his peers.

Within moments, the door closes, and I find myself sinking further into the mattress. The sheets are no longer bloody, so Jada might have changed them when she got rid of my dress.

However it happened, I'm grateful. Clean sheets are like a clean slate.

The medicine is kicking in fast like Jada promised, so my thoughts are groggy by the time Callan returns to the bedside, casting me into shadow while the door slides closed behind him, shutting off the humans from view.

"Who is she?" I ask, my voice soft and a little slurred.

"Ex-military," he replies. "She's trained in combat medicine. Each of my human guards is handpicked for a skill they possess. Brock is a sniper, Dermot and Sean are close combat fighters, Paul is a strategist. Many supernaturals discount the strength and skills that humans possess." His expression is flinty. "I don't."

"They're your friends," I say before he can turn away toward the chair again.

His focus is piercing. "They'd die for me," he says. "And the feeling's mutual."

I'm stunned. "You'd die for them? Why?"

"Some humans have the heart of a dragon," he says. "Even if they can't shift into one."

As he turns back to the chair, I catch the faraway look in his eyes, the sudden hunch in his shoulders, and I'm surprised to finally break through the calm sunshine exterior to catch the drifting scent of desert sand and burning heat... the far-off echo of remembered gunfire... explosions of metal and clay...

I try to catch my breath. "You fought in a human war."

He stiffens, remaining with his back to me, as he murmurs, "How the fuck did you—?"

He falls quiet, and I don't explain how I know. He already asked me why the angels sent me after him, and I told him it's because I sense guilt. I guess I didn't explain that sensing someone's nature comes hand in hand with understanding the events in their life that have contributed to who they are.

He remains silent for so long that I start to drift off before he says, "Supernaturals avoid human wars, and particularly human warzones. I saw my chance to live free of my dragon's curse. Away from other supernaturals. A place where I could move about without fear of exposure." He shrugs. "I thought that if I died in a human war, what of it? But those humans out there, they kept me alive."

My eyelids are drooping and my voice is a bare whisper as I take a guess. "They think your fear of touch is a symptom of the war."

His response is vehement. "It isn't a lie. I can kill the people I care about simply by accidentally brushing up against them. It scares the fuck out of me." His chest suddenly rises and falls more rapidly, his fists clench and unclench, and I'm shocked to realize that... he really is afraid. Maybe more shocked that he admitted it. I never thought an alpha would admit any weakness.

Again, he breathes out slowly, a controlled exhalation, and I can practically hear him counting to slow his breathing down and get his fear under control. "My dragon is an uncontrollable weapon. Flashbacks are a part of my life. I live under the constant threat of exposing the existence of dragons, or of killing someone I love. Some days, I wonder if my dragon will turn on the humans too. So I limit my contact with them as well. It's why I rarely leave my home."

The Serene Commander called Callan Steele a recluse. The angels couldn't identify him, let alone find members of his clan. His appearance at the concert hall was a rare event—one he must have devised. Knowing the risk he took... all those people he could have bumped into...

Although, thinking back, he had arrived late, kept his distance from me, stayed to the side of the balcony, and then waited for the rest of the audience to clear out before he left.

It was still a massive risk. All to capture me.

Now, here I am. In his home. Ironically, this is the place the angels have been looking for. If it weren't for my wounds and the fact that I'm his prisoner, my goal to identify and find Callan Steele would be coming together perfectly right now.

Inwardly, I scoff at myself. Some fucking goal.

"I do everything I can to ensure that my dragon doesn't hurt someone I care about," Callan says, his expression hardening. "Just as I will do everything in my power to ensure that you never again hurt anyone I care about."

The determination in his speech can't cut through the weight of the medication that's making my breathing even and peaceful. "What about your sister?" I ask. "And your clan? Would you die for them, too?"

Callan's response is a faraway rumble and I'm asleep before I hear what he says.

CHAPTER NINE

Music filters through my senses, a gentle harmony of violins and a piano, and I'm disoriented again. Did I fall asleep at the theater? Was it all a nightmare?

My eyes fly open, my body immediately answering my call to move and a second later, I'm crouched on the bed, eyes wide, ready to defend myself.

"Easy." Callan rises from the seat opposite me, his hands outstretched. "Take a breath, angel, and don't do anything reckless."

I was expecting to find the medical apparatus still attached to me, but I'm free of all lines and bandages. A soft T-shirt covers my body to my hips, and after a quick pat-down check, I ascertain that I'm wearing underpants but not a bra.

Pressing my hands to my cheeks, I discover that the cut on my face feels nicely sealed, although my skin is still tender. When I flip up the bottom of the shirt, I find the knife wound uncovered so I can see that my skin is neatly knitted together and appears to be healing well.

Most importantly, I don't ache so badly anymore.

But to be healed to this extent means I must have been passed out for a while. Definitely for days.

Quickly scanning the room for threats, I find only Callan. I can't identify a device from which the soft music is playing. The rest of the room is as bare as when I first arrived.

Actually, more bare.

Weirdly, the cage is gone. *But... where?* It's not the kind of structure Callan could have removed with a click of his fingers. Come to think of it, I don't remember seeing it when Jada was here, either.

"Where is the cage?" I demand to know.

A pleased expression grows on Callan's face. He gives me the smallest smile as he leans back into his chair. "It's good to see you're feeling better."

"Not good for you," I say, noting that he didn't answer me. Maybe the cage is concealed in the wall somehow and can be returned if he wants it. But the human is gone, so the absence of chains around my wrists is unsettling.

I shiver as the cold environment registers again. "Why is it so cold? Why are there no windows? Is it because of your fire?" My brow furrows. "What day is it?"

He continues to sit calmly. "It's good that you're asking questions."

"Answers would be better."

He inclines his head. "I'll answer every question you ask, for as long as you don't fight me."

I narrow my eyes at him. "It's an interesting deal you're trying to make. Answers in exchange for peace." I shake my head, prepared to spread my wings and fight my way free. "I'm not sure that peace is in my nature."

My focus shifts to the place in the wall that conceals the exit. I may have been partially delirious when I woke up the first time, but I memorized its location.

Callan's shoulders tense as he follows my line of sight.

Even in his human form, he's one of the largest people I've ever met. I have no guarantees that I'll survive a fight with his dragon. Going along with him seems safest for now. Especially since I'm not bound, which means I'll have more opportunities to escape if I get my timing right.

"Why am I not in chains?" I ask, eyeing him suspiciously.

He leans forward, his expression clear, not a speck of malice in it. "Because I don't want you to swap one cage for another."

I'm surprised he remembered what I said to him about the cell the angels keep me in.

I retort, "This room may not have bars, but, trust me, it's a cage."

He shrugs as he rises to his feet. "Given that this is my home, I guess that puts us in a cage together. Are you hungry?"

I'm starving, but I'm also wary.

Without waiting for me to respond, he strides to the wall, presses his hand against it to open the door, and disappears through it.

I expect the door to close behind him, and I'm stunned when it remains open. Is he playing mind games with me? Will the door slam shut as I approach?

Sliding off the bed and dropping to the floor, I eye the opening warily before I take a few steps toward it. Then another few.

The cold air from the far room wafts through the opening and I take a step back to scoop up the blanket from the bed and wrap it around my shoulders before I finally step up to the door.

Will it slam shut when I'm only halfway through and hurt me? But if that were his intention, then why go to all of the trouble of healing me?

A mountain of horrible possibilities assails me before I launch myself through the door, skidding on the other side, staring back at it.

Nothing untoward happens and the scent of food overwhelms me. My stomach lurches when I spy the table within the sunken lounge on the far side of the room. It's full of plates, covered in food.

Damn, I'm hungry.

Callan is strolling casually toward the lounge, but the moment that I turn to consider the front door, he seems to sense it.

Stopping in his tracks and turning back to me, he says, "I've taken measures to ensure you can't leave. You won't get through the door before I stop you. Put escape out of your mind, angel. Come and eat."

I know he's fast, but I'm closer to the door than he is. He told me to put escape out of my mind, but it's all I can think about.

I have nobody to blame for my current situation but myself. The Serene Commander told me that Callan Steele would be at the concert hall, and he was. It's my fault that I misidentified him. I need to get to safety and make a new plan.

Getting out of this building is my first goal.

I don't stop to second-guess my chances.

Turning my back to him, I pull the soft shirt up over my head, my loose hair swinging against my naked skin before I tie the shirt around my breasts to cover them, deliberately securing it low so the material won't hinder my wings.

He doesn't move toward me, and he sounds more curious than alarmed. "What are you—?"

I glance at him, my muscles tensing, and his posture changes, his shoulders squared.

"Don't do it," he says, a warning in his voice.

Bursting into action, I run as fast as I can, my feet barely touching the floor before I leap. My black wings thump out at my sides, and I angle downward, a single beat pushing me forward, my fists outstretched, the momentum giving me the strength I'll need to punch through the door.

There's a glint of gold from multiple points at the edge of my vision and then—

Whoomph!

I scream when I hit what feels like a brick wall, the backward pressure wrenching me away from the door and into the air. Hot bands wrap around my wrists, ankles, and even my stomach, and a startlingly cold object hits my back—the same sensation that forced my wings to retract outside the concert hall.

Fuck! No!

It all happens so fast that I struggle to process it. My wings fold back on me, and the golden bands spin me in the air like I'm some kind of puppet until I come chest-to-chest with a raging dragon shifter.

Callan hauls me up against him, his arms closing around me, his wings spreading out at his sides, fire rushing from his lips and exploding around us. The shirt I wrapped around my breasts singes at the edges while his shirt disintegrates completely, burning off his chest.

His skin is hard, his grip harder, dragging my body closer while the golden bands around my wrists tug at my arms, forcing my back into an arch.

"I'm not letting you go." His voice is low, the snarl of a beast.

My eyes water with the heat of fire raging around us. The first time I was encased in his flames, I held my breath, afraid to inhale, but this time, anger overrides my survival instincts. Callan's presence does nothing to smother my rage—in fact, my anger is growing faster within me now that he's shifted.

I throw my head back with a challenge. "I thought you didn't want me to swap one cage for another."

"My home doesn't have to be a cage," he says, his wings sweeping the flames. "Stop fighting me, and give in to the fact that you're mine now."

I shiver as I realize that Callan's dragon is fully in control of him, and the dragon's intentions are simple: trap me, keep me.

I'm not sure if my shiver is caused by apprehension or delight, because the wild heart of me is responding to the roughness of his hold, his voice, his intense focus on me.

With every breath I take, I inhale liquid fire. I'm shocked to realize that, this time, I didn't hold my breath. More shocked that the flames aren't burning me from the inside out, but instead, they're warming me the same way that Callan's presence normally does. I strain against the golden chains, but this time, it's to pull toward him.

The chains ease up a little, allowing my arms to return to my sides while the loose ends curve outward and back around his hips. He told me that they're made from dragon's gold, and only the dragon who owns the gold can control them. Right now, they seem to be doing his bidding without any outward action that I can see.

His arms shift, too, one hand rising up to cup the back of my head, while his other arm supports my back, keeping me aloft with him in the air.

It's only now that I realize the fire extinguishers haven't triggered. My quick glance upward tells me that—surprisingly—his fire isn't reaching the ceiling or the walls or even the sunken lounge behind him.

My breathing intensifies, growing panicked, as I realize that every time I inhale...

I'm pulling his fire into my body. I'm containing it.

His lips curve into a smile that only strengthens the mysterious glint in his eyes.

"Keep inhaling, angel," he says, shifting to press his hand to my heart, right against the scorched edges of the T-shirt I tied around my chest. "You'll stay warm this way."

Warm doesn't come close to describing how I feel right now. Every part of me feels alive. It's like I reached beyond myself and touched a spark that, somehow, feels both very familiar but also very new.

Despite the fire I'm dragging into my body, I don't exhale it again.

I can barely speak. "How am I doing this?"

His expression softens a little. "I don't know, but I'm determined to find out."

The chains rest downward now, hanging from my hands toward the floor, leaving me free to press against Callan—or to thrash against his hold if I want to.

I hesitate. Uncertain now.

There's more to this dragon than I thought.

There's more to *me* than I thought.

His voice is low, an intoxicating growl. "Stay with me." His upper hand strokes across my back in swirls that make my skin tingle. "I'll give you everything you need."

"Except my freedom," I murmur, a heated breath.

"Give me a day and you won't want your freedom."

What could he possibly give me that would entice me to remain his prisoner? Nothing could outweigh the Serene Commander's promise of redemption for my soul.

Could it?

I speak carefully, not much more than a whisper. "At the end of the day, if I want to leave, will you let me?"

He shakes his head. "You won't want to leave."

I search his golden eyes since he didn't give me a clear promise to let me go. If he's lying, I can't tell, and that's what scares me most.

For once, I have to take a chance without knowing the true nature of the person I'm dealing with.

"I'll give you one day," I say. "Just one."

CHAPTER TEN

Callan lowers us to the floor, his golden wings circling the air around me without touching me.

His hand slips from my chest as he retracts his wings and steps back. At the same time, the chains unfurl from around my body, opening so they don't grate against my skin before they glide up into the air.

I follow their path back to the corners of the room nearest to the front door, where they adhere to the ceiling and blend, color-shifting, into the silver surface. A clever camouflage. I don't know much about dragon's gold, but so far, it's clear to me that it behaves like a living entity, and I don't understand how Callan controls it.

Now that the chains are positioned near the door again, they will no doubt be ready to catch me if I break my promise to stay for the day.

The wire contraption lifts off my back, releasing my wings, and I finally get to see it, surprised at how finely crafted it appears. It's like a golden spiderweb the width and breadth of my shoulders, a mesh trap. Like the chains, it adheres to the ceiling above the front door.

Callan rolls his shoulders, his eyes closing briefly as his wings fold back so far that I can't see them anymore and his skin loses its sheen. His hair appeared brighter when he shifted, but now it returns to the darkest brown.

I'm left standing in the middle of the floor, unbound, barely dressed. Despite the freezing air, I'm warm just like he promised.

Callan's eyes glint with fading gold. "That fire in your heart right now. It's mine."

I don't deny it. Lifting my hands and arms to study them, I imagine I see a new sheen glistening on my skin, but it could just as easily be a reflection off Callan's body.

He takes a step back, remaining shirtless while his dragon fades completely. His shift is slow and smooth. The Grudge and Scorn dragons I've fought shift rapidly—the Grudge awkwardly, the Scorn sharply, like a flicking blade—but watching Callan change back to his human form is like watching the sunlight change angles. He's as warm in my senses now as he was when he was exhaling ribbons of flame.

I remind myself: I'm staying with him to find answers.

"What is that music?" I ask as the quiet violins continue to play in the background.

The corner of his mouth twitches up. "Do you like it?"

"It sounds like the Philadelphia Orchestra."

"It *is* the Philadelphia Orchestra."

I tilt my head.

"A recording of them," he clarifies. "Since you seemed to enjoy it so much the other night."

I had. It was the most beautiful sound I'd ever heard. It still is. He called me observant, but he must be, too.

He turns toward the food, his posture more relaxed than before. "Come and eat. I'll answer your questions."

My stomach growls so loudly that there could be a small dragon hiding within it. I bounce on the balls of my feet for a moment, trying to decide if I should untie my shirt and pull it on again—but the edges are visibly singed, and the material could now have holes in awkward places.

I stride toward the food, getting a good look at the layout of the sunken lounge for the first time. It's carved into the floor in a rectangular shape with a step down on the closest edge and seats cut into the marble around the other three sides.

"I wasn't sure what you'd like, so I had everything made for you," Callan says, gesturing to the table that sits in the middle of the sunken area.

It holds every conceivable breakfast food. There are the basics like toast, pieces of fruit, and jugs of various juices, along with every sort of egg from scrambled to sunny side up. Also sausages, bacon, and a multitude of cereals, together with milk, and finally a pot of coffee, which I've never tried.

My eyes grow wide as I consider my choices. The angels keep me on a simple diet. I've smelled bacon but never tasted it, so it's the first food I reach for after I slide onto the marble seat opposite Callan. I leave the coffee for now because I'm not sure how my body will react to the stimulant.

While I fill my plate with small samples of food, Callan leans back in his seat, his pose casual. He doesn't say anything as I pick the foods I want to try. I don't take too much of anything since I have no idea if I'll like them—or if my stomach will tolerate them. I don't want to spend the next few hours vomiting because I've eaten something too rich.

"Giving me access to cutlery is a dangerous thing to do," I say, turning a butter knife over in my hands as I continue to assess my food options.

He doesn't seem perturbed. "No more dangerous than giving you access to a sheet or a water faucet."

I scoff, remembering my threat when he first took me to his bedroom. I use the knife to butter my toast instead of flinging the blade at him.

It's beautiful toast. Thickly cut and crispy at the edges.

Swallowing the first bite, I'm unable to hide my appreciative sigh, but I quickly refocus. "You promised me answers."

"I'll start from the first." He continues to watch me carefully as he speaks, a scrutiny that makes me feel like I'm a puzzle he's trying to solve. "The cage swivels back into the wall; it's a mechanism to conceal it from my human friends. My home is cold because I run hot—the air-conditioning helps me regulate my temperature. There are no windows because I can't risk being seen if I shift unexpectedly—and because these walls are specially designed to contain my fire. As for the time of day, it's morning. You were asleep for three days. Four nights, to be exact." He rubs his chin. "I think those were your initial questions."

I swallow carefully. I wasn't expecting him to remember exactly what I asked when I woke up, and I file away his attention to detail, since perhaps dragons have sharp memories.

"Explain dragon's gold to me," I say.

He makes a non-committal noise and I wonder how much detail he will give me, considering anything he tells me could help me escape the chains in future.

He holds his hand up and without him uttering a single word, a band of gold peels off the wall behind him, its golden hue only becoming apparent as it reveals itself.

Fuck. I consider the walls with renewed distrust, since this new band wasn't one that caught me before, and it makes me wonder how many more are hidden around the room.

This band is shorter than the ones near the exit. It floats down to Callan's open palm and wraps itself around his hand before he closes his fist around it.

"Dragon's gold is created over hundreds of years and passed down through families. It starts with ordinary metal that must be hoarded until it becomes a living substance that listens and senses the will of its owner. Every dragon keeps their hoard in a vault, the location of which is known only to them."

That matches what I already knew—that dragons hoard gold and jewels—and partly explains what was a surprise to me—that the gold could come alive.

"If it will only obey you, how did I break it the other night?" I ask.

Callan's expression hardens. "I don't believe it was because of you, but because of Sophia."

I'm baffled. And disappointed. If it had something to do with Sophia, then it might not happen again. I keep my question nonchalant. "Why do you say that?"

"Because Tyler doesn't treat his gold well. He forces it into the shape of jewelry at his whim and lays cold jewels over the top of it. Gifts for Sophia. As you probably know, dragons hoard jewels too, but again, we need to keep them for many years and treat them with care before they take on living properties and can exist symbiotically with the gold.

"I have only a few pieces of jewelry made from my gold and those were crafted over the course of several years. It's important to only choose the metal that craves stability, combine it with stones that have been carefully honed, and even then, you have to lay the gold and the jewels side by side and allow them to unite on their own." He leans back. "No good relationship can be forced."

I scoff, since every relationship I've ever known has been forced. "That doesn't explain why I broke my chains."

"Sophia's bracelet," he says. "The one she was wearing. It would have triggered my gold to want to get away from her. For a few moments, its needs were the same as yours. When you pushed her away from you, its needs were met, and after that, it resumed its loyalty to me."

I hide my disappointment now that there's little likelihood

that I'll break through the gold again. Assuming he's telling me the truth.

My next question is more careful because, once again, I'm not sure how honest he will be. "Why does your dragon react to touch?"

Callan gives me a smile, but it carries a steely edge. "If my dragon perceives a threat, he wants to destroy it. It seems that as far as he's concerned, every supernatural is a threat."

He leans forward again, his cinnamon eyes raking across my face. "We aren't so different that way, you and I."

I give him a reluctant nod, unable to disagree. "Has your dragon always been this way?"

Callan shakes his head. "It didn't start until I turned eighteen. Until then, I hadn't shifted at all, and I wasn't sure if I would. Some dragons never do. We don't know why, but it's happening more and more as our species dies out."

I pause my chewing, remembering the way Tyler had thrown himself in front of his wife when Callan's fire had raged through this room. I knew that modern dragon shifters had limited shifting abilities, but not that some couldn't shift at all. "Is Sophia one of those dragons who can't shift?"

He nods. "She is."

"That must be difficult," I say carefully. "Does she cast a dragon's shadow in moonlight?"

"She does not."

Hardly a dragon. That's what the Serene Commander would say if she could hear this conversation. *Barely worth the effort to destroy.* In her eyes, this would be more evidence that these shifters are mere imposters.

I shake it off and direct the conversation back to Callan. "When was your first shift?"

"When I least expected it," he says. "I lived my life like any human with far too much money at my disposal. I dated, partied. And then one day, Zahra hugged me like she had a hundred times before."

He picks up an apple and turns it over in his hands. "My dragon surfaced and nearly killed her. Luckily, her wings are as strong as mine and her reflexes are second to none. She was able to protect herself. As soon as I realized I couldn't control my shift, I took myself far away from her and our family."

"Is that when you went to fight in the human war?"

There's a new tension around Callan's eyes. He grips the apple so hard that its surface bursts, but he doesn't seem to care about the pulp squeezing between his fingers. "The old alpha took advantage of my absence."

"What happened?" I ask quietly.

"He thought my father was conspiring against him, so when I left, he went after my family. He killed my step-mother—Zahra's mother—then my father. You've experienced what a dragon can do with his fists, so you'll understand how angry I was when I heard about it."

I try to suppress my shudder, to not feel the rage he must be feeling right now. "How did Zahra survive?"

"She escaped. Badly injured. She flew halfway around the world to find me and tell me what had happened."

At first, I assume he means in an airplane, but then my eyes widen. "Wait… She flew? As in, using her wings?"

He gives a terse nod. "When she couldn't find me, she spent some time in Japan, learning from the old dragon masters. By the time she figured out where I was, she was strong enough to challenge the alpha herself." His voice lowers. "But by then, she had a reason not to."

I'm curious to learn more about his sister, but before I can ask, he continues. "I came back, challenged him, and burned his heart to ash."

My lips part with a quickly indrawn breath. "Who was he?"

"His name isn't important. What matters is that he was

Martha's husband and Sophia's father. Also important is the fact that Tyler married Sophia—despite her inability to shift—because he thought the old alpha would pass the leadership on to him. Instead, the Dread became mine."

I chew my thoughts as intensely as I savor my food. I recall the tension between Tyler and Callan outside the concert hall, and then the way that Martha had ordered Callan to get me—the 'wild animal'—under control. Also, the way Sophia had turned up at Callan's home despite what was clearly an order to stay away that night. "So Tyler covets the leadership, Martha pretends she still has power, and Sophia…?"

"Sophia is caught between her mother and her husband," Callan says. "She has no power in either of those relationships, so she acts out as a result."

I put my fork down and carefully consider Callan across the table. "Now you have me."

He taps the table, still studying me carefully, both of us scrutinizing the other, and I suddenly struggle to swallow the food in my mouth.

"Now I have you." For the first time, his irises morph to pure juniper green, a color that suddenly reminds me less of a burned field and more of snow-covered fir trees in winter. Their leaves are sharp.

His dragon's snarl sounds in his voice. "You're the angels' greatest weapon. You're the only angel—the only supernatural, other than another dragon—who has succeeded in killing my kind. My plan was to make it clear to the angels that even their greatest weapon can die at my hands. That they should fear me."

I can't eat another mouthful. "You planned to send my charred heart back to them."

"Ultimately, yes."

I'm cold despite the warmth of the flames I inhaled that still heat my body. "Ultimately?"

His smile is icy. "Before that, I planned to use you to lure them out. Kill them one by one until they learn that coming after me or my people means death."

I remember the way he'd placed my hair clip beside my purse—the way he asked me if the angels would come for me. He didn't believe me when I said they wouldn't. He *wanted* them to come after me.

"But now you've discovered that your fire can't hurt me," I whisper. "My heart will not be burned by you."

His gaze is shadowed, and yet somehow, it heats me to my core. "My instinct is to keep you alive," he says. "To keep you at my side. No matter what it takes. Even if it means enticing you to stay by whatever means possible."

He told me that if I stayed with him, he would give me everything I need. It's a seductive promise. A wicked promise.

It lulled me into sitting down and eating with him.

It doesn't mean he won't kill me eventually. After all, he could drive a dagger into my heart instead of burning it.

As if he reads my thoughts, he says, "I could have killed you at any time in the last three days while you slept. I'm not sure that you would have had the same restraint if our positions were reversed."

I give him a quick shake of my head. "You would be dead."

Probably.

"Where does that leave me?" I ask.

"You're a mystery I intend to solve," he says. "And a power I need to control." His voice becomes steely. "Make no mistake, angel. If I can't control you, I have to kill you. I'd rather convince you it's worth your while to stay."

"To what end?" I whisper, my throat constricted. I'm not afraid of a fight with him, but I'm questioning my path. The more time I spend with him, the more I'm sensing his emotions beyond the initial warmth and calm he exuded. Right now, I glimpse a storm, a battle of his inner nature, and I wonder at the tension between the compassion and care he exhibited when he spoke about the humans, and the rage he shows when he speaks of his clan.

He snarls as his rage wins. "To whatever end I want."

My stomach tightens, a small thrill passing through me at the dangerous tightrope I'm about to walk, the same rebellious thrill I felt covering my eyes with my hands instead of my blindfold when the Serene Commander last visited me.

I suppose, in some ways, I'm covering my eyes right now, ignoring my orders by accepting the challenge Callan poses to me.

For me, the world is a forest. Callan Steele may be a sharp tree that casts a long shadow, but I'm the wolf that prowls beneath it. Staying with him gives me the chance to gather all the information I need to destroy his clan, annihilate the other clans, and earn my place with the angels.

His gaze heats, his focus falling to my lips when I allow myself to smile.

"You promised it would only take a day for me to decide I want to stay," I say. "The clock is already ticking, Callan."

The tension leaves his shoulders and a slow smile brightens his eyes, his irises becoming cinnamon brown again. "First, I want your name."

I allow my smile to widen, all the while promising myself that he will discover my true name if he tries to kill me.

"The angels call me 'Lana,'" I say.

CHAPTER ELEVEN

"*L*ana." Callan tries out my name, but some of the fury returns to his gaze. "Not your true name."

"Of course not. My true name was given to me in the old language. A pretty name like *Lana* doesn't belong to me."

He looks baffled and I'm not sure why.

"Stand up," he orders me, as if he expects me to obey him immediately.

"No."

He takes a breath. Pauses. As if he's preparing for a battle of wills. "Humor me."

I narrow my eyes at him, uncertain where he's going with this.

I slip out from behind the table into the slightly more open space in front of the step into the sunken lounge. In a flash, his gaze descends from my head, pausing briefly on my eyes, my burned makeshift bandeau, the healing wound on my side, down past my fists, slowing at the curve of my legs before flashing back to my face.

I lift my chin, snarling at him, not bothering to pull the hair away from my eyes.

"You're right," he says, his growl making me shiver in a way I wasn't expecting. Warm. Enticing. "You belong in a wilderness. *Lana* doesn't fit you." He tips his chin. "Tell me your real name. In the old language."

"No."

The corner of his mouth hitches into a confident smile. "You'll tell me soon enough."

I tip my head and purse my lips, but I also smile. "I like these challenges you throw me. It's like you think you can win them."

"I know I can," he says, his smile growing. "With time and patience."

I glower at him, but he changes the subject on the next breath, not giving me time to argue. "Have you had enough to eat?"

I catch up fast to the change in topics. "Yes."

"Good." He jumps lightly from the sunken lounge, strides to a panel in the wall, and glides his fingers across it in a pattern I quietly commit to memory.

A new door opens, and I find myself rising to my feet, stepping out of the lounge area and to the left so I can see into the space that Callan has revealed.

"It's yours if you want it," he says when I draw level with him.

"What?" I'm stunned. The room inside is the most opulent bedroom I've ever seen, the kind I imagine the Serene Commander sleeps in.

Unlike the two rooms I've seen in Callan's home so far, this one is filled with furniture—a large bed covered in silken sheets, soft blankets, and at least five plump pillows; a wooden chest at the base of the bed, also covered in pillows; a chair and writing desk at the side of the room; and bedside tables with ornate lamps on top of them on both sides of the bed. The floor appears to be polished oak, and the right-hand wall is painted the softest, most calming green.

On the far wall, there are two open doors. One leads into a tiled area that appears to be a bathroom, although my depth perception tells me it's nearly as big as the bedroom. The other door opens into some sort of dressing room by the looks of the hanging space and the floor-to-ceiling mirrors. It's also enormous.

The only similarity between this room and Callan's bedroom is the poles at each corner of the bed that reach all of the way up to the ceiling.

"This room isn't fireproof," I say.

Callan nods. "It's your space. I'll only enter it with your permission."

I arch an eyebrow at him, wondering how truthful that promise will end up being.

"You can change anything about it that you want. All you need to do is ask. A different color scheme, new furniture. You decide."

I fight how unexpectedly overwhelmed this gesture makes me feel. My cell under the Cathedral was mine, but it was surrounded by bars and could be invaded by the Serene Commander at her whim. If Callan's true to his word—still a big *if* in my mind—then this room is really and truly *my* space. The first space I've had to myself.

"Okay," I whisper. Definitely not a bad start to making me want to stay.

When I step into the room, I glance back, testing his resolve not to come inside. He remains outside, a smile playing around his mouth, as if he reads my mind and my distrust.

The floor isn't as hard beneath my feet as I was expecting, and the pillows are so silken that my fingers glide over them soundlessly as I pass by.

My smile fades a little when I enter the dressing room. It's bare—not an item of clothing in sight, which is going to be a problem—but more than that, the mirrors force me to acknowledge my current state of undress and my disheveled appearance.

I'm wearing nothing more than a pair of black underpants and a shirt tied around my chest. My hair is knotted where it hangs over my right shoulder nearly to my waist. And my face is pale, although the bruises aren't as bad as I thought they might be.

Self-consciously, I adjust the top of the bandeau and pull some of the material out so it hangs to my stomach and hides the healing wound. Then I attempt to run my fingers through my tangled tresses to smooth them out. Unsuccessfully.

"I'm not used to mirrors," I say, emerging from the dressing room.

Callan remains at the door. "I can have them removed if you like."

My response is instinctive. "No." I bite my lip and glare at the floor for a second while I compose myself. "It's okay."

I've never had a reason to care about my appearance. My clothing has always been a pragmatic choice and so has my hairstyle. All I needed was my hunting clothes and a hair tie to keep the strands out of my face. All I wanted was to do my job efficiently.

But now, I need to know what I look like to others. I need to know if I appear vulnerable or hurt or... defiant.

When I look up again, I find Callan studying me, his focus traveling from my bare feet up to my face. It's a lingering look that brings heat to my cheeks, but there's an element of wariness in it that makes me hold my breath.

He's sizing me up the way an opponent would.

He saw me in action, but he must wonder how someone as slight as I am could kill Grudge dragons.

"Do you want the room?" he asks, a demand for confirmation.

"Yes," I say before I can second-guess my choice. It doesn't mean I'll stop fighting him, though.

He looks pleased. "Then it's time to get you some new clothes," he says, a firm declaration before he disappears around the door.

A moment later, I hear what sounds like the soft contact of his hand swishing against the wall again.

There must be some kind of intercom placed in the wall because Jada's voice sounds a second later. "Yes, Callan?"

"Bring up everything we discussed. I've left the door open for you."

There's a hint of excitement in her voice. "We'll be right up."

I exit the bedroom and keep my distance from Callan. I feel exposed without proper clothing now that humans are about to join us. Jada knows I'm an assassin, but I'm not sure what she'll make of the slightly burned shirt tucked around my chest. I really want to spread my wings, remind myself how strong they are and wrap them around myself, but of course I can't risk the humans seeing me like that.

Prowling toward the screen on the back wall, I watch it shift to a cityscape again, this time with the sun rising slowly behind it and turning the pictured buildings golden.

"The image can be anything you want," Callan says, prowling up behind me, dangerously close, but I don't step away.

"A mountain," I say.

He strides to the far right of the wall, presses the screen, and flicks through a menu before stepping back again.

I hold my breath as the scene in front of me morphs into a snow-capped peak, the blue silhouette of a vast mountain range behind it. A lone eagle soars through the air, a small but unmistakable speck in the distance.

I'm so enthralled that I don't step away when Callan approaches me again, a low murmur on his lips. "What else do you want, Lana?"

"Coffee," I say, at which he raises his eyebrows since coffee was already on offer this morning, but I clarify. "In a café."

It's a request that I know will challenge him because he said he rarely leaves this building, and I can't imagine him letting me go anywhere without him. That would risk losing control of me and he made it clear that if that happens, he has to kill me.

Despite not knowing if I even like coffee, I wonder what it would be like to sip coffee in a café like I'm another person, living another life.

I continue without pause. "I also want a walk along the river at sunrise." Another request that I hope will challenge him to leave this building with me. Then I point at the screen. "And to climb a mountain like that one."

He's pensive for a moment before his lips curve into a confident smile. "I can make that happen."

My brow furrows, but I'm more curious, than suspicious, about his confidence. Before I can ask him how he plans to give me my wishes, the door behind us opens, and Jada enters with the four human guards who were with her the other day.

The men are pushing multiple large carts and it quickly becomes apparent that they're clothes racks. Large ones. Stuffed with clothing. Shoeboxes. Accessories like belts and scarves. In addition, several transparent trays of jewelry sit on a shelf at the top of one of the racks.

My jaw drops a little at the sheer volume of clothing they're wheeling toward me.

A woman I've never met trails along behind them, her heels clicking on the marble floor. She has bright-red hair swept up on top of her head and perfect makeup that brings out the depth of her brown eyes, the shape of her lips, and the contours of her cheekbones. Diamonds drop from her earlobes and her fingers glitter with rings. She's wearing a flowing, white skirt and a crisp, blue shirt.

It doesn't seem like she's been here before because she peers all around as she follows the others, paying more attention to her surroundings than to me.

Jada strides ahead of the woman but doesn't crowd me. "Surprise," she says with a soft smile, her brown eyes twinkling. "Every woman's dream wardrobe is now at your fingertips."

I try to bring moisture to my suddenly dry lips, not sure how I feel about another unexpectedly overwhelming situation.

So many clothes.

Jada sets about instructing the guys where to put the clothes racks within my bedroom and I catch their names briefly: Brock, the dark-skinned man I saw the other day; Dermot with pale skin, very pale blond hair, and close-set eyes; Sean with tanned skin, brown hair, and a short-cut brown beard; and Paul, with olive skin and a scar across his chin. Brock is the tallest, standing nearly as tall as Callan, but the other three are only mildly shorter and they're all polite as they quickly reappear from within the bedroom.

It's impossible to miss the curious glances they give me or the hint of wariness in their expressions, although not one of them looks me up and down in any way that could be interpreted as insulting.

At a guess, I imagine Callan has told them as much about me as he told Jada: I'm dangerous, but he wants me alive.

Jada returns to my side. "How are you feeling today?"

I resist the urge to tug on the bandeau, wishing to heaven I was at least wearing shorts or a skirt. "I'm much better."

She clears her throat and stands between me and the others. "No doubt you'll feel even better once you have some new clothes."

Before I can respond, the new woman gasps and finally rushes toward me.

I take a hasty step back while Jada edges between us, which I'm sure is for the other woman's safety, not mine.

"What happened?" the redhead exclaims, reaching around

Jada toward the top of the shirt that's bunched above my breasts. She spins with a glare at Callan. "That's a designer shirt!"

Jada leans back toward me with a whisper. "Probably cost about $200. Maybe more. It was the first comfortable thing I could find for you to wear."

My brow furrows again since I'm not sure how you simply 'grab' a designer shirt for someone.

Callan shrugs as he returns the redhead's stare. "Campfire," he says. "It's not a big deal, Tish."

The woman—Tish—looks around the bare room. "A campfire? In here?" She scowls at Callan when he remains silent. "Fine. Keep your secrets."

She swings back to me, wipes her expression clean, and holds out her hand with a smile. "Hi, I'm Tish. I'm here to help you find your style."

"I'm Lana," I say, aware of the others listening in since they didn't know my name before now, either. "You're here to… what?"

She gives a high-pitched giggle that grates on my senses. "Jada said you might be a reluctant customer, but don't worry. I'll make sure you look beautiful."

She scoops her arm around my waist and pulls me toward the bedroom. "Let's figure out what suits you."

Her touch is so sudden that my reflexes nearly kick in. I stop myself before I sweep her feet out from under her and knock her on her backside.

She seems oblivious to my tension, but Jada notices it, judging by how closely she keeps pace with us, watching me carefully while Tish propels me through the bedroom door.

Within seconds, the redhead has waved at Callan as if she's shooing him away. "How do I close this door?" she asks, fumbling around the wall on its right-hand side.

Jada reaches out and presses a barely perceptible panel at eye level and the door slides shut—not so fast that I miss Callan's expression. His arms are crossed over his broad chest and his lips are pressed into a slightly worried line.

I imagine he may be rethinking his methods of convincing me to willingly stay. After all, I'm an assassin, not a runway model. If he wanted to make me happy, he should have filled the racks with hunting clothes and daggers.

I grit my teeth and tell myself that I need ordinary clothing, reminding myself again that it matters how I look to others. If I look and dress like the Dread, I'll be more likely to blend in.

Tish stops me firmly in the middle of the room in front of the bed and looks me up and down, muttering to herself, "Black hair, blue eyes, slight frame, long legs. That's good, but..." Her lips press together. "Not the best cleavage I've seen."

My arms fly across my chest. No, my breasts are not the amplest in the world, but being smaller makes it easier to run and hunt, especially since bust support was never at the top of the Serene Commander's list when she gave me underwear.

It takes all of my willpower not to break Tish's hand when she leans in to brush her fingertips across my face.

"Don't worry," she says. "These bruises are nothing that a little bit of makeup won't fix." She spins from me to scrutinize the racks of clothing, seeming oblivious to my glower as she continues to mutter to herself, pulling items out and placing them on the bed.

Now that the door has closed between me and Callan, I discover just how solid the walls must be, because suddenly, my senses aren't dulled anymore.

I'm startled by the contrast between the two women in the room with me. While Jada is like a tree with strong roots and her scent is warm and earthy, Tish is like an insubstantial cloud, the kind that blows one way or another depending on the push of the wind.

Right now, her excitement is sharp, practically biting, but I'd be a fool if I thought she was excited about dressing me. She's a thief. I know it from the scent of cloves that clings to her. The smell is a cloying result of the envy that often motivates theft, and she's fucking full of it. But that doesn't explain to me why her levels of excitement are quite so high right now...

I watch her carefully, planting my feet on the wooden floor, my focus becoming pinpoint as I consider the way she ruffles through the clothing, the way her bracelets jangle and her rings glitter, and the softness of her voice as she talks to herself.

Proving how perceptive she is, Jada seems to read the attack stance in my body language. "Have you had a chance to have a shower yet, Lana?"

"Good idea," I say, quickly striding to the room on the left of the bed and closing the door before Tish can utter a protest.

"But—"

Thank heaven, the door locks.

I exhale slowly as I press my hands to the wooden surface. Without hesitation, I unfurl my wings, needing their weight. This room may be ridiculously large, but I'm grateful it can accommodate my wings. I release them slowly and don't let them touch the walls or floor so they won't scrape noisily along the tiles.

Turning to the room, I discover that the bath is enormous. So is the shower area. It has multiple water outlets and I'm not even sure which one I should use. A set of shelves on the wall at my back is filled with towels, soaps, and shampoos, and a long vanity with two sinks in it stretches across the wall on the right side of the room.

Once again, I'm self-conscious about my wild appearance in the mirror, but now it only builds anger—an anger that Callan isn't present to dampen.

I'm not a shelf ornament. I wasn't designed to look pretty.

I snarl at myself and lift my wings, suddenly appreciating the scorched shirt, remembering the gleam in Callan's eyes when he said I belong in a wilderness. *Truth.*

This is me. No matter how I might need to dress up from this moment on, underneath it all, I am wild.

CHAPTER TWELVE

I choose soap and shampoo before I fold my wings out of sight and take a guess at which of the water faucets to turn on in the shower area.

Jada must have done a great job of cleaning my wounds because it's only when I put my head under the stream that the water runs red.

Three shampoos later, the water is finally clear.

With a sigh, I press my hands to the tiled wall, mentally preparing myself to go back out and face the wardrobe onslaught.

Minutes later, I'm wrapped in a bathrobe, my hair is towel-dried, and I've pasted a smile onto my face that looks more like a snarl.

I check myself in the mirror and my smile fades.

Fuck, it's no use trying to look friendly.

With a sigh, I give up and emerge to find that Tish has picked out multiple outfits for me and laid them all on the bed.

But first she hands me a basket of underwear.

"Choose the ones you want to wear right now," she says. "These are in a variety of sizes so you can get the fit right."

I peer at the items, plucking out a pair of what can only be underpants but aren't constructed of more than a few strings and a triangle of lace.

"Um...?"

Jada is sitting on the edge of the bed and looks like she's holding in a laugh. "I wouldn't wear those, either," she says with a wink. "Not unless you're planning to take them off quickly."

"No," I say, pushing them back at Tish.

With a huff, she takes away that basket and hands me a new one—her backup plan, I suppose. This one contains items that are recognizable as underwear, even if they're also decorated with patches of lace.

I choose underpants and a bra in my size, return to the bathroom, and quickly emerge again, this time with underwear on under my bathrobe.

"Great," Tish says. "Let's try this outfit first." She gestures to a set of clothing that I don't hate: black jeans and a scoopnecked rose-colored shirt.

I turn my back, sweep the bathrobe off my shoulders, and reach for the shirt, but I freeze when Tish gasps.

Looking back to her, I ask, "What's wrong?"

"That's not something I see every day," Tish says, staring at my back.

My scars.

I swivel fully to her, but not before I pull the bathrobe closer around my chest to continue concealing the wound on my side. I sense her nature sway as if she's being billowed in a wind she didn't expect and she's not certain where it's taking her.

Jada slides off the bed, but I stop her before she can speak.

"Are my scars going to be a problem?" I ask Tish, my voice devoid of any emotion.

"No," she squeaks, visibly recalibrating. "Not a problem. Let's avoid low-backed clothing... shall we?" As she sweeps several of the shirts up from the bed, she continues with a mutter, "Because *nobody* needs to see *that*."

She returns the low-backed shirts to the rack and pauses there as she goes about choosing replacements.

I control my exhale, using my breathing to get my anger under control. My scars are ugly and brutal. They were intended to be so. But I don't need anyone rubbing my face in it.

I glance at Jada, only to find her standing very still, glaring hard enough at Tish's back to tear strips off her.

When Jada catches my eye, I mouth, *It's okay*.

She presses her lips together as if she's refraining from uttering a few choice words.

Determined to get this over with, I pull on the black jeans. They're a good fit and so is the top. Without waiting for Tish to give me permission, I take off the outfit and hang it in the dressing room.

My first set of new clothing.

An hour later, I have ten practical outfits. Half are casual, while the other half are the kind I could wear out. I also have three black evening dresses of varying lengths—although heaven knows where I would wear them. Only one dress on the whole rack had a high back, so two of the evening dresses are useless to me. Tish pointedly suggested I wear a shawl around my shoulders.

Multiple pairs of shoes of all styles—boots, heels, and flats— now sit on the shoe racks in the dressing room, and one set of drawers is filled with accessories: belts, scarves, and hair ties. The other chest of drawers contains underwear, along with pajamas and casual clothing—sweatpants, sweaters, and soft T-shirts.

Finally, I'm dressed in a pair of skinny blue jeans and a white wrap-around shirt with a collar. Tish hands me the matching heels, but I put them on the floor since I'd feel silly wearing them around the living area.

"Now for the real beauties," Tish says as she reaches for the jewelry cases. "These are apparently family heirlooms, but Callan is letting them out into the world for you." She widens her eyes at me, her voice hushed. "Which makes you very special."

I don't feel so special when she presents me with two golden bracelets. One is a solid band inlaid with three little sapphires. The other is an interlinked chain with a ruby heart dangling from it.

I remember what he told me about dragon's gold being turned into jewelry. If these are family heirlooms, chances are high that they're made from dragon's gold. Which means they're instant, wearable shackles that won't raise human eyebrows.

It's a stark reminder that he can give me a beautiful bedroom and more clothing than I need, but I remain his captive.

"It's too much," I say, attempting to avoid wearing the bracelets, certain that once they go on, they won't come off again. "I can't wear those. What if I damage them?"

"Nonsense. You can't say *no* to priceless items like these." Tish is already reaching for my left hand and clipping the band over my wrist. Within seconds, the gold chain with the ruby pendant dangles from my other wrist.

"There." She steps back. "So elegant." Her brow furrows. "Other than your hair."

I press my lips together and swallow a retort. At least she didn't mention my bruises or my scars again. For someone whose job it is to make me look beautiful, she manages to make me feel like shit.

"Here," she says, patting the side of the bed.

I obey her, but I do so reluctantly. Within moments, she has procured a hairbrush, has sat down beside me, and is attempting to run the brush through my knots. I get through the moments by imagining myself knocking her on her butt again and again with every painful tug of the brush.

She doesn't seem to notice my tension, but she also doesn't understand the risk I pose to her. In contrast, Jada watches me closely.

"You don't have to wear anything you're not comfortable with," she says quietly, reaching out and tapping the bracelet on my left hand while Tish grumbles about the clumps in my hair.

I turn the golden band so that the sapphires face upward. I don't have a choice. Callan controls this metal by will alone. Fighting against them now will be a waste of energy.

I need to pick my battles.

"It's fine," I say.

What isn't fine is the constant clatter of Tish's own bracelets at my ear every time she draws the brush through my hair.

My reflexes fire and I grab her wrist on the next pull, stopping her a little more harshly than I intended.

She jumps, but I grip her firmly, suddenly very focused on the piece of jewelry she's wearing: a golden band with an emerald charm. It's just like the one that Sophia was wearing. In fact, the small scratch at the edge of it tells me it's *exactly* the one Sophia was wearing.

"Where did you get this?" I ask Tish.

"It was a gift," she says.

I continue to grip her wrist. "From whom?"

"A friend," she says. Despite her light response, her firm tug against my hold betrays her sudden fear. Any reasonable person would be tense if they were grabbed and held, but once again, her nature sways within my senses, this time sharply.

I immediately let her go, just as suddenly realizing what I couldn't put my finger on until now. She's not excited, she's *desperate*. Why, I'm not yet sure.

For a brief moment, I consider if she's a dragon, but I don't think so, since Callan was vehement about not letting any dragons into the building until he was ready. Unless he *is* ready now…

I shake myself because there are too many unknowns and no way to work through them. Even if this room had windows, it's daylight outside; there isn't a trace of moonlight for me to confirm if Tish casts a dragon's shadow.

Of course, if she isn't a dragon, then she has somehow acquired dragon's gold. Even though she's a thief, it's unlikely that she would steal this particular piece and wear it so openly. She said it was a gift from a friend so Sophia must have given it to her—but that seems strange, given how long it takes to cultivate dragon's gold, making it priceless.

No matter how Tish got the bracelet, I need her to leave because her duplicitous nature is jarring my senses.

I give an overly dramatic yawn. "Thank you for your help with my clothing, Tish," I say. "But I'm very tired and need to rest now."

She smiles. "Of course. I'll leave you to it."

She pauses at the door. "Are you coming, Jada?"

"I'll stay and help Lana settle in," Jada replies before Tish exits the room and closes the door behind her.

The air clears as soon as she's gone, and I can breathe again.

I drop my smile as I turn to Jada. "How well do you know Tish?"

"She works for a married couple that Callan knows: Tyler and Sophia. There's friction between them and Callan, but I don't know why." Jada grimaces at me. "Or where you come into it."

She shakes her head. "Or why he'd ask Tish to come here today. I know she's brilliant at styling people—and you look amazing in all of those outfits—but fuck, she's a bitch."

An unexpected warmth fills my chest as Jada speaks and it takes some of the edge off my frayed emotions.

I pick up the hairbrush and continue where Tish left off, working my way through the tangles, wincing when I meet knot after knot. Lying in bed for three days really messed with my hair, and before that I was thrashing to free myself.

"Here, let me help," Jada says, reaching for the brush. "I used to brush my sister's hair all the time. She had fine hair like yours."

"Had?" I ask quietly, picking up on the past tense immediately.

"Yeah."

Jada is quiet for a long time as she works her way through my hair, and I respect her silence. I don't know what it feels like to have family, but I *feel* her pain now. It's deep, like a thorn that won't come out; a dull ache.

She finally pauses. Her voice is shaky, but she seems determined to speak. "It was a hit and run. Nearly five years ago. Right after we all got back." She takes a deep breath. In and out. "Kelly was always afraid that I'd be the one to die on her, not the other way around. I had to identify her body and… I saw a lot of shit in combat, but somehow, seeing her all broken like that…" She takes another deep, shuddering breath. "If it wasn't for Callan and the guys…"

Her hand trembles where it rests on my head and I catch her palm, drawing it into mine, looking her in the eyes when I say, "Do you know who did it?"

She shakes her head. "Kelly was dating some guy at the time, but it was early days and she hadn't told me his name. They were out on a date and it happened after. I was crashing at her place while I was looking for my own place, and she didn't come home that night, but I didn't think anything of it because, you know, she was on a date. I got the call at dawn."

My hand tightens around hers as I continue to maintain her gaze. "If you find out who did it, tell me. I'll kill them."

She stares back at me, her deep brown eyes widening. Her voice is quiet when she says, "Even after you disarmed me so fast the other day, there was a part of me that didn't believe what Callan said about you. But now I do."

I release her hand, and she lifts her chin, blinking away the moisture in her eyes as she clears her throat and refocuses. "If there's beautiful hair beneath this bird's nest, I promise I'll find it."

I snort. "You'll have to find another home for the birds."

She shrugs and plays along. "Don't worry. They can nest in the piles of clothing you didn't choose." She inclines her head at the clothes that either didn't fit or didn't work for me. "I'll ask the guys to take those away when you're ready."

My forehead creases. "Where did all of this clothing come from so quickly? And how did Callan furnish this room so fast?"

Jada shuffles a little. "He didn't. I mean, not for you."

It takes me a moment to realize I'd made an assumption that wasn't correct: I thought Callan created this room just for me. "It was already like this."

Jada confirms with a short nod.

"Does his sister stay here sometimes?"

Jada blinks at me. "His sister? No."

I stare at her blankly. "Then why would he have a room—"

I stop myself, but it's too late.

Oh, I'm fucking naïve.

Once again, I don't understand the parts of the world that revolve around lust and sex, and I've only now realized that this room is designed for both. But I'm not sure how that fits with what Callan told me earlier about keeping people safe.

Jada clears her throat again. "Callan may fear touch, but that hasn't stopped him from having female visitors. This building has everything you could want. There's a lot to entertain." She flushes, speaking quickly. "Sometimes, these women sleep over, but don't ask me what happens after dark. Or *if* anything happens after dark. I don't want to know. And again, he pays me not to ask awkward questions."

Thinking it through, I say, "You said earlier that you grabbed that designer shirt. That's because you already had all of this clothing on hand, didn't you?"

She nods before she waves at the clothes racks. "These are just the clothes that are in your size. There's always something here for a woman who didn't think she'd be staying overnight."

Callan made it clear that he doesn't risk harming humans or supernaturals. If I take him at his word, then this room is for sleeping and the clothes are for wearing, not taking off. I may not know enough about lust, but I understand greed. If Callan has as much money as I think he does, then a woman might be more than willing to overlook the lack of sex for the material gain.

That is, assuming he didn't lie to me. After all, his dragon doesn't currently react to human touch, so he could have human girlfriends.

Ultimately, it only matters to me if there's someone in his life who could make my life complicated in some way or another. "I hope he hasn't broken anyone's heart?" I ask, a leading question.

Jada relaxes a little. "The lives of the rich." She gives a shrug before she gestures around us. "The women who step into this room... I'm pretty sure their hearts aren't the breaking type."

Is mine?

It's an unwanted question.

"Did you know that Callan was wealthy when you met him?"

"Hell, no," she says. "He enlisted when I did. We trained together. He's a true friend. I never had a clue about any of this. None of us did until we got back, and he offered us new lives."

"Callan told me he rarely goes out—is that right?"

She nods. "He usually only leaves the building when we can control the environment around him. Never into crowded situations that we can't control. Having said that, he owns a number of clubs around the city, which he sometimes visits—but again because he can control the environment there." She grins and gives me a wink. "You may not believe it to look at us in uniform, but we're actually pretty good at blending in."

"But he must go out without you sometimes." I'm testing her because he was out the other night without any of his human guards.

Her smile fades. "Sometimes. Not often. Usually to the clubs he controls. I don't like it because I worry about him. He has a lot of secrets, and in my experience, secrets mean enemies." She shakes herself. "But he's a grown man."

She pulls the brush through my hair one more time and I'm startled to realize that she's done already. Patting my head, I find my hair is smooth and soft to touch.

She's a miracle worker.

"Before I forget," she says, reaching into her pocket and pulling out a small tube. "This gel is for your wounds. It will help them heal without scarring."

I turn the tube over in my hands. I don't normally scar. The wounds on my back are an anomaly, but I appreciate her gesture. "Thank you."

She gives me a small smile. "Callan made it clear that you're important to him. That means you're important to me." She reaches for my hand. "I tend to be a bit protective of the important people in my life. If you need anything, let me know."

"Thank you. I will."

Her hand is warm on mine. She clears her throat. "I have to get back to work. Come out whenever you're ready."

She closes the door behind her, and I stare at the space she leaves behind. I'm left with the tang of copper across my tongue, the evidence of blood on her hands, but it's mingled with the scent of fallen leaves, the earthy cycles of a leaf through life and death. She has undoubtedly taken life, but it doesn't trigger my rage like I expected it would.

I make a vow to myself that no matter what happens between Callan and me, Jada won't get caught in the middle.

CHAPTER THIRTEEN

hen I emerge into the quiet living area, I find everyone else is gone and Callan sits within the sunken lounge contemplating the mountain scene on the opposite wall. He has pulled on a new shirt and sweats.

"Dragons once lived in mountains like those," he says, his hand rising from the table. "There was a range—it's gone now, but they called it 'the Crystal Peaks.' It was where dragons flocked. One dragon in each generation was gifted with all of the knowledge of our race and the responsibility to ensure that humans and supernaturals abided by the old laws. They called that dragon 'Vanem Dragon.' It means 'dragon of light.'"

I nod. The Serene Commander told me a little about dragon history. The Vanem Dragon was the pinnacle of dragons, the strongest and wisest. A 'true' dragon, as she would say.

Callan gestures at the scene. "The dragon masters still live in the mountains, searching for a cure for our dying race. So we can fully shift again."

"Do *you* search for a cure?"

He focuses on me. "I've abandoned the possibility of ever

achieving a full shift. But I won't let my people die out." His jaw clenches. "Or be slaughtered."

His fierce gaze rakes over me and I know, from having caught myself in the mirror, that I look anything but threatening right now, especially with my long, straight hair tucked demurely behind one ear.

His focus stops on the bracelets around my wrists and some of his tension evaporates.

"Better," he says, and I presume his comment covers my entire appearance, not just the jewelry.

I hold up my wrists so that the bracelets catch the light. "What do these do?"

"They allow me to track you. And they'll bind your wrists if I need them to."

Unflustered by his continuing scrutiny and determined to not show him how I really feel about the bracelets, I lean back against the wall. "Why did you invite one of Sophia's employees to your home today, Callan? It can't have been purely for her expertise in fashion."

His lips curve, but his eyes narrow. "What did you make of Sophia's human friend, Tish?"

I fold my arms. "She's desperate, although I'm not sure why. Her loyalty shifts to whomever she perceives can give her the most of whatever she needs: money, attention, possibly even sex. She can be easily manipulated and won't hesitate to tell secrets for personal gain. She'll go right back to Sophia and tell her everything that happened here."

I'm increasingly cold as I catalog all the things Tish saw today: my burned shirt, the scars on my back, the bracelets I'm wearing—although presumably, she doesn't know that they're made from dragon's gold. "Is that what you wanted her to do?"

Callan's expression doesn't change. "Tish is in financial trouble. According to my sister, Tish and Sophia have been spending a lot more time together in the last few weeks—more than a purely business relationship would require. What did you make of her bracelet?"

"It was Sophia's. Could Tish know that it's dragon's gold?"

Callan shakes his head emphatically. "We don't reveal our true nature to humans. The consequence is death."

"For the dragon?"

Shadows grow in his eyes. "For the human."

The fire I swallowed earlier isn't warm enough to keep me from shuddering.

"The dragon is punished severely but allowed to live," Callan explains. "Our low numbers mean we can't afford to lose a life. Unfortunately, that makes some dragons less inclined to be careful, and the old alpha wasn't as strict as I am. I've made it clear to my clan that I won't tolerate the loss of human life."

He inclines his head at the control panel that I can now make out on the wall next to my door. "That's why I have passcodes on so many doors. It's why I can lock this place down with a single code. It's also why every other Dread dragon in this city lives in a building without natural light and takes extreme precautions against discovery. We never walk the street at night. We always remain under cover."

Which is also why it was extremely difficult for me to identify and find them.

"If the bracelet is gold, and Tish needs money, maybe Sophia gave it to her to help her?" I say.

Callan rubs his chin. "That was my first thought, but it wouldn't be worth as much as Tish needs, and dragon's gold is dangerous to humans. It can make them very ill."

"How ill?" I ask.

"If worn for long periods of time, it can lead to death."

I'm a little startled. My brow furrows. "A dangerous gift." Not the kind someone would normally give a friend. "She might have thought Tish would pawn it, not wear it."

"Maybe." Callan's eyes glint, and for a second, I see a flash of gold, but I dismiss it as a trick of the light. "Or maybe Sophia has recklessly endangered the entire clan and needs to be dealt with."

He peers at me as if he expects me to give my opinion, and it dawns on me, with startling clarity, why he invited Tish in the first place.

"You think I can give you answers."

He inclines his head. "You sense guilt. I want to know what Sophia is guilty of before I pass judgement. Is she guilty of caring for her friend so much that she would do anything to help her? Or is she deliberately pushing my boundaries? She's the daughter of the former alpha and one of our most vulnerable members since she's unable to shift. Is she trying to make me punish her because it will undermine my leadership by proving to my clan that I care more about humans than I do about them?"

Fucking politics. "I can't tell you any of that from this room," I point out.

A smile plays around Callan's mouth, but it suddenly feels dangerous. "True. Which leaves me with a dilemma: keep you here or take you out."

He rises suddenly, stretching his neck. "Speaking of taking you places, I promised you coffee in a café."

"You did." I'm curious how he's going to come through.

Callan points me toward the front door. "This way."

I follow, but my footfalls become wary as we approach the exit and draw nearer to the dragon's gold that I know is concealed against the walls.

"It's fine," Callan says, opening the door. "The gold will comply with my will and let you pass this time."

I don't entirely believe him until I walk through the door unscathed. Then I have the chance to properly see the hallway outside for the first time. It's just as cold as the room I left behind and both ends of it have screens instead of windows. They both show mountains.

Because there's no natural light or windows, it's impossible to tell the time of day. Oddly, it's not as disconcerting as it could be. My cell under the Cathedral was blocked off from the outside world, too, so I'm not unfamiliar with the way the hours can blend into each other.

Actually… I'm surprised to realize that I'm more at peace here than in my cell, separated from the outside world and its pall of emotions, but with more space to move around in than I have under the Cathedral.

"How does this building not have windows?" I ask.

Callan strides to the elevator door, which has only a down arrow beside it, indicating that we're already on the highest level.

"There are windows around the outer rooms so this building looks normal from the outside," he replies. "These core rooms are completely obscured. I had the structure designed so it's like two buildings within one. There's an outer rim of shallow rooms that look like ordinary apartments while the inner core, where I live, is sealed off from the outside world."

"No sunlight," I murmur, following him into the large elevator as it opens. "Or moonlight, for that matter."

He gives me a sharp grin before he hits the button for the fifth floor, which is a little unexpected.

"If you designed this entire building to conceal your existence, then… do you live alone?"

"All other staff come here only to work, but Jada, Brock, Dermot, Paul, and Sean live on the second floor. They understand that there are rules, and I pay them—"

"Not to ask questions," I finish for him.

"If I didn't trust them, they wouldn't be here."

"Then what are the other floors for?" I ask.

His smile turns mysterious. "You'll find out in time. In the meantime, you'll have to make do with where I invite you to go. For instance…" He gestures as the elevator doors open. "A café."

I step into what looks like a provincial French café, complete with cobblestone floor and neat, round tables. A youngish man —maybe in his late teens—sits behind the counter and jumps up when we appear. He's wearing an apron and is tall and lanky with tousled, light-brown hair.

He immediately calls across the room. "The usual, Callan?"

"Sure," Callan says, before he turns to me. "What kind of coffee do you like?"

There are kinds? I shuffle a little, suddenly feeling stupid, and Callan's smile grows, but it's not unkind.

"How about a latte?" he asks. "Not too strong, and not too bitter."

I don't know what kind of coffee that is, but I nod. "Sure."

Turning back to the barista, Callan says, "A latte for Lana, thanks."

The barista gives me a wave with a casual, "Hey, Lana. I'm Matt," before getting to work.

Before stepping into the café area, I glance farther down to the left along the corridor that sits on that side of the café. It looks like there are more rooms off the corridor, which makes sense since the floorspace is larger than what's taken up by the café.

Without touching me, Callan extends his hand, gesturing me forward to one of the tables where a newspaper is laid out beside a computer tablet. He takes a seat and promptly scans the newspaper first, then the tablet.

I sit down stiffly, eyes wide, then narrowed. "How do you have your own café?"

Callan glances up. "There's a whole world inside this building. You might enjoy the library on level seven. Or the home theater on level six." He watches me from beneath his lashes as he speaks, as if he's testing my response to each suggestion. "Maybe the gym on floor eight. Or the pool on the first level."

I don't give anything away, but the library and the gym pique my interest.

"You have everything you need to entertain a guest," I say, drawing conclusions based on my meager understanding of human life. "But maybe I'm not so easy to amuse."

"I didn't expect that you would be." He doesn't back down. "But you might change your mind."

I might *have* to change my mind, considering he's made it clear that I either stay of my own volition or he ends me.

Matt slips a coffee in front of me that has a frothy top with the pattern of a leaf on it. In contrast, he places a tall glass of some sort of green concoction in front of Callan.

"Enjoy your coffee," he says to me.

I peer up at him, so thrown by my surroundings that I say the first thing that pops into my head. "I don't know if I will. I've never had coffee."

Matt's eyebrows rise. "This one's my best brew," he says with a confident smile.

Callan puts the newspaper down, and I have the sense that although he genuinely wants to read it, he's determined to keep watching me. "Matt works for me in the day and takes classes at night."

"Okay, but..." I wrinkle my nose at Callan's drink. "What is *that*?"

"Everything a growing dragon needs," Callan says, one corner of his mouth hitching up into a grin.

Matt laughs, and I have no doubt he has no idea that Callan means it literally.

It's time to test how much spontaneity Callan will tolerate. The only way I'll discover more about him is to test his boundaries. The more often I can catch him off guard, the more likely he is to reveal things he would otherwise hide.

I spin to Matt but point to the tall, green drink. "I want one of those, too."

Callan looks surprised, but I give him a hard stare.

"What?" I say. "You think you can ply me with delicacies, and I'll swoon over them. It's nice to try new things, but I also want what keeps me healthy." I lean toward him. "Besides, I notice you're not drinking coffee."

Callan's response is a deep rumble. "I don't need stimulants."

Matt is still hovering, but Callan gives him a quick nod. "A juice for Lana, too."

When Matt heads to the counter, Callan throws his head back and drinks the glass of green liquid in one long go, all without taking a breath. He places the empty cup down on the table and inhales deeply.

I turn my coffee cup around in my hand, wanting to try it, but determined to wait for the green drink first.

Within moments, Matt is back with a glass for me. Abandoning all hesitancy, I throw the liquid back, drinking as fast as Callan did. I don't recognize most of the tastes, but it's far more palatable than I was expecting. Apple, spinach, cucumber, mint; those are the flavors I isolate among others I've never tasted before.

Placing the cup down with only a few drops left, I run my finger around the rim and lick the final liquid from my fingertip. "Not bad," I say, looking up to find Callan fixated on my lips.

I'm not sure why.

My stomach flutters, my heart skips a beat, and again, I'm not sure why.

A hint of a smile touches Callan's lips. "Do you want to try your coffee?"

Feeling unusually flustered by his scrutiny, I lift the cup to my mouth, feel the little bubbles of froth on top of it burst against my lips, and give it a taste.

It *is* bitter, and I'm disappointed.

Placing it back on the table, I stare at the delicious-looking caramel-colored liquid for a moment before I shake my head, feeling a little forlorn. "It's not for me."

Callan laughs, but it's a deep, throaty sound. "Coffee is an acquired taste."

I throw an apologetic smile at Matt where he hovers nearby. "I don't intend any offense."

"None taken," he says with an easy grin. "A juice for you tomorrow, then?"

Tomorrow is a long way away in the circumstances, but I answer politely, "Yes, thank you."

After Matt scoops up the empty glasses and the coffee cup, I return my attention to Callan, but I lower my voice. "You promised to convince me that I want to stay. The gym is where I'd like to go."

He looks me up and down and, again, it draws a physical reaction from my body—a flush of heat through my cheeks and stomach. Maybe it's because his consideration is so relaxed now compared to the tension of our previous interactions. Somehow, he seems to chill out drastically around his human friends. In contrast, it seems to be when he's alone with me that his dragon surfaces.

"Don't you want to change first?" he asks.

I glance down at my clothing. I'm used to working out in jeans and a shirt. It's not like the Serene Commander gives me workout gear. "No need."

"All right then."

Once we're back in the elevator, Callan folds his arms and settles against the back of the elevator without pressing a button. Watching him carefully, I choose the eighth floor.

I roll up my sleeves on the way. The crisp cotton shirt won't give me the most flexibility, but there's an easy fix to that if I'm willing.

Unlike the café level, on level eight, the elevator lets out into a hallway with a door and a touchpad on the opposite wall. Callan inputs a numbered code, speaking it aloud this time.

"Remember this pass code," he says. "You'll need it for the library, too. Only you and I know it. I don't want humans to see me bench press more weight than I should be able to, so there's never any staff on this level. There's a smaller gym for them near the pool on the first level. The downside is that you'll have to clean up after yourself."

He doesn't explain why he has a lock on the library, too, but right now, I'm more focused on what's in front of me.

"I don't have a problem with cleaning up," I say, striding into the gym.

It's a large space with every sort of workout apparatus I could imagine neatly arranged around the edges of the room—from weights on the right to treadmills on the left. A large tumbling area sits in the middle, but it's the far side of the room that pulls my attention.

Five dummies in vaguely human shapes are positioned in a row with lots of space around them while the back wall is covered in wooden weapons.

I head straight for the dummies, testing the flex in their bases and the firmness of their padding. "Will it be a problem if I break these?" I ask Callan, who keeps his distance.

"I can easily get more."

I can't stop my smile. *Now* I'm in heaven.

Without thinking much about it, I pull off my shirt, leaving myself only in my bra and jeans. Wadding up the shirt in my hands, I survey my training weapon options, deciding that a wooden short sword should work well.

Pitching the shirt to the floor and choosing a sword, I spin, just as Callan takes a step toward me, leaving us only inches apart.

My eyes flash up to his and I'm suddenly wary of the golden hints in his cinnamon irises. I'm slowly starting to recognize the different hues and what they mean. Juniper green is when he's angry. Cinnamon brown is when he's relaxed. Golden flecks indicate that his dragon is surfacing and that's when I'm not sure what he'll do. Or how I'll react.

"I'm curious about something, Lana. Or, *not*-Lana," he says, a low rumble.

My breath catches and I'm suddenly drawn to his lips, remembering the flames that curled around his face and chest. "What's that?"

"You undress yourself in front of me as if you don't think I'll notice." He pauses, his focus intensifying. "Why is that?"

"Because you won't," I whisper, staring up at him, my certainty fading when my response seems to evoke a storm that heats his gaze.

He decreases the gap to a dangerously small distance between us and his voice lowers further still. "If I could touch you, I'd show you just how much notice I take."

CHAPTER FOURTEEN

 $\mathcal{I}$ force myself to take a step back, even though I'd rather take a step forward. The longer I'm in Callan's presence, the more I can sense his moods, and his current frame of mind is like...

Chasing after a dragonfly as it flits across crystal-clear water. Alluring but with footing that is altogether too uncertain.

"I want to use my wings," I say, attempting to explain why I took my shirt off.

A glimmer of a smile plays across his lips, a light in his eyes that only increases as I test the weight of the makeshift weapon I'm holding.

"Then by all means, go ahead," he says, stepping to the side, the gleam in his eyes only growing as he finds a spot to lean against the wall and observe.

The anticipation of training in a space like this helps me push aside my self-consciousness. I'm not afraid of showing him what I can do. He knows my reputation, so he shouldn't be surprised.

I start small, jabbing the wooden weapon lightly at the nearest dummy to assess the impact. It feels as if it would take a lot of effort to actually impale the dummies, and that's good because I want to give myself a workout. I need to know that my body is still strong.

Swinging to the dummy behind me, I lunge and drive the side of the sword at it before I stand up straight again. I stretch my neck from side to side, and remain mindful of the distance between Callan and me. I don't want to accidentally come into contact with him.

Satisfied that I'm in the clear, I slash the sword back and forth through the air, concentrating on getting a feel for how it handles. Not as nicely as a real sword, but it will do for now.

Inhaling, exhaling, and centering myself, I swing to the dummy again, this time concentrating on my foot placement, making the movement fluid.

And so I begin.

Within seconds, I lose myself to the rhythm of attack, gliding smoothly between dummies, my movements silent and stealthy as I make contact, spinning between them, each strike a quick *thud*.

I increase my speed, testing my stamina in this open space. My hair flies around my face as I release my wings to gain air and plow down on a dummy before landing and spinning to the next one. Then back, each blow harder until the whacks of the sword are loud in my hearing.

I don't stop to take breaks, breathing through the exertion of my muscles and pushing on. Completely lost in the rhythm of the kill now, I'm hardly aware of the way my wings release and retract, lifting me, giving me momentum, or pulling me back, balancing me.

My forehead is beaded with sweat and my chest is heaving, but I push myself further because it's only here in the movement of battle that I find true peace. A pinnacle I reach when my intentions are clear and simple.

A sort of weightlessness.

I keep going until my muscles are aching and then, with one final spin, I ram the sword into the neck of the nearest dummy with all of my strength, taking off its head.

The pieces of the dummy fly wide and I stop where I am, my arm extended, my feet planted in a lunge position, and my wings spread.

I draw my feet together smoothly as I retract my wings, take a deep breath, and then… I allow myself to flop onto my back. Sprawling on the mat with a laugh, I stare up at the ceiling for a moment, coming back to myself when Callan towers over me.

His expression is unreadable. He may as well be made of stone, but I'm too full of peace to worry.

"Okay, you got me," I murmur. "I love this room."

His intense gaze burns down on me. "I'd like to try something," he says, his voice rough, "but it could lead to disaster."

My reaction is more reserved this time as I quickly refocus and prop myself up on my elbows. "What is it?"

He reveals the long fighting stick he was holding behind his back. With a flick of his wrist, it becomes apparent that there are two of them.

"Fight me," he says.

My stomach lurches. "You have the advantage," I say. "I'm tired."

He shakes his head at me, as if he doesn't believe it. "You're barely puffing. That was a warm-up. Humor me."

When he asked me to humor him earlier this morning, he gave me a onceover that made my toes curl. He does the same now and it's incredibly distracting.

I reach out to run my hand along the bottom of the staff he offers me, my fingertips skipping over the smooth surface.

"We have to be careful," I say. "I would hate for this room to be burned."

"Everything fun comes with a risk," Callan says.

A thrill rides my spine, but I arch my eyebrows nonchalantly at him before I dart upward and scoop the second staff into my hand so fast that I nearly pull him off-balance.

He regains his footing as quickly as I expected.

Without taking my eyes off him, I wipe the remaining sweat off my brow with the back of my free hand and step steadily toward the tumbling mat and the open space behind me.

Extending the fighting stick as I go, I say, "Prepare."

He casually drops his weapon onto the edge of the mat before he removes his shirt, revealing his perfectly sculpted chest and stomach muscles. Again, my stomach flutters, a distraction I'm not used to, but again, I refocus.

After scooping up his weapon, he doesn't waste any time with formalities, striding toward me, the stick raised.

I immediately defend myself and the two rods *clack* against each other. I sense the testing pressure of his first downward blow, which I match.

"Don't go easy on me, Callan," I say as the weapons strain against each other with increasing force.

He laughs. "I thought you said you were tired."

I answer him with a flick of my stick that shoves his weapon upward. In the next instant, I spin for increased force and whack his shoulder.

He hunches in time to take the blow, and I'm intrigued by the bruise that forms—and then fades just as quickly—across his skin.

"Your dragon heals you fast," I say, my weapon ready but hovering. A hint of envy grows within me, but it's only a trickle and I push it away.

"I'm lucky that way." Callan watches the sway of my stick, his intense focus increasing.

Going on the attack, I drive him around the mat, our fighting sticks striking so loudly against each other that I'm sure they're going to snap. He matches my speed and strength, until my muscles strain in an effort to defend myself.

All of my envy is gone and in its place is exhilaration. I've never had a sparring partner. At least, not one I didn't intend to immediately kill.

After a quick flurry of exchanged blows—neither of us landing a single hit—my wings burst outward. Bouncing on the balls of my feet, I tuck my wings and somersault over his head, landing and spinning, intending to give him a good whack across his shoulder blades. If I could have used my feet, I would have kicked him mid-flight, but that means contact with his body, which I won't risk right now.

He turns as fast as I hoped he would and deflects the blow.

Jumping backward to increase the space between us, I speak as he prowls after me. "Can you shift at will?"

More than anything, I want to know if he can fight me in the air. The ceiling in this room is high enough that we'd have space…

"Not without dousing my environment with flames," he says, tapping my fighting stick with his since I've slowed down to question him. It's a goading strike that tells me he wants to keep fighting. "It's all or nothing. In that respect, I'm like other dragon shifters."

His response confirms at least one thing I knew about dragons: They can't partially shift.

"You said some dragons can't shift at all," I say, avoiding the blows he attempts to make on either side of me.

"Our magic is dying," he responds with a snarl. "Eventually, we'll be gone forever."

No more dragons.

I'm surprised by the sadness that wells inside me at that thought. Despite my determination to destroy the clans—these dragons that aren't full dragons—it saddens me that one day, nothing of the ancient dragons will remain on this Earth.

I shake myself before he can land a hit on my shoulder, refocusing on the fight.

With a soft exhalation, I go on the attack again. The room fills with the sharp cracks of wood as we leave the mat. We work our way around the space in an increasingly fast flurry of movement during which he proves just how agile he is.

He's as fast as me.

As strong as me. Dammit, *stronger*.

But my wings give me an advantage he doesn't have.

Or at least, I assume they will, but it seems he's learning how I move.

Just as I aim a quick blow at his stomach, he knocks his fighting stick down on mine, closes his free hand over the end of my stick, and disarms me, a move I wasn't expecting.

Using both sticks like poles, he pushes them against the cartilage at the top of my wings and drives me back toward the wall. I should have been more aware of my surroundings—that I was so close to this side of the room—but I was focused on what was in front of me: *him*.

In any other situation, I could easily fight back, use my legs to push him away from me, but because of the reduced space between us and the threat of imminent contact between our bodies, I don't want to risk it.

I allow him to push me against the smooth surface, the two rods pressed against my wings while his chest stops inches from mine.

"You've made it clear that you like this room," he says, a soft, low statement. "Stay very still if you don't want it to burn."

"I have no intention of moving," I reply, despite the urge to reach out and chase the bead of sweat dripping down his face with my fingertip.

My chest rises and falls more rapidly after the workout and so does his, both of us taking deep breaths. The scent of his body is once again like a field of burned grass, and his juniper-green eyes rake over my face.

It's the color of his eyes now that makes me wary—and also intrigued because he doesn't seem as angry as before.

"You're stronger than you should be," he says.

"I'm stronger than you would *like* me to be," I reply with a smile and not a hint of concern.

"I never thought I'd say this to anyone who wasn't a dragon, but you really could have ripped Tyler's head off his shoulders the other night."

I shake my head. "Too messy. Too much blood. Breaking is cleaner."

"I'm not saying you would have. I'm saying you *could* have."

My jaw tightens and a heavy sensation settles in my chest. "Yes."

"Angels are skilled, I'll give them that, but ordinary angels don't have the strength to take us on. Their expertise is in aerial combat. They can't hit a dragon like a ton of bricks like you can."

They, he said. As if I'm not one of them.

I'm not sure where he's going with this and I'm suddenly uncertain enough that I push back against the rods keeping my wings pinned to the wall, my feathers swishing against the wooden poles.

He presses back, keeping me where I am.

"Perhaps it's the weight of my corruption," I say, my smile gone. My old friend *despair* pushes at the edges of my mind again as hard as I push back against it.

"What makes you believe you're corrupt?" Callan asks, a furrow in his brow and a sharp light in his unmistakably green eyes.

I'm surprised that he has to ask.

"I know I am," I say. "Other angels hate killing. They believe in goodness and love. They can't harm another being except in self-defense or through righteous decree. I revel in the hunt. I *want* to kill—"

"It's not life you want to destroy," he says. "It's guilt. You told me so."

A snarl rises to my lips because he speaks as if he knows me. "Is there a difference?"

"Of course there's a difference." His fists tighten so hard around the sticks that his knuckles are turning white. "Would you kill a child?"

My eyes widen and my response is instant. "Never."

"Then you're not corrupted."

"But…" Sudden emotional pain strikes through my chest, a tumult of rage and fear that his presence does nothing to dull. "Why are you saying this to me?"

I want him to be angry, to try to cage me, because then I can fight back. I can't fight against his assertion that I'm not wicked, but I also can't accept his argument. The foundations of my self-perception are well-established within my mind.

I am not *good*. I am not light and peace. I am the bloodied weapon that needs to be used during times of war and is hidden away during times of peace so others can forget how the peace was won.

As hard as I search his eyes, I can't fathom the nuances of his expression, the shifts in the color of his eyes, the emergence of cinnamon and the storm between his emotions—rage and calm —the way his forehead creases one moment and clears the next, as if he's somehow both infuriated and intrigued by me.

I grit my teeth and repeat myself, demanding an answer. "You have to kill me if you can't control me, so why are you saying this to me?"

"Because I need you."

His low murmur freezes me. I feel as if he poured molten lava over me and then followed it with a bucket of ice and now my world is cracking apart in the extremes.

Nobody needs me. They want my skills or my strength, but they don't need *me*.

He can't be any different.

I push away his exact words and add in what he means: He needs me so he can defeat the angels. He needs me to discern the motives of those who would challenge his leadership. He needs me to stop killing his people.

My eyes burn, and I'm both shocked and hateful of my sadness—but mostly that he can see it.

I blink hard against the moisture gathering around my lashes. Somehow, he managed to cut my heart with mere words. Something even the Serene Commander hasn't been able to do.

He speaks carefully. "I thought my plan for you was clear cut. But then you survived my flames. You revealed to me that you're a prisoner *because* of your power. Caged. Beaten. And convinced that your need for justice is a corruption."

His hands slip closer to my wings, as if he wants to run his fingers through them. "Open your mind, *not*-Lana, to the possibility that you're meant for more than one purpose. That your path may not be pre-determined. Then you might realize that you have real choices to make." His jaw hardens and his eyes are nearly pure green as his proximity heats me. "Then we might not have to kill each other."

He takes a small step back from me and, even though he doesn't yet release my wings, the increased distance between us leaves me feeling like I'm twisting in the wind.

What does he want from me, if not my death?

I tell myself I shouldn't care.

He is my enemy. A monstrous enemy.

Except that… he's not any more monstrous than I am. With every layer of his life that he reveals to me, I'm questioning everything I believed about him. Callan Steele. Dread dragon. Protector of humans. Fearsome clan leader. I can't put him in a silo because the reality is far more complicated than that.

I want to close the gap between us, but I force myself to remain still when I'm confronted by the realization that he's warmer than he was before. The air shimmers around his bare chest, as if a shift into his dragon form is at a trigger point.

He speaks in a rumble that is reminiscent of a burst of flames across ash, compelling me to listen.

"I'm giving you an hour to yourself," he says, surprising me. "I want you back on floor fifteen for lunch. Be aware that the bracelets are connected to the dragon's gold that is hidden throughout this building. If you try to leave, the bracelets and the gold will trap and stop you. Keep in mind that by trying to leave, you could risk exposing our existence to the humans. I think you understand the consequences of that."

He said he would die for the humans. They obviously mean a lot to him, and having spent even the smallest amount of time with Jada, I understand why.

"I'm surprised you're willing to take that risk," I whisper.

"At some point, I have to take a chance with you," he says. "I'm giving you a taste of freedom—of what it means to willingly stand at my side. It's up to you what you do with your time."

The sticks slide away from my wings, a careful movement on his part.

I remain against the wall as he places the weapons back on the wall and scoops up his shirt. He doesn't pull it on, striding away with the fabric gripped in his big hand.

The door closes behind him and I'm left in complete silence.

I don't know how to process what he said to me. He told me to open my mind. He told me he doesn't believe that I'm corrupted.

Yet I must be, because I've *killed*, not *saved*. Time and time again.

I wrap my arms around my stomach, slide down the wall, and stay there for a long time.

I try to cut through the complexities of my current situation and focus on the simplest things: He doesn't want to kill me, and now that I've spent time with him, I don't feel enough hatred toward him to want to kill him. Yet. But he also made it clear that if he can't control me, then he doesn't have a choice about ending me. My existence threatens his people. One of us will have to kill the other unless… one of us *bends*.

I've never bent. I've never been like a tall stem of grass in the wind. I've only ever struck back.

Maybe… a first step is time. Patience.

If I tell myself this is the long hunt, then it won't go against my basic nature. I'm simply biding my time. Observing my prey. Exploring his world. And as for my need to free myself from my cursed nature, it's only a delay. After all, I've been a hunter all of my life. What are a few more days—a week, even a month—for a creature like me?

My reasoning may not hold for long, and it may have holes in it, but it's the only way I can reconcile accepting these bracelets around my wrists and not fighting against the chains that will entrap me if I try to leave.

Picking myself up, I retract my wings, retrieve my shirt, and clean up the pieces of the dummy I broke.

It's only when I'm turning away that I notice a single feather on the dark surface of the mat. It's not unusual for me to lose a feather every now and then. Some of the older ones fall out all on their own, and I must have lost it during the fight. But when I crouch to pick it up, the strange sheen on this one makes me pause.

When I turn it into the light, its surface has an opalescent shimmer that I've never seen on my feathers before. A rainbow of colors glimmer across the soft, black shape, becoming stronger at the tip.

Twice now, I've survived Callan's fire and I shouldn't be surprised that it would have affected my feathers. In fact, it would be more surprising if it didn't, but I'm not sure what to make of this.

I slip the feather into my pocket, and at the same time, I wall up my churning thoughts and lock them away behind a single goal: to survive.

CHAPTER FIFTEEN

By the time I emerge from the gym, I have only half an hour left of the time Callan gave me, but I know where I want to spend it.

Hurrying to the seventh floor, I expect to find a library filled with shelves, but, once I use the passcode to step beyond the hallway, I discover that this library is not like any I've ever seen.

Instead of bookshelves on which the books are filed away, there are four leafless trees positioned in a diamond shape within the room. Every branch of the trees is lined with books whose pages are open so that it appears as if the structures have grown books instead of leaves.

When I touch their branches, I'm struck by how lifelike they feel and the way the books' pages seem to rustle in a wind I can't hear. Even though I'm sure the trees are not real or living, my senses buzz in a way that tells me they're magical. Or at the very least, the books are.

My jaw drops even further when I prowl around each of the trees, leaning in to see what the books reveal. They range from ancient texts that I can't read to modern books of lore, all with gorgeous illustrations. There are many books on angels, which doesn't surprise me, since Callan would have tried to find out everything he could about my species.

When I investigate the books on the other trees, I discover that each tree is dedicated to a form of magic. The far back tree contains books dealing with creatures of dark magic; the tree on the left deals with elemental magic; the one on the right is all about old magic; while the closest deals with light magic that belongs to angels and dragons.

Carefully releasing my wings, I fly up to see the books on the highest branches of the light magic tree, focusing on one that shows a group of angels with pure-gold eyes, their blonde hair braided back and pulled into tight, high ponytails.

The caption beneath the image states that these are Sentinels.

I've never seen one. Only heard about them.

The Sentinels are the strongest angelic warriors and also the purest. They're chosen to guard the angels' most precious items —from ancient jewels to items of rare magic.

The Serene Commander once told me that I'm as strong as a Sentinel, but she spoke with bitterness. At one point, she had apparently begged the Celestial Ascendant—the angel whose role it is to monitor the legions of angels on Earth—to order the Sentinels to help eradicate the dragons. The Celestial Ascendant refused because the Sentinels can't leave their posts.

The women in the image are all dressed the same as each other: high mahogany boots beneath knee-length flowing white dresses. Their bodices are covered with mahogany leather breastplates, and the skin around their eyes and temples is painted to look like mahogany wings.

They each hold a golden spear and wear a band of flat gold about half an inch wide across their foreheads.

Reaching out to turn the page, I find an entry on the Celestial Ascendant, the purest and most powerful angel on Earth, and I become so engrossed that I lose track of time. It's only when the bracelets around my wrists grow warm, and the ruby heart on one of them begins to glow, that I realize my hour is nearly up.

Reluctantly, I retract my wings and return to the fifteenth floor.

When I arrive, I'm surprised that Callan isn't anywhere in sight. I was expecting to find him waiting for me.

The room is well-lit, but in the distance, I catch the flicker of candlelight on the table within the sunken lounge. As I approach, I can see that two places have been set with cutlery, wineglasses, and folded napkins—just like in a restaurant.

I'm thrown by how civilized it all looks—and suddenly conscious of how sweaty the clothing that I blithely used as gym gear is.

Since Callan isn't waiting impatiently for me, I race into my room to freshen up and change into one of my nicer outfits: a soft, mesh midi skirt with black accents and an off-the-shoulder black, long-sleeved shirt.

I take a moment to retrieve the loose feather from the pocket of my jeans and place it in the top drawer of one of the bedside tables for safekeeping. Then I tie my hair back in a low ponytail that hangs across my left shoulder, before I prowl back into the living area in bare feet.

This time, I find Callan sitting within the sunken lounge, flipping through something on a computer tablet. He's dressed more formally than he was this morning in a collared shirt and long, gray pants. His dark hair is slicked back. At first glance, he looks relaxed, but his expression is reserved when he looks up.

We left things in a tense place, and I'm prepared to tackle our situation head on, but he stops me with a polite question before returning his attention to the tablet.

"Did you enjoy the library?"

I pause at the top of the steps into the sunken lounge. "How did you know I went to the library?"

He glances pointedly at the bracelets, and I suddenly recall that they allow him to track me.

"I know the location of every piece of dragon's gold that belongs to me," he says.

Stepping down into the sunken lounge and taking my place at the table opposite him, I answer his initial question. "I enjoyed the library as much as the gym."

He sets aside the tablet and looks right at me, and I'm struck with the sense that he was already paying more attention than I thought he was. His focus follows my hair across my bare shoulder, up along the curve of my neck, and across my face.

I didn't really answer his question. Evasion has been second nature to me for so long that I hardly notice I'm doing it.

"I enjoyed it a lot," I clarify.

"Good." He studies me with a new intensity and I'm not sure what he sees.

My lips part as I try to figure out what to say, how to explain to him that I'm prepared to accept a truce. For now. "You asked me to—"

I'm interrupted by the opening of the far door and Matt wheels in a cart with two plates covered in metal domes.

I press my lips together and hold my thoughts, although Matt's presence doesn't do anything to reduce Callan's scrutiny.

The young man doesn't seem to notice. He sets the food down in front of me with a cheery smile. "I'm your waiter today. Can I offer you a glass of wine?"

I stare up at him, but Callan tips his chin in the affirmative, and Matt pours me a glass of red wine before he gives me a smile. "Enjoy your meal."

"Thank you," I murmur, staring down at my plate. I recognize the salad on the side but not the square of some sort of layered food containing what looks like meat and pasta interspersed with a white sauce.

As soon as Matt leaves, I poke the layered food. "What is this?"

Callan gives me a quizzical look. "It's called lasagna. You've never eaten it?"

Cutting a very small portion off the corner, I dab it to my tongue before hesitantly chewing.

My jaw drops.

I take another piece, larger this time, and chew it just as carefully. Slowly. Savoring the combination of flavors bursting across my tongue. Like nothing I've eaten before.

It's rich. I'll probably have a stomachache if I eat too much of it, but... I moan, a sound that draws Callan's renewed scrutiny. "By the heavens, this is *good*."

Callan laughs, some of the tension disappearing from his shoulders—but not all of it. "What the fuck did the angels feed you?"

"Not this," I say, shoving another mouthful in. "I want more of this. Every night, please."

His response is soft as he puts down his fork. "Every night, huh?"

To say that I would be here every night, let alone one more night is a big leap.

But this is me. *Bending*.

Forcing myself to abandon the delicious food and taking a deep breath in an attempt to calm the suddenly rapid beat of my heart, I start the conversation we need to have carefully but without guile.

"We're enemies," I say, acutely aware that I have his full attention and even more aware that he's bracing for what I'm about to say.

His fist is tight around the knife he's holding, but I continue to speak as if there isn't a threat of death between us.

"We're destined to end each other," I say. "It's unavoidable and inevitable, but that doesn't mean it has to be today. Or even tomorrow."

I pause, then take another breath, grateful that he doesn't interrupt. "This morning, you said it would only take you a day to convince me to give up my freedom. You told me I wouldn't want to leave. You gave me my own room and all the clothes I could want. Your home is a palace compared to my cell. But the thing is, none of that matters to me. I came into this world with nothing, and nothing will ever truly belong to me but my choices."

His eyes splash with juniper green, the burned grass that I associate with danger. "What is your choice now?"

"I am what I am," I say. "I was built to exact justice where it can't otherwise be found. I can't promise you that I won't rage against members of your clan. I can't promise that I won't want to exact swift retribution, come what may. But I can promise you... that I'll wait."

His brow is furrowed, his jaw tense. "Wait for what, *not-Lana?*"

"For the day when... *if...* I discover that you deserve all the darkness that my real name embodies. That's the day I'll stop waiting." I rid myself of all my doubts. "That's the day one of us will have to end the other. Until then, I'll wait."

He considers me for a long moment.

I don't look away, even though it surprises me when he's this quiet. It's such a startling contrast to the ferocity of his dragon, but perhaps... that's his battle. I remember the look in his eyes when I realized he was clamping down on his dragon's fury, controlling it. Sheer willpower.

It makes me wonder if Callan wasn't as strong as he is, if his dragon would rage without end. An uncontrollable rage. Like my anger when I'm drowning in a sea of peoples' cruel intentions and all I want is to destroy them all.

I bite my lip the longer he doesn't respond, but I tell myself not to speak.

I haven't promised peace. I can't.

I've promised time.

Finally, he leans back, his increasingly cinnamon eyes following the curve of my cheeks to my bottom lip, then back to my eyes.

"Then we won't be killing each other today," he says.

"Despite the power imbalance between us," I say, tapping my forefinger against the bracelet on my left hand to emphasize my captivity. "We won't be."

The tension slowly leaves his shoulders. His jaw relaxes, and this time, his smile is… slow but real. "Good."

His skin shimmers for a moment and I focus in on his cheeks and neck, along with the visible patch of chest where his shirt is open at the top, noting the slight iridescent sheen on his skin, remembering the flicker of gold through his irises earlier.

He said he can't partially shift, but the change in his skin tone can't be anything else. It's subtle, but then, that's what a partial shift is. Changing irises, shifting skin, the beast's growl in his voice.

"What is it?" he asks, his voice rough, even though the tension doesn't return to his expression.

I shake my head, sure that I'm imagining it, even though I really want to reach out and touch his skin—show him what he looks like to me.

"Nothing," I whisper. It can't be anything.

With a slightly curious look, he lets it go before he leans back in his chair. "I want you to come out with me tonight," he says, a sudden proposal. "I own a club with a safe space where humans won't take notice of us. I want to take you there."

Despite his apparently relaxed countenance, anxiety grows within me. "Why?"

"Because the Cohort will be there tonight. They need to see you."

I catch on quickly. "They need to see that you're in control of me."

He dips his head in the affirmative.

"Taking me out will reveal the location of your home," I say. "Unless you plan to blindfold me again. Even if you do, it's a big risk to take."

He shakes his head. "It's only a risk if you lied about giving me time. If you lied—which I don't believe you did—then you should know that I have other homes. I can abandon this one at a moment's notice if I need to. The only people you could really hurt are my human friends." He leans forward. "I don't think you'll do that."

He's right: I wouldn't. My apprehension dissolves. "Then I'll go with you."

His smile returns. "Wear a dress."

"I'll wear whatever I want," I snap back.

He laughs, but his pleased expression fades a little as he says, "That's fine, but you should know that I'll have to—"

He doesn't finish before Jada's voice sounds through the intercom on the wall—the same device Callan used when he asked her to bring up my clothing this morning.

"Callan? Are you there?" Her tone is urgent. "Your sister's on her way up and she looks fucking angry. What the hell did you do to piss her off?"

Callan freezes where he sits. He looks as surprised as Jada sounds, which makes me think that Zahra never barges in— certainly not in a furious mood, and certainly not now when he told her he wanted privacy.

He spins to me, and his focus is suddenly on my wrists. "You can't appear to be moving around freely. She isn't ready for that and I don't want another fight to happen between you. I need you to understand that I don't have another choice."

I eye him warily. "Choice about what?"

Before I can protest, he raises his hand and a band of dragon's gold flies from the wall on my left, wrapping around my left wrist and yanking me from my seat.

An indignant cry passes my lips as the band wrenches me into the space at the side of the table next to the step. The gold's contact with my skin is as sudden as the first moment that I was chained in the alley, and my instinct is to fight back.

I grab at it with my free hand. "No!"

The band snakes around my other wrist before I can evade it. It wraps around my arms in a figure eight that leaves a loose end before it tugs me straight down to the floor.

I fall into a kneeling position, my back hunched over.

Callan crouches beside me. "If Zahra's angry, then her dragon has control. The bracelets won't be enough to assuage her. A fight between you won't end well this time."

At the corner of my vision, the fine, web-like clip for my wings flies toward me, shocking me when it manages to slip beneath the base of my shirt and slide all the way up across my shoulder blades. It's cold and makes me shudder before it settles against my back and bites into my skin.

I snarl up at Callan as he strides past me, but he doesn't pay any attention to my anger.

"Come with me," he orders. "Quickly."

CHAPTER SIXTEEN

At Callan's command, the gold around my hands yanks me upward. I have a choice between being dragged up the step and along the floor or accepting the situation and hurrying in the direction I'm being pulled. Toward Callan's bedroom door, where he slaps his palm against the access panel.

He catches the loose end of the chain as it tugs me through the now-open door. I glare at him, but he doesn't say a word. He pulls me toward his bed and wraps the end of the chain around the nearest post so that I'm tied to it again.

He pauses then, and the briefest shadow of regret passes across his face before he turns away. "Stay here."

As if I have a choice.

He leaves the door open, and I guess it's so that Zahra can verify that I'm still a captive. He didn't chain my feet this time, but they're not much use to me right now.

With a sigh, I sink to the edge of the bed where I lean against the post, trying to get comfortable. Closing my eyes, I expand my other senses, using my hearing to the fullest extent.

As it turns out, Zahra isn't in the mood for a whispered conversation.

As soon as Callan opens the door, her voice cracks through the room, emphasizing the extent to which sound can echo within the empty space.

"What the fuck, Callan?" Her heels clack loudly on the marble floor, but she doesn't walk far enough to be visible to me through the open door. "Of all the fucking stupid things you could do. You haven't brought her before the Cohort, but you ask Sophia's human friend to come and play *dress up?*"

"It wasn't like that," Callan replies, sounding far calmer than I was expecting.

"Not like that, huh?" She sounds like she wants to pummel him. "Let's see... Dresses. Shoes. Jewelry. Ribbons for her fucking hair! What part am I getting wrong?"

Ribbons. There weren't any ribbons.

"Are you done?" he asks, less patient.

"No!" she cries. "I'm not done. I'm *scared*, Callan. I'm fucking scared for my daughter right now. Your enemies will exploit any weakness. You know that!" Zahra barely pauses for breath. "Sophia told everyone that the angel survived your flames—"

"Lana," he snaps. "The angel's name is Lana."

"Fuck, Callan, are you listening to me? Sophia's telling everyone that you can't kill the angel. And if you can't kill the angel, then none of us can. She says that we're vulnerable and that *you're* the one bringing the danger to us."

I sense him move. Imagine him shaking his head.

Sense Zahra reach out despite needing to keep her distance.

"You burned Sophia's hair, Callan. She hasn't bothered to cut it or fix it because it's visual proof that you nearly killed her. She's gaining traction and it's not just the Cohort who are listening to her now; the entire clan is taking notice."

Callan says something in reply, but I don't hear it because a closer sound makes my eyes fly open. A small presence I'm shocked I didn't detect until now.

A little girl.

She stands just inside Callan's room.

Her hair is straight and black but cut short at her shoulders. She has a perfect rosebud mouth and large, angular eyes. Her skin is light brown and her irises are the same cinnamon as Zahra's.

She can't be much more than five years old.

Zahra mentioned a daughter and I guess I'm looking at her.

"Hi," the little girl whispers, the quietest sound.

I edge closer to the post I'm tied to, trying to move in front of the chains to conceal them, but it's impossible without turning my back on her.

"Uh… hello," I whisper back.

I'm surprised when she walks right up to me, little footsteps, slightly unsteady, as if she's carrying a great weight. Her large eyes widen as she stares up at me.

"You're an angel," she says, another whisper.

I stay very still.

"Do you have soft feathers?" she asks.

I clear my throat and find my voice. "Yes, but I can't show them to you. My wings are clipped right now."

"Mine too," she says. "It hurts."

I'm a little surprised. Not that it hurts her—I know how much the clip aches—but that this little girl has formed wings already when dragons as old as Sophia have never shifted.

"Why do you have to wear a clip?" I ask her.

She climbs onto the bed beside me, grunting softly with effort. "My wings like to fly, but we must *not* show the humans." She settles in beside me. "They'll kill us dead."

"Yeah." I'm surprised by how articulate she is, every sound pronounced, even though she's whispering. I infer from what she said that she can't control her wings yet. The weight of them within her body might also be why she's a little unsteady. If she's wearing a clip, I can't see it through the back of her blouse, but I guess that's the point.

"Have you come to help Uncle Callan?" she asks me, her serious eyes turned up to mine.

I chew my lip for a moment before I ask, softly, "Why does Uncle Callan need help?"

"No hugs," she says, her hopeful expression falling. "He needs hugs."

"Yeah," I whisper. "I guess we all do."

Outside the room, Zahra's voice is no less furious. "They'll come after Emi first, you know that!" She suddenly stops and an intense silence falls outside the room. Then she asks, urgently, "Wait… Where's Emi? She was right here—"

Her heels clack sharply against the marble floor, rapidly approaching. "Emika?"

She stops a few paces away from the doorway, her eyes flying wide when she sees her daughter sitting next to me.

"Emika! No!" Zahra's focus flashes to me and the fury in her voice is so much like a whip that I wince. "Get the fuck away from my daughter."

It's not like I have anywhere to go. Slipping off the bed, I swing around the pole and crouch on the other side of it, as far from the child as I can.

Up on the bed, Emika has frozen, her little shoulders tense, her breathing suddenly rapid as her mother storms into the room.

Emi bursts into tears when Zahra sweeps her up into her arms. "Mama!"

Zahra swings to me, clutching Emi close. Her cinnamon eyes are wild and bright with bronze hues, a bronze sheen glistening across her light-brown skin. I process what looks like a partial shift while focusing on the problem in front of me.

"Stay the hell away from my daughter," she says.

I remain crouched and perfectly still. "You're scaring her," I say, my voice barely audible above Emi's crying.

"She *should* be afraid!" Zahra cries. "You're here to kill her."

I shake my head, edging upward, an instinctive response. "Your daughter's innocent. I don't kill the innocent."

Zahra's narrowed eyes tell me she doesn't believe me and there's nothing I can say that will alleviate her fear. A mother's fear. Her need to protect her daughter at all costs.

Adjusting my position, I sink to the floor again, aware of Callan's looming presence within the doorway. At the same time, I sense a strange new tension between the bracelets on my wrists and the golden bands clamped around my arms, a growing heat between them.

Zahra swings away from me, preparing to leave, but I won't stay quiet. "Your daughter will grow in fear if you raise her to be afraid."

Zahra tenses and snarls back at me. "You're lecturing me on being a parent?"

I refuse to look away. "If you tell your daughter often enough that she should be afraid, then she'll believe it. If you tell her she isn't strong enough, she'll believe that, too. If she thinks she can't trust anyone, then she never will. Eventually, anger will be her only defense and by then, it will be too late for her to learn any other way."

Zahra's expression has fallen, her brow is intensely furrowed, and her lips are parted, but she doesn't immediately hurl a retort back at me.

"I'm not lecturing you," I say quietly. "I'm speaking from experience."

The color in Zahra's cheeks drains and for a brief moment, there's a hint of pity in the shape of her lips, but then she's like stone. "My daughter will not become like you."

I drop my focus to my bound hands, my shoulders hunching even further. The clip across my wings pulls against my skin and I fight to conceal my discomfort. "If you're sure."

As Zahra turns away, slower now, I glance up at Emi, her little face visible over Zahra's shoulder but half-covered by her hair. Her cheeks are blotchy, but her cries have subsided into whimpers. I search for fear in that brief moment of eye contact, praying I don't see it.

She wasn't afraid of me when she first stepped into this room. I don't want her to be afraid of me now.

Her mother whisks her away before I know for certain.

"The Cohort, Callan," Zahra says pointedly to him when she stops just outside the door.

Despite the care he gives to the gap between them, his response is clipped. "It's already arranged, Zahra. I'm taking Lana to the Hollow Rose tonight. If you'd waited another ten minutes, I would have had the chance to tell you."

She deflates a little, but not much. "Promise me you know what you're doing."

This is the moment that, if Callan could touch her, I imagine he'd reach out, grip her shoulders, and look her straight in the eyes. As it is, all he does is make eye contact. "I have this under control."

"I hope that's true." She pulls Emi closer, keeping her out of my line of sight.

"Zahra," Callan says before she can step away. "I won't let anything happen to you or my niece."

She bites her lip. Quieter. "I believe you. I'll be there tonight." With another glance at him, much less fiery than before, she disappears from view.

I listen to her footfalls as they recede, then to the opening and closing of the door.

Callan leans back against the doorframe, his shoulders hunched, his focus down.

"She wants to trust you, but fear is clouding her judgment." I speak softly, but the truth as I see it sounds sharp in the silence. "Emika is the reason Zahra didn't challenge the old alpha, isn't she?"

"Zahra was pregnant when she left the dragon masters. She's

never gone back, and she doesn't speak about Emi's father." Callan raises his head. "Dragon children rarely grow up with both parents. Zahra was the rare exception. Her mother raised me too."

I chew on my next question, uncertain whether or not to ask it. "What happened to your mother?"

"She was human."

I'm surprised. "How is that possible when humans aren't allowed to find out about dragons?"

His jaw tightens. "Because human women don't survive the birth of a dragon child." He meets my eyes. "My mother never knew what my father was, or what she was carrying. We develop like human children in the womb. You won't see anything on an ultrasound. It's not until moonlight touches us outside the womb that our true nature is triggered and after that, we develop as dragons.

"In the past, dragons justified female human deaths because our species is dying out." His voice is low and harsh. "It's a barbaric practice and I outlawed it."

I'm quiet for a moment before I say, "Your human mother is why you have an affinity for humans."

"Maybe," he says. "Or maybe I believe it's wrong to kill an innocent person, no matter their species."

He's angry, but for once, he's not angry with me or the angels.

"You hated your father," I whisper.

He exhales a heavy breath. "I loved my father. I hated his choices."

I process that for a moment. "What about Zahra? I'm assuming her mother was a dragon."

"One of the strongest." He nods. "She chose my father after I was born." He grimaces. "We can't all have children, so Zahra's mother waited to choose her mate from one of the males who had proven he could bring a child into the world."

I'm not sure if I'm aghast or somehow not surprised at the brutal pragmatism involved in choosing a mate.

Callan clears his throat. "Zahra has purer blood than any of us. Which makes Emika one of the strongest dragons to be born in generations."

"But Zahra chooses to be your *beta*," I say carefully.

"Only in name. And only for stability. She wouldn't challenge the old alpha because she knew her daughter could be used as leverage against her. She stands at my side because otherwise, there would be a constant power play between us, and the Cohort would use that against both of us. Again, to the detriment of her daughter."

I consider him carefully. "Is Zahra strong enough to kill you?"

He takes a long moment to answer me. "Yes."

Finally peeling himself off the wall, he crosses the distance and crouches to me. "That's why I never want a fight to happen between you and her."

I remember the fight she and I had when I first arrived and the way she tried to trap me. I understand his concern now. If her intentions had been different, that fight might have gone very badly.

His hand hovers over the golden bands securing me to the bed post. His focus remains down, his lips pressed tightly together, his shoulders tense again. He's far closer to me than he should be and for a dangerous moment, I'm sure he's going to drop his hand to my arm.

"You're bruised," he says, his fingertips hovering near the edges of the golden bands, where they bite my skin.

I give him a crooked smile. "On the bright side, bruises on me will be a better look for your friends tonight."

His eyes flash to mine and they're pure green, an angry glare that surprises me.

I hurry on before he can say anything. "I think we both know that the bracelets won't be enough tonight."

He speaks with the same fury that he exhibited when he told everyone to get out the first night he brought me here. "Fuck them."

"Callan," I say, trying to make it easier. "I'll pick a dress that looks good with gold."

Some of his fury abates and his forehead creases. "You fought these chains when Zahra arrived before. Why have you stopped fighting them now?"

"Because I understand you and your sister a little better now."

With a small movement of Callan's fingers, the bands slip away from my arms and glide up through the air and then out through the open door behind him. He leaves the bracelets on me like before. The clip is slower to rise from my back, and I need to hunch over so that it can slip out from beneath my shirt.

He withdraws, returning to his feet, and I stand slowly with him.

"We'll leave at eight," he says. "Until then, stay on this level. I have something I need to take care of before we go."

When he leaves, the silence is real. So is the warmth of the bracelets around my wrists, reminding me of the strange tingling between them and the golden bands.

I have a whole afternoon to myself and the space around me is much larger than my cell, but the silence is familiar. I spent long hours in my cage in silence like this and it allowed me to hone my senses.

Now that Callan's gone, I need to test my skills and reassure myself that it's only his presence that messes with my ability to assess my surroundings.

I retreat to my room, sit cross-legged on the floor with my eyes closed, and run through my breathing exercises, slowly sinking into a meditative state before I expand my senses and allow all of the sounds and smells around me to flood in.

For hours, I fill my mind with the soft *whoosh* of the air conditioning and the quiet buzz of electricity running through the walls, and then, when my senses are floating free, I allow my mind to sink.

Below the floor, taking in the empty space beneath me. There's another level there, but it contains nothing. No furniture, no interior walls. I sink farther still and discover the next floor down is the same. After that, it gets fuzzy and I know I've pushed my abilities as far as they can go.

I'm surprised that there's nothing below us, but perhaps Callan has left a few floors empty as a buffer. Curious now, I allow my mind to float upward, sensing the continued whir of the building's electricals and becoming aware of a larger space above this level that I wasn't expecting.

Just as my mind rises toward what I expect to be the roof cavity, I hit a layer of power that bursts across my senses like fireworks.

Fuck! A magical barrier!

I jolt away from it within my mind, my whole body tingling.

The shot of adrenaline surges through me and I struggle to gain control of my response, taking a deep breath and sinking back to my body.

I'm uncertain about what I touched. It's another level, that's for sure, even though the elevator apparently only rises as high as this floor. And it's protected by magic so strong that I couldn't sense anything beyond it.

I focus on the present, on relaxing my mind and banishing the shock I experienced. Gradually returning to my immersive state, I allow myself to settle.

An hour later, I'm ready to try again, prepared this time to touch the ceiling more carefully.

This time, I'm interrupted by the suddenly overloud sound

of the elevator rising, the grinding of its opening door, and the buzzing of the control panel outside the living area.

The warm scent of sunshine lifts the fog.

Callan is back and I'm suddenly conscious of the time.

I take deeps breaths and reel in my senses, dampening my hearing and the smells around me. It's a slow process since I'm so fully immersed, but I hurry a little because Callan's firm footfalls are headed toward me and they're like booming hammers in my amplified hearing. Combined with a softer thumping sound I can't identify.

I open my eyes, adjusting back to normal as he appears at my door. He's holding a metal case, which he places down in the doorway. It must have been bumping against his leg—the soft thumping sound I heard.

"Is it late?" I ask.

He studies me where I continue to sit cross-legged, my hair falling across my shoulder, the mesh skirt pooling around me.

"It isn't late," he says. "Are you hungry?"

I take stock of my stomach. "A little."

"I'll get some food." He leaves the case in the doorway and within minutes, the mouthwatering scent of roasted potatoes filters through the air. I realize that I'm more than a little hungry.

Callan doesn't tell me what's in the case, and I decide to ignore it for now, heading out to the sunken lounge to eat with him.

After a quick meal, I return to my room and stand in my dressing area to consider my choices. I reach for my only high-backed dress first before I push it aside and reach for one of the low-backed gowns instead.

It will reveal my scars. But it will also show the clip that I'll have to wear across my shoulder blades, which seems important. I hate the feel of dragon's gold against my skin, but I understand the need for it. Callan's position is not secure. He took a huge risk inviting Tish here today—a reckless risk, actually, since he could have simply handed me some clothes. It's a risk that could still backfire on him.

For a moment, I worry about humans seeing the clip, but Callan said they won't take notice of us and worst case, the clip is pretty enough that it can pass as jewelry.

Swiftly removing my clothing, I pull on fresh underwear, choose a bra that will work with the dress, and then slip into the gown.

It reaches my ankles but has a long slit up the left leg. The bodice is shaped across my breasts and cut down to my sternum with a gap between the two sides so that the skin between my breasts is bare. The sleeves are soft mesh bands that sit across my shoulders. It's simple, but it works.

When I turn and consider the back, which leaves a large triangle of skin visible, I tell myself that my pride can handle it. What are scars but proof that I'm a survivor?

Emerging from the dressing room, I study the case that Callan left, which still sits in my doorway. He didn't say anything about it, but I can only assume it's meant for me.

Placing it on the bed, I release the clasps and stare down at the golden pieces nestled on velvet inside it. I recognize the spiderweb clip secured to the inside of the lid. The remaining pieces are wide bands made of thin gold. Delicate in a way that surprises me.

There are what look like four armbands. Also a necklace made from a curved band with a chain at the back and with multiple fine strands of gold attached to a single spot at the front. And a much larger circle of gold that is far too big for my neck or arms, so I'm not sure where I'm supposed to put it…

Callan's presence is warm when he appears in the doorway behind me. He's dressed in gray pants and a collared shirt that's open at the top and with the sleeves rolled up to the bottom of his large biceps.

"That one's for your waist," he says.

"Oh."

I straighten and turn toward him.

He doesn't step foot inside my room—just like he promised —but all it takes is a turn of his palm and the largest circle of gold rises up out of the case and floats toward my waist, settling across my hips before the chain attached to the back of it secures it tightly around me.

Next are the armbands, two of which settle around the tops of my forearms, and I discover that the other two are not for my arms after all when they settle around my ankles. Then the necklace rises and floats into position around my neck, sitting across my clavicle. I stay very still as the chain at the back of it clicks together.

The loose, golden strands connected to the front of the necklace fall softly between my breasts.

Last of all, the clip settles against my spine. It's the most uncomfortable and I wince a little.

"You didn't give me these to look pretty," I say. "Show me."

He clicks his fingers.

The waistband suddenly splits, dropping lines toward my ankles that adhere to the rings around them. At the same time, the loose strands between my breasts whip out and connect with the armbands, pulling my arms inward.

I jolt, off-balance, anticipating the shortening of the bands that would pull me to my knees, but Callan clicks his fingers again and the bands release me. "You don't need to see the rest," he says. "My clan should be satisfied with seeing so much gold on you."

I turn and catch sight of myself in the mirror within the dressing room, appreciating how much the chains look like normal jewelry.

Callan inclines his head. "It's time to go."

"Just a moment." On impulse, I hurry back into the dressing

room and snatch up one of the shawls, a sheer black one that I drape across my shoulders. It should leave the clip visible while concealing the worst of my scars.

"Will Jada be coming with us tonight?" I ask when I return to Callan.

He shakes his head. "My human friends never accompany me to the club."

"Okay, then." I take a deep breath and prepare myself.

CHAPTER SEVENTEEN

We descend in the elevator and exit into the parking garage, after which Callan gestures to a dark gray two-seater sports car. When I slide into it, the scent of new leather is overpowering. I'm immediately aware of the tinted windows, and I press my fingertips to the dark surface.

"It keeps the moonlight out," Callan explains, slipping into the driver's seat and turning the ignition before reaching for the garage door opener.

The vehicle makes a beautiful growl as we speed from the garage, although Callan drives more carefully on the road.

It's my first view of the exterior of Callan's home and the street sign confirms the radius in which I thought he lived— only five blocks from the river and not too far from the concert hall.

The city is shrouded in night, but the streets are alive with people and sparkle with artificial light as we pass a mix of modern and older buildings on our way farther downtown.

Soon enough, we turn onto a busy street and the neon sign ahead announces the Hollow Rose. A side street we pass is filled with patrons lining up to go inside. Callan turns into the next alley and drives down toward a garage door. A security guard opens it and waves us through.

"Human?" I ask.

"Everyone who works for me is human."

The lives of the rich.

Inside, the parking garage looks a lot like the one beneath Callan's home. I recognize the sleek sports car and the sports motorcycle that Davison and Byron drove away that first night.

I exit the vehicle slowly, trying to dampen my senses instead of expanding them. A steady thump of music thrums through the ceiling above us, and I'm already mentally preparing for the explosion of sensory input I'll experience once we enter the club. The only saving grace is that Callan's presence will dull my ability to sense guilt and constrain my rage. Nightclubs are generally not good places for me.

My heels tap on the concrete while my dress swishes quietly around my legs.

"Who is in the Cohort?" I ask, attempting to distract myself.

"The eight strongest Dread dragons, including me as their leader," Callan replies, locking the vehicle and striding after me. "You'll recognize some of them tonight." He speaks as if they're old acquaintances and not my mortal enemies. "Byron, Davison, Tyler, and Martha. Zahra, of course. There are two others you haven't met: one female, one male. They're cousins. Beatrix and Felix Lamonte."

"Will they all be here tonight?" I ask, steeling myself.

"Without a doubt. You should be prepared for them to have brought other clan members with them, too. It's only when I summon the Cohort to my home that our meetings are private."

A man waits at the bottom of the elevator and Callan greets him casually—their interaction relaxed enough that I assume he's not a dragon. It quickly becomes apparent that he's one of the club staff when Callan has an exchange with him about drink orders for 'the balcony,' wherever that is.

We step into the elevator, I take up a place in the back corner, Callan stands in the other corner, and the staff member presses the button for the second and third floors.

He leaves us at the second floor, stepping into a dark hallway.

When the doors close again, Callan says, "We're going straight to the balcony upstairs to avoid the crowd and the dance floor."

The volume of sound increases as the elevator rises and I brace for the inevitable sensory overload.

I'm surprised when the elevator lets out into a small entry room that's lined with glass walls so that I can see directly through to the room ahead—except that it's not so much a room as what looks like an enormous balcony, like Callan said. It's also lined in glass and has a view through to the ceiling of what must be the dance floor below us. Lights flash and smoke effects waft through the distant air. The floor beneath my feet thrums with the beat of music. I'm glad to discover that I can't discern the scents of the people within the club from here, because otherwise my senses would be going haywire.

The balcony has eight tables set out at intervals. One of them is set much farther apart from the others on the right-hand side with a clear path to it from the glass entry room.

The benefit of the glass atrium is that Callan can see beyond it and make his presence known so that nobody accidentally steps into his path. The downside is that everyone can immediately see us.

It only takes a second for Zahra to identify us, given that she's sitting at the nearest table.

She stands up, dressed in a low-cut V-neck dress in an earthy color. She's wearing nearly as much jewelry as I am—a band around her left arm, a chain around her neck, and an anklet—but I'm sure her gold is not for the purposes of restraint.

While Callan pauses at the transparent door onto the balcony, I quickly sum up the dragons at each of the tables. Each of the Cohort members sits with other people. Davison is with two men and a brunette, who appears to be wearing more jewelry than I am. Martha, the oldest of the group, is sitting at a table behind Tyler and Sophia, surrounded by four women.

Tyler's scrutiny is particularly sharp, a searing glance down my body, while Sophia's expression is shadowed. She's as elegantly dressed as Zahra, but her bracelet is noticeably absent from around her wrist and her hair... *heavens*. My focus lingers briefly on the short, clumped patch at the side of her head—clearly visible just like Zahra said—before I quickly size up the man and woman sitting together at the next table.

Probably the Lamonte cousins. They're both tall and lithe with high cheekbones and dark hair. It's impossible to accurately tell eye, hair, or skin coloring in this light, but the woman —Beatrix—has straight, dark hair cut at an angle along her jaw and is wearing heavy eye makeup that accentuates the dark eyes that dominate her face, while the man has longer hair that's swept back into a sleek bun. They have a sort of cruel beauty about them that makes me grateful for Callan's presence.

Otherwise, I'm sure I'd have to kill them.

I stand clear of Callan's position while he opens the door and holds it for me to step through.

The steady, distant hum of music from the dance floor alleviates what would otherwise be dead silence.

"Well, fuck me," Beatrix says, loudly enough to be heard before she stands and glides toward me. Her feet are bare. I spy her heels, discarded beside her table.

She breezes past Callan—although she's smart enough to veer wide of him—and reaches out to skip her fingertips across the top of my shawl, around the armband on my left arm, and over to my hair, which she flicks. "Beautiful killer. All chained up. What a pity."

I'm frozen as she leans in and inhales deeply. She lets out a moan, her voice rising. "Fuck me twice! This bitch smells like the night air after it rains." She spins to Callan with wide, bright eyes. "Can I play with her?" She gleams at him. "Pretty please?"

Callan swings to Beatrix and takes a step toward her.

She jumps back lightly and bursts into a heady laugh. "Oh my. Possessive. Now I *really* want to mess with her."

"Fuck off, Beatrix," he growls.

She pouts. "Not nice. You should learn to share your toys, Callan."

But she's already edging away to a safe distance. Batting her eyelashes at Callan, she slinks back to her cousin, who leans forward across their table with a predatory grin.

He purses his lips at me and kisses the air. When Beatrix drops into her seat and leans in to whisper something into his ear behind her cupped hand, he laughs loudly and turns back to his drink.

Nearby, Sophia is giving Beatrix a death stare while Martha huffs and everyone else who was staring at me finally turns back to their drinks and conversation.

I let out the breath I was holding.

Callan inclines his head at the empty table on the right. I follow him, attempting to appear appropriately obedient, all the while remaining aware of every move the dragons are making, every laugh, every clink of jewelry, every glance in my direction.

We pass Zahra on the way. Like the others, she isn't alone at her table, sitting with two men and two women, all of whom are elegantly dressed, their eyes bright with curiosity, but any hint of fear disappeared when Beatrix attempted to rile me up and I didn't respond.

Zahra remains at a safe distance from Callan but leans in to deliver a quiet message. "Keep Lana away from Byron. He's in a foul mood."

My instincts prickle. Byron was the one who tried to stab me in the SUV.

"Also, don't be surprised if Tyler approaches you," Zahra continues. "He's had too many drinks already, so he's not at his smartest."

Callan seems to take her warnings seriously, giving her a firm nod before continuing on to his table.

When I take a seat in the chair he pulls out for me, I scan the room for Byron, finding the dragon with the scruffy beard in the shadows of the far corner, the only one sitting alone. His table is set apart from the others, like Callan's table, but its surface is littered with empty shot glasses. He stares into another one that's half full. The other dragons appear to be ignoring him, but I don't miss their cautious glances. They seem almost as wary of him as they are of me.

Within moments of us sitting down, a team of waitstaff appears, rapidly clearing out the empty glasses and setting down new drinks for everyone, including me, before they quickly disappear again. None of them pays any attention to my back or the clip that rests against my skin.

True to Zahra's prediction, it's only minutes before Tyler approaches with Sophia on his heels.

Just as they're doing with Byron, the other dragons keep us in their sights while maintaining the appearance of being busy with their own conversations.

Tyler pulls up a chair closer to me than I would like and sprawls in it.

"You finally brought her out." He speaks to Callan, but his gray-blue eyes are pinned on me.

Callan's expression is icy, his biceps bunching when he leans forward. "It took time to tame her."

In the next breath, he shifts his attention to Sophia. "How are you, Sophia?" he asks, far more gently than he spoke to Tyler. "Not hurt?"

"I... uh..." She pats her hair. "A little singed—"

Callan swings to me. "Lana." His voice changes again. This time stony. "Give Sophia your shawl."

I freeze a little. The material is covering my back, but I knew what I was doing when I wore a low-backed dress, and I see exactly where Callan's going with this.

Without objection, I stand, slip the scarf from my shoulders, and step carefully around the table, aware of Tyler's gaze on my form. Reaching Sophia, I fold the shawl slowly and hold it out to her.

She stares up at me from her seat as if I'm trying to give her a stick of dynamite. That I've already lit a match to.

"For your hair," I say contritely. "Since it was my fault."

Sophia's hand darts out. She snatches the scarf, leaving me to back away from her.

I'm painfully aware of the scars on my back, and even more aware of Sophia's cruel smile when I catch her staring at them as I walk back to my seat.

There's a drop in the conversation behind me, a sudden silence from Beatrix's table, before the conversation resumes, hushed now.

Sophia wraps the scarf around her hair and tucks her bangs neatly into it. She's smiling at Callan now and I guess she must be satisfied that my humiliation is greater than hers. "How thoughtful of you, Callan."

I'm a step away from my seat, just past Tyler, when the blond-haired dragon grabs my wrist, stopping me. Rising to his feet, he pulls me into his side in one swift movement so that my shoulder is jammed against this chest. His arm curls around my waist.

He reeks of cheap beer, oddly disconcerting since I assumed he could afford expensive liquor. His lips nudge my earlobe when he whispers, "I don't think you're tame at all."

I'm frozen, uncertain how Callan is reacting because I can't see him from this angle, but even more unsettled by the way Tyler's hand strokes my waist. Right in front of his wife. Because she's behind me, I can't see her, either, but my skin tingles, as if the intensity of the anger coming at me from multiple angles is going to cut me some new scars.

I'm starting to question whether the onceover Tyler gave me at the theater was fake or very real. All I know for sure is that he's trying to goad me into lashing out. I keep my expression blank. Get through the seconds by imagining myself punching his face and breaking his nose, remembering the moment in the alley when his body dropped within my hands and his neck was ready to break.

He waits another beat, another second for me to react, but when I don't make a sound or a move, he lets me go.

I continue back to my seat.

Callan has barely moved, but when I sit, I notice his left hand has dropped to the edge of his chair and the metal surface has buckled where he grips it.

Across the distance, Beatrix pouts at her table, her voice floating through the suddenly tense silence. "If Tyler gets to play, why can't I?"

Callan's fingers stretch at the side of his chair, a forced relax-ation, and in the next second, he lets out a laugh. "Because we all know you don't play nicely, Beatrix." He reaches for his glass without looking at me. "Do you see?" he calls to the group. "She's completely tame."

He glowers at everyone before he breaks into a grin. "Now get the fuck on with enjoying yourselves!"

The tension eases and conversations resume. At the table to the left, Zahra tips her glass to her brother before turning back to her friends. Even Martha seems to relax, arching her eyebrows at Callan, as if she didn't think he could do it, but he did.

I'm prepared to continue with the charade. For now.

CHAPTER EIGHTEEN

For the next hour, I sit quietly and observe while members of Callan's clan come and go from our table. Their conversation seems casual, but I quickly come to recognize that they all want or need something—mostly to do with business. Help with a deal they're trying to make. Assistance with a security issue. Advice about which human is more likely to accept an enticement—that one should probably shock me, but it doesn't.

Callan seems to have connections everywhere, both human and supernatural, a labyrinth of contacts. A witch on the east side of town who is willing to create potions. A panther shifter in the north who will take care of little problems that require a bit of muscle. A human willing to speed up certain paperwork.

When Davison approaches, Callan asks him, "Any update on the relocation of the wolf shifter pack?"

My ears prick up. A pack of wolf shifters went missing four months ago and I assumed the Dread were responsible for killing them since the wolf shifters were occupying prime real estate within the city.

Davison replies, "They're all settled outside of town."

"That's good news," Callan says. "Transfer an extra payment through one of the shell companies. The alpha's fucking proud; he won't accept the extra help if he knows it's coming from me."

"Consider it done."

Davison pushes back his chair, pausing only to glance at me, his focus running across the golden band around my neck. He plants his hands on the table and leans toward Callan. "It's good to see her controlled, Callan. The rumors were starting to fly."

Callan tips his chin and Davison steps away.

I remain sitting as stiffly as my 'controlled' situation demands. "Wolf shifters?" I ask quietly.

"One of their pack members racked up an extremely large debt," Callan says as he continues to scan the room. "He owed money to a Scorn dragon you never want to get into trouble with. I took care of it and pulled some strings to get the wolves out of the city. They'll have a fresh start now."

The next dragon approaches us—one of Zahra's friends—and I don't have the chance to ask any more questions.

If Callan's telling the truth, then the wolf shifters are alive and well. I fold my hands across my lap, wondering how many other situations I've misinterpreted.

As the night draws on, Byron is the only one who doesn't approach our table, remaining at his own, slumping further and further the more he drinks.

The longer I sit quietly, the more the dragons seem at ease around me, to the point where, another hour later, they hardly look at me.

All the while, the thrumming beat plays on my senses and the air around me grows warmer the longer I sit beside Callan. I need a moment of space, even though I recognize that stepping away from him carries other dangers.

"May I use the bathroom?" I ask him when I see my chance.

He hesitates before he inclines his head toward the far side of the room. "Down that corridor."

I keep my movements small and slow as I rise from my seat and walk straight toward the dark opening at the side of the room, not veering off the path but aware of all the eyes suddenly on me—Callan's in particular.

Turning the corner into the dimly lit corridor where I'm no longer visible to the dragons, I exhale and try to stretch the tension from my neck and shoulders before I hurry onward.

The bathroom is also dimly lit, but it's clean. Locking myself in a cubicle, I close my eyes for a long minute, centering myself, taking as much as I can from this moment of peace away from the dragons. The blissful seconds tick by until I'm forced to acknowledge that I can't stay in here forever.

Steeling myself to go back out there, I emerge, start washing my hands, and then pause as I discern light footfalls along the corridor outside.

Beatrix waltzes into the bathroom and I keep my focus down, intent on washing up and getting back to Callan before my anger rises.

She seems to have other ideas, gliding right up to me and leaning against the basin so close to me that I have to angle left to avoid knocking her with my elbow.

"Those are some scars you have. Poor little Night Sky," she croons. It seems that she's decided to give me a pet name that matches with how I apparently smell.

When she reaches out to flick my hair again, I can't stop myself. My reflexes are a storm of movement. I grab her hand, twist her wrist, grab her other shoulder, and yank her twisted arm behind her back. I ram her face-first into the tiled wall with a *thud*.

The air *whooshes* out of her lungs. "Fuck!"

Pinning her to the wall, I snarl into her ear. "Patronize me one more time..."

"Get off me," she snaps, a hint of fear in her voice. Up close, I inhale her scent, the sharp tang of sour lemon mixed with the heavy scent of cloves, but no copper.

Liar. Thief. But not a killer. I'm surprised by the last.

"Get the hell off me before someone comes in and you undo everything I did for you," she snarls.

"What are you talking about?" I'm surprised enough that I ease up and allow her to shove me off her—not that I try to hold on.

She spins and presses her back against the wall, as far away from me as she can get, her chest heaving. She takes a moment to touch her fingertips to her cheek with another curse. "You nearly split my skin. Do you have a fucking death wish?"

I grit my teeth. "What do you mean, *everything you did for me?*"

She stares at me, refocusing. "I did you a favor," she snaps. "You walk in and they're ready to tear you to shreds. I made you look weak. I took the fucking heat off you." She checks her fingertips again, whispering, "*Bitch.*"

I narrow my eyes at her, reflecting on her performance earlier. It had certainly defused the initial tension. "Why would you do that for me?"

She gives me a hard glare, her big, dark eyes wide. "I might not be Callan's biggest fan, but there's no fucking way I'm letting Sophia get her way. That bitch is nothing but a damn distraction."

"From what?"

I stand my ground when Beatrix lurches right up into my face. She suddenly smells icy, the scent of fear.

Real fear.

"Byron," she says, lowering her voice. "Tell Callan to watch him. He's getting reckless. I've seen him walking the streets at night, right in the fucking moonlight. It's like he doesn't care if he endangers us all."

A sense of dread stirs in my stomach as I peer into her eyes. "Why are you telling me this?"

She pulls herself upright. "Because if you were here to kill us, you would have done it already. The fact that you haven't tells me…"

When I remain silent waiting for her to continue, she sighs. "I don't know what the fuck it tells me." She rubs her forehead. "Just do me a favor and warn Callan, okay?"

"I will."

At that moment, voices sound outside the door. I recognize them as Sophia's and Martha's and they sound overly bright, a little too loud.

Beatrix's eyes widen. "Fucking bitch brigade is here."

Just as Sophia pushes the door open, Beatrix backhands me. It's a hard hit—stronger than I was anticipating—and I bang into the wall behind me, knocking my shoulder on the paper towel dispenser. Beatrix plows after me and shoves me up against the tiles, her hands biting my shoulders, her face close to my neck as she inhales deeply—and loudly. "Hot damn, Night Sky."

Behind her, Sophia makes a disgusted noise and Martha huffs. "Beatrix, take it elsewhere!"

Without letting up on my shoulders, Beatrix tips her head back to see them, as if she only now noticed they were there. "What?" she singsongs. "Like you're so pure."

She eases up on me, dances her fingertips up and down my arms, and then releases me. While she checks herself in the mirror, running her thumb across the corner of her lip as if she's fixing her lipstick, I keep to the wall and make myself look clumsy while I'm at it.

Beatrix blows a kiss back at me as she saunters out. "Thanks for the fun, Night Sky. Don't tell Callan." She pauses beside Sophia and widens her eyes dramatically. "I'd hate for him to burn my hair."

Out she sashays, leaving Sophia fuming. "That bitch!"

"Sophia," Martha warns, indicating me with a sharp nod of her head to remind Sophia that I'm still present.

"Like I care," Sophia snaps.

She strides right up to me and shoves me against the wall just like Beatrix did. This time, it's like being pushed around by a butterfly, and I have to exaggerate the impact of my back hitting the tiles.

"Stay away from my husband," Sophia says, grabbing the side of my necklace. The piece of jewelry already has a tight fit, so the increased pressure pulls it against the other side of my neck. It's slim enough that it threatens to break my skin. My wince is real this time.

"Sophia!" Martha snaps. "Do *not* leave a mark on her."

Sophia doesn't seem to care. Her face is close to mine, her breath remarkably clear of alcohol. "I see the way Tyler looks at you," she whispers. "The same way he looks at my so-called friend."

My forehead creases. Genuine puzzlement. Then it clears. "You mean Tish."

"He thinks I don't know that he's sleeping with her, but I'm not stupid. If he'll screw a human, then he'll screw an angel." She gives me another shove before she backs off, rubbing her wrist where her bracelet normally rests. "Stay away from him or I'll do more than clip your wings."

I straighten my dress, check briefly for any sign of blood on my neck, and veer wide of her and Martha. "Excuse me."

I'm only a step outside the bathroom when I sense another presence, this one lurking in the shadows of the corridor to my left.

Oh, fuck, what now? All I wanted was a moment of peace...

I don't make a sound when I'm pulled into the shadows and a big hand covers my mouth, but the press of a sharp blade against my side is frighteningly familiar.

"High and mighty Callan," Byron whispers into my ear, a low, threatening sound. "He's fucked you up pretty good, hasn't he? Just like he promised. Dressed you up in death."

I attempt to speak against his hand, which, like Tyler's breath, reeks of alcohol.

"No, no, hush," he whispers. "Don't speak. Just listen." His right arm tightens around my waist and his blade presses harder against my ribs, but this time, it hasn't yet cut skin.

"You have to look beneath the surface," Byron whispers. "Look where you're not supposed to look. You see all this? Money. Booze. Cars. But who does the dirty work, huh?"

His hand slips on my waist, the knife grating against my dress, but he's so unsteady that the blade turns sideways and lifts the material instead of cutting it. "I'm the one who takes care of problems. Are you still a problem, Lana?"

I attempt to extricate myself and that seems to be all it takes to knock Byron off-balance. He stumbles backward, taking me with him, but he's so drunk that his fall against the wall breaks his hold on me.

I jump away from him, spinning to keep him in my sights.

He lifts an unsteady finger and points it at me, then at himself.

I back away, watching in case he comes after me. When he doesn't, I take the chance to check my dress and ascertain that it's uncut.

I fight the impulse to run to the end of the corridor, keeping my speed steady as I return to the balcony. The music is louder now and the dragons are mingling beyond their tables. On the far side, close to the glass wall, Beatrix is dancing with several others while Zahra is in conversation with Davison's friends.

Callan has remained at his table, although this time, one of Zahra's friends is sitting opposite him. The breath Callan releases when he sees me is visible across the distance before he turns back to the woman.

I stride toward them, only to be stopped again by Tyler, who's sitting on his own at the table nearest to my path back to Callan.

"Lana." Tyler pats the seat beside him.

I give him a cold, hard stare. My tolerance for being accosted is now running very low. I grit my teeth and force myself to give a polite response. "No, thank you."

When I move past him, he snags my arm, keeping his voice down. "I said, sit the fuck down."

Actually, he hadn't said anything like that. I bite my tongue before I say so.

A glance tells me Callan hasn't noticed yet, and nobody else has, either. If I could fight Tyler right now, I'd get him off me in two seconds flat, but as it is, nobody is paying attention to me, and I need to keep it that way.

I allow him to pull me into the chair he patted.

"There, see. Not so hard after all." He scooches across to me. "I only want a second of your time. While my wife is busy fixing her hair."

He grins as if he told a joke, but his contempt for Sophia makes me run cold.

"She was supposed to be your ticket to the top, wasn't she?" I ask.

He jolts at my abrupt question, but a retort quickly forms on his lips. "I was promised control of the Dread if I married her."

"So now you have a wife you despise and no power to make the marriage worth it."

He leans in close and I realize just how loose his lips have become when he mutters, "And no children."

Oh.

He brushes the hair from my face, his knuckles grazing my neck. "Only one child has been born to our clan in five long fucking years." He stares at me. "One descendant. Just one. We need to start looking beyond our own kind." His fingertips brush my jawline. "And since you seem subservient now…"

I stiffen.

Stay away from my husband, Sophia said. If only he'd fucking stay away from me.

"Maybe you could come visit me sometime?" Tyler says.

That's it. I'm done being polite.

I turn right into him. "Or… how about I climb up onto your lap and we can go at it right here, and see what everyone thinks of that?" I lean in close enough to him that my lips touch his ear. "I wonder what the consequences would be? Would Callan come raging over here and claim what's his?"

Tyler stiffens, but his response is a sneer. "He won't risk starting a fire. He couldn't do a fucking thing."

"Okay, maybe… but I wonder how long you'd let me touch you before that little voice in the back of your head starts asking if I'm going to rip your cock off?"

Tyler laughs, a harsh sound. "You can't hurt me." His eyes flash to mine. "If you shed a single drop of dragon's blood, the gold you're wearing will—"

"Immobilize me. I know."

"No," he whispers, a sudden light entering his eyes. He runs his finger across the golden band around my waist, then the one around my neck. "These particular bands will cut you to pieces."

I freeze. *What?*

He licks his lips, studying my reaction. "You didn't know?" A smile breaks out on his face as he continues to stroke the necklace. "This one will slice your head from your shoulders. And this one at your waist, will sever you in half. Nice, clean cuts. But what a mess." He inclines his head toward Davison's table. "Don't worry, Davison knows how to clean up nasty situations like that."

I tell myself that Tyler must be lying about this jewelry, but then I remember the way Beatrix had checked her cheek when I shoved her against the bathroom wall, exclaiming that I nearly broke her skin, asking me if I had a death wish. And Byron said Callan had dressed me up in death.

It's no wonder the clan has accepted my presence here so easily tonight. Beatrix said she did me a favor. She stopped anyone getting in my face and risking my retaliation.

But Callan… He didn't tell me that I'm wearing a death trap.

My heart is beating faster and cold panic threatens to overwhelm me. A mere scratch can draw blood. An accident could draw blood. A small mistake could end me. I may be strong, but my skin and bones aren't made of metal. The golden bands are suddenly very heavy against my skin.

Too tight.

I fight against the instinct to try to rip them off. *Now!*

Desperately, I push away my fear and focus on extricating myself from my present situation. I need to get away from Tyler as fast as I can.

"Okay, I guess you've got me there," I say, as if I don't care about the golden bands. "But how about this one: Sophia sees us and starts screaming about how you're fucking a human and trying to get that human pregnant."

The last is a guess on my part, but the way Tyler stiffens confirms my theory.

"Callan's mother was human," he says. "His father understood what we had to do. We don't have a choice anymore."

"But Callan disagrees," I say. "Sure, he might not want to expose his power here in this place, but if he deems your crimes worthy of death, he'll come after you. You won't stand a chance."

Tyler's hands harden on my shoulders. "Get the fuck away from me."

"Gladly."

I rise from my seat, aware of Callan's furious scrutiny across the room, but his anger fills me with ice now.

I can handle assholes like Tyler. I can handle bitches like Sophia. What I can't handle is that Callan put this necklace on me and acted as if I looked beautiful in it.

My chest hurts because it feels like a betrayal.

It *is* a betrayal.

I told him I'd give him time, that I wouldn't strike until I was sure he deserved my darkness.

That time might have already arrived.

CHAPTER NINETEEN

It's 2 o'clock in the morning by the time we leave, a dark part of night. The time when nothing good happens.

I made it through the rest of the evening by sitting silently near Callan and keeping my hands and feet to myself, avoiding contact of any kind with anyone. Callan's focus was increasingly on me and I wished I could see the color of his eyes, but the neon lights hid their hues from me.

If he didn't tell me about the bands, what else has he lied about?

By the time we finally exit the building, get back in the car, and Callan drives out onto the street, I feel like I want to tear out of my own skin.

Callan speaks quietly over the engine's purr as we drive toward his home, which is also in the direction of the river.

"I promised you a walk by the river before sunrise," he says, scanning the road ahead. "We could go now."

"No!" It's a sharper response than I intended, but it's beyond me how he thinks I'd want to stay in these chains a second longer than I need to. I attempt to soften my voice and focus on balling up my panic for a little longer. I tell myself to hold on. "I really need to get out of these clothes."

A slight crease forms in his forehead, but he doesn't speak again, and I sense his mood shift, tension growing in his jaw and shoulders.

I constrain my fear by planning my next steps, focusing on the analytical.

The first thing I need is to get out of these bands. The second is to force Callan to let me go. The third is to go back to the angels and…

I can't think past that moment.

As soon as he pulls into the parking garage and stops the vehicle, I jump out of the car and stride ahead of him.

He's slower, pacing after me like a beast at a prowl.

"Lana, what's going on?" he asks.

I clench my teeth and consider asking him to get me out of the chains here, but I don't know if there are security cameras in the parking garage and I can't risk the humans seeing the magic at work.

He doesn't push me for an answer, and I tell myself that I just need to make it to the fifteenth floor.

Long, agonizing seconds.

We exit the elevator, Callan enters the passcode, and I hurry inside the living area, waiting another beat for him to close the door.

"Get them off me." I hold out my arms. I'm shaking and I hate it, but my heart is pounding, and I can't slow it down. "Get these bands off me unless you intend to kill me already."

Callan hovers opposite me, a towering form, a perplexed crease in his forehead.

He waves his hand, and the necklace and waistband unclick and lift off my body, along with the anklets and armbands, leaving me only wearing the bracelets again. The other pieces float toward the wall on my right, where they line up in the air.

I back away from them, trying to breathe, feeling as panicked as I was at the theater. I should gather my wits and fight my way free now, but there's a dark, hurt part of me that wants answers. "Why would you do that to me? After I promised not to fight you, how could you do that?"

Callan is half-poised, still standing in front of the door. His right hand rises as if he's going to reach for me, but he drops it. "Lana?" He's cautious. "*Not*-Lana. What are you talking about?"

"I'm talking about the death trap you so casually put me in, Callan." I point at the pieces. "I'm talking about your fucking dragon's gold!"

He shakes his head, his brow furrowing as he looks from me to the gold, and it's as if he doesn't know what I'm talking about.

Then, just like that, his expression clears. But instead of guilt or anger, he looks as if I punched him. "You thought the pieces could kill you."

I snarl. "That's what they're designed to do, aren't they?"

"Not anymore." He takes a slow, cautious step toward me. "Yesterday afternoon, when I left you alone, it was because I was coaxing the death out of those bands. My clan would only accept your presence if they thought I had complete control over you. I should have told you so you weren't blindsided. That's on me." He takes another step toward me. "Lana, I will never ask you to wear gold that could kill you."

I stare up at him. *Is he lying to me?*

When he first captured me in the alley outside the concert hall, he promised he would fuck with me. Is he playing me now? Has he been plucking at my emotions ever since I got here?

He saw the scars on my back, heard me talk about cages… I gave him enough information for him to know how to gain my trust.

"How am I supposed to believe you?" I cry. "We're enemies! I can't trust you!"

He's as still as stone, not moving a muscle now. "I wish there was a way to prove it to you."

"Oh, there is," I say, making a decision, knowing that what I'm about to do could hurt me badly.

But I'm at rock bottom with no good options.

With a scream, I launch myself at the gold, snatch the necklace from the air, and slap it against my left arm. In the next instant, I swing my right hand into Callan's face, connecting with his nose.

The second before I make contact, his eyes widen, but he doesn't try to get out of the way.

Crack!

Callan's nose breaks, blood splatters the floor, and I brace for the consequences.

His fire explodes around us, his dragon's skin shimmers across his face, healing his nose instantly, and his wings thump widely in the air, but all I care about is the band on my arm...

It doesn't tighten. Doesn't cut me. It warms a little in the flames.

I stare at it, my eyes burning with tears.

He was telling the truth.

Callan's silhouette is awash with flames. He speaks in a low rumble while the fire swills around his face and torso. "You were willing to lose an arm to find out if I was lying to you."

"I'm willing to do a lot of things," I say, hot tears running down my cheeks, proving that I'm capable of crying after all. "You think I'm wild? You've obviously never seen an animal chew off its own paw to escape a trap."

"Which trap do you want to escape from, *not*-Lana?" His eyes are pure gold, fiery, but I can't read his emotions right now. "The cage the angels put you in, or my home?"

Once again, I'm inhaling his fire, and this time, it feels too much. It's like there's a well inside me and it's already full and now the heat is beyond what I can control.

"My own body," I say. "My wings. My hands. My soul. That's the cage I want to escape."

He doesn't touch me, but the gap between us feels very small now. My black dress billows in his flames. His gaze follows the strands of my hair as they fly around my face. Above us, the fire has nearly reached the ceiling and soon we'll be surrounded by a snowstorm.

"Tell me something, Lana," he says. "What did the angels promise you in exchange for killing dragons?"

My response is a bare whisper. "I was promised freedom from who I am. They can change me."

"How?" he asks.

I falter. "I don't..."

I don't know. The Serene Commander never told me how she intended to help me, only that she would.

"How?" he pushes, a hint of anger growing in his voice that makes it growl like the fire around me. "A magic spell? A bath in holy water? Or do you think the Serene Commander would share her soul's light with you?"

My jaw clenches. "Don't mock me."

His eyes become hard, golden but with hints of cold green. "You believe that the angels can give you the purity you crave, yet they're the ones sending you out to put blood on your hands. You believe I would wrap you up in gold that could cut you to pieces, and yet, ironically, you're the one who came to kill me."

He beats his wings and scoops me up off the floor, pulling me against him, the contact between our bodies creating an intense heat that shimmers in waves and strikes me to my core.

"You're willing to believe the worst about yourself," he says, "but you won't accept the simplest truth."

"And what is that?" I demand to know, tendrils of fire wafting across the air as I breathe. "What is this basic truth you want me to believe?"

He pauses, tipping his head a little, and I'm not sure why until the clip that was subduing my wings floats off my back. My black wings immediately shoot out at my sides, giving a strong beat. I'm surprised because it wasn't a deliberate move on my part, more instinctive than anything else, as if my body has its own ideas about what I should do right now.

Callan lets me go so that we face each other across the amber air, our wings beating slowly to keep us aloft. He follows the curve of my face to my dark wings where they glimmer, gilded feathers glistening.

A rueful smile passes his lips. "I want you to believe that you were perfect to begin with."

At that moment, the fire reaches the ceiling, and the snowstorm erupts, the sudden cold beating down on me, harsher than the fire.

I drag my wings to my sides and drop to the floor. The bracelets I'm wearing grow dull with every cold droplet that hits them, but my skin tingles beneath the metal, a constant pulse as regular as my heartbeat.

My chest feels hollow.

I hunch over my knees, my wings draped on the ground.

The fire has died and, with it, the storm in Callan's eyes. "If I could be sure that you would stop hunting my people, I would let you go," he says. "But that choice is not open to me right now."

He crooks his finger at the golden jewelry that had sat around my body and it sails through the air, trailing after him as he turns to his room.

I remain where I am for a long time after his door closes, huddled within my wings, before I crawl to my room and climb onto the bed. I don't bother closing the door. This it the closest I'll get to an open cage.

I turn off the light and try to block out the pain in my chest.

CHAPTER TWENTY

I dream of death.

Quiet thuds. My fists.

The tearing of sinew and muscle. My hands.

Final breaths, indrawn, exhaled, rattled, gasped... every dragon I've killed.

Their deaths blur together, but each one had a common factor: the overwhelming taste of copper across my tongue when I fought them, the twisted shape of their dragon's shadow, and the knowledge that they were killers. Monsters.

I am no better than them.

I gasp for breath, jolting upright in my bed, trying to reach for the lamp at the side of it to shed light on the darkness of my room.

My hand slips on the switch; I struggle to grip it. In my panic, I knock the lamp onto the floor with a crash.

I'm covered in sweat. So slick with it that I feel like I'm drowning. Giving up on the light, I shove at the covers that are twisted around my legs and arms, finally throwing them off enough to slither to the floor.

"Lana?" Callan's voice breaks through the mire. His silhouette is visible in the doorway through the sweaty strands of my hair. He's dressed only in shorts, and his form seems to fill the whole doorway.

He looks half-asleep, his hair tousled, one hand resting on the doorframe as he pauses there. He said this was my space, but it looks like he's about to break his word.

"No!" My vehement shout cracks through the darkness. I gasp for air, my breaths rasping. "Stay out."

I don't need his help.

I don't *want* his help.

I want to be left alone like I usually am.

His voice is firmer now, more demanding. "Lana. Let me come in."

I manage to string more than two words together, my snarls increasing. "What are you going to do, Callan? Hug me? Console me? Tell me again how perfect I must have been before I became a killer?" My voice rises to a scream. "How are you going to help me, Callan? You can't even touch me!"

His fist collides with the doorframe and the splinter of wood cracks through my hearing more sharply than my own scream, stopping the breath in my chest.

"No, but I want to," he says.

Then he's gone.

Still gasping for breath, I stare at the emptiness that fills the doorway, the faint glow of his bedroom light now revealing the crushed frame.

He didn't break his word. He stayed out.

It doesn't change the fact that I'm burning up, that sweat drips down my face and chest, and that this is no panic attack. Something is very wrong with me...

Crawling around the bed, I force myself to make my way on hands and knees into the bathroom, where I manage to drag myself across the tiles to the shower. With difficulty, I strip off the black dress, leaving myself only in my underwear.

With a final heave, I reach up to turn the shower on full cold.

I tip my head back under the stream, trying to reduce the heat in my body. The water pours over me and it should be helping, but instead, my tremors increase. It's more than anxiety, more than fear. This heat within my chest is burning me from the inside, so hot that the water pouring onto me is turning into steam.

Fucking steam.

I flashback to Callan's shifts yesterday and when we got back from the club, to the way I'd inhaled his fire, to his growled declaration that the fire within me belonged to him. That it was…

His fire.

Oh… fuck.

Fuck, fuck, fuck!

Suddenly, I'm screaming, and I can't stop.

Now, panic rushes through me as I turn the water off and throw myself back toward the bathroom door, only succeeding in slipping on the floor tiles and crashing into the wall.

With a heave, I pull myself upward, releasing my wings and trying to use them. The outer edge of my right wing smacks the wall next to me, but I use it to leverage myself upright, beating my wings, even though they thump against the wall, finally rising off the floor while water sloughs off me.

With another beat, I rise as high as I can—which isn't that high—and I focus through my fear on the bathroom door and the open bedroom door beyond it.

I need to get through both doors and into the fireproof living area. Fast.

With a single, strong beat of my wings, I angle forward and into a dive, wrapping my wings around my body so I can fit through the bathroom door first. At the same time, I throw myself into a spiral, the momentum spinning me across the bedroom.

Even with my wings tucked around me, the angle toward the bedroom door is too sharp and my shoulder hits the splintered edge. I crash sideways through the opening, trying to tuck my feet, but I'm not fast enough.

My calves hit the doorframe, my body rockets in the other direction, and I slide wildly across the marble floor, one wing tucked around me, the other spread wide while I desperately try to pull it in.

I tumble right into the sunken lounge, where I smack my cheekbone against the edge of the step, hit the hard edges of the seat, and land at the bottom beside the table. It feels like every bone in my body crunches, but broken bones are the least of my concerns right now.

My voice is both fierce and furiously wretched as I try to push myself upright, screaming through the heat that I can't control. "*Callan!*"

His footfalls are already pounding toward me. Near enough that he must have darted back out of his room the moment I started screaming in the shower.

"The doors!" I scream, unable to be coherent. "Doors! Shut!"

He needs to close the doors.

"Don't worry about the doors." His arms close around me and I don't know if it's his fire or mine that billows around us.

I scream against the glistening scales forming across his chest, the force of the heat I'm exhaling driving him backward. He takes me with him up into the air as his wings spread wide, the golden webbing beating the flames.

With every scream, the pressure inside me releases, but the fire I'm exhaling is hot and angry, a wild force that drives fear into my heart.

"I can't..." I choke around the flames and the scorching heat in my throat. "I can't stop."

I wrap my legs around his waist, my fingers clawing his shoulders as I hold on with all of my might, trying to anchor myself. I've lost control and it scares me—more than losing a fight or losing my freedom. I need control. Even if it's as small as refusing to put on a blindfold. Or driving a stick through a dummy's head. Or insisting on drinking green glop.

Gleaming fire swirls around us, billowing toward the walls. The doors to both our bedrooms slam shut and a small part of me is relieved. That bedroom is the first slice of comfort I've experienced—as much as it also makes me feel out of place, and it isn't exactly *mine*, it's a place I don't want destroyed.

The walls around us gleam in the heat waves and I expect the extinguishers to go off again at any moment.

My heart pounds and my screams abate, the pressure outside my body somehow equalizing with the pressure inside me so that I can finally start to regain some control.

Callan has remained impossibly quiet, his chest rising and falling against my cheek, and I finally throw my head back to find his focus fixed on me.

Ribbons of fire twirl from his mouth, dancing through the narrow space between us. The heat touches every part of me from my bare toes to my bruised calves to my surprisingly unbroken arms. I was sure they took the brunt of the fall into the sunken lounge.

Securing me against him with one hand supporting my back, he brushes his thumb against my cheek. It's a light touch, barely making contact.

"Why does fate keep bruising this spot?" he asks, the lowest rumble that sounds less like Callan and more like the beast his body relentlessly shifts into.

Tyler busted up this same cheekbone on that first night. Now I've hurt it again crashing down into the lounge. I guess my face saved my arms.

I take a breath, only to inhale his fire again, and the heat feels uncompromising and unending. I take it in and in and in… and breathe it out and out and out…

Daring to reach up to brush the underside of his jaw, I trace the angle of his face, the slight cleft in his chin.

A desperate need for knowledge rides me. "What is happening to me?"

"I can only think of one way to find out for sure, but it's too dangerous," he says, another low rumble that doesn't sound like him.

"More dangerous than this?"

The golden hue of his irises shifts, darkening as if his human form is fighting his dragon form.

"Yes," he says, and this time, his human voice dominates. "It's a last resort."

My fingers pause at the side of his jaw while his palm remains pressed to my cheek. The bracelet with the ruby heart finally slips down my wrist a small way, its metal surface gleaming in the fire.

"I'm not afraid of last resorts," I say. "I'm more afraid of this."

His wings beat more slowly while his thumb brushes my jaw. His touch makes me tingle and I'm suddenly aware of the hard press of his stomach muscles between my legs, the roughness of his skin against my thighs, and the warmth of his chest against mine.

"This?" he asks, glancing at the fire, before he follows the movement of his thumb to the corner of my lips. "Or this?"

"Both," I say. An honest answer, since I'm not sure what to do with the tightening in my lower stomach and the urge to trace his chest like I'm tracing his jaw.

I tip my head back just a little and use my thigh muscles to lift myself—again just a little. I could use my wings to raise myself higher, but I hurt them during my dive and my instincts tell me to keep them close to my back.

Very slowly, I draw nearer to him, my lips the barest breath away from his, the heat between us increasing, although I'm aware now that I'm not exhaling flames anymore. Just inhaling his fire.

The tip of my nose brushes the side of his nose first before I turn my face a little, my bruised cheek near to his cheek. I close my eyes, hold my breath, and lean in, lightly brushing my face to his before I quickly withdraw.

His hold on me tightens before I can lean back completely.

"Why did you do that?" It's a quiet request. More human than dragon.

"I don't know," I whisper, another honest answer. Despite the quietness of my response, my voice sounds louder in my ears now that the rush of our fire is dying down.

I've seen people kiss, so I know what kissing is, and I've spent enough time in dark alleys and dingy nightclubs to have seen people fuck, so I know what that looks like too. But touching my nose to his before turning my cheek into his… I don't know what that was.

I'm uncertain now and feel strangely vulnerable about it. More exposed than about the fact that I'm only in my underwear.

"It felt like the right thing to do," I say.

He gives a single nod, as if he agrees, before he brushes a few strands of my hair back from my face. "Why wouldn't you let me help you before?"

"Because I don't need anybody."

"Don't or can't allow yourself to?" he asks, his gaze steady, and I appreciate the complete lack of judgment in his eyes.

I lean toward him again, but I stop myself before making contact. Again, I answer him honestly and I blame it on the remnant heat shimmering around us, drawing on my truths like a poultice. "Can't. I have to be self-sufficient. Or I won't survive."

His hand trails across my shoulder and down my back and his voice is soft and low, brushing across my hearing while his fingers trace the shape of my shoulder blades. "But you did need me."

The fire has died down now. His and mine. Both contained.

I shake my head. "I *used* you as a shield."

He doesn't seem perturbed by my assertion, but the golden hue in his eyes brightens and fades as his beast pushes forward with a hoarse growl. "Lying doesn't suit you."

My eyes widen, but the roughness of his accusation doesn't scare me, since I'm more accustomed to violence than to kindness.

I edge upward again. "Is it possible to feel both hate and need at the same time?"

His hand tightens on my back, pulling me closer, and I'm aware of the increased speed of my breathing, the press of my chest against his, and the growing heat between my legs.

Just as his head lowers to mine, his lips a breath away, he gives himself a small shake. Clasping me closely, he tucks his wings against his sides and drops lightly to the floor with me in his arms.

I'm not alarmed when he strides toward his bedroom instead of taking me back to mine. There's a part of me that feels reckless enough to tempt fate and see where the next few minutes take me. Sometimes, surviving means taking a risk. Wrapping my arms around him and fully retracting my wings, I keep myself steady while he opens the door.

His room is lit only by the glow from our bodies now, leaving dark the outline of his bed.

When he reaches it, he lowers me onto the edge of it so that I'm in a sitting position, his hands trailing across the outside of my thighs before rising to stroke my back, then my shoulders, as he guides me backward.

Just when I think he's going to rear up over me, he slips to the side behind me, pulling me into him, fitting my back to his front. His upper arm slips across my chest at the level of my shoulders and his wing folds over me like a blanket from my shoulders to my feet.

His lips brush my shoulder. "Sleep now."

I don't think I can. Not like this. Not when my whole body is buzzing with sensations I don't fully understand. When I make the slightest move to turn around, his arm tightens and his wing grows heavier.

"Sleep," I murmur to myself.

I sense Callan smile where his lips press to my neck, then to my shoulder, then back to my neck. "Sleep," he says.

Easier said than done. I wiggle my toes, focusing on relaxing the muscles in my legs, letting go of the tension in my stomach, then my shoulders, breathing out slowly, holding my breath, breathing in slowly. Finally, I focus on the warmth of Callan's chest, the different textures of his skin now that he's shifted, and the impossible strength in his arms.

When his breathing deepens, so does mine.

CHAPTER TWENTY-ONE

hat feels like a second later, I open my eyes to a soft glow coming from the far corners of the ceiling. The artificial light is the same hue as sunrise—even though I'm sure it must be the afternoon now.

Callan's wing is no longer wrapped over me, but his arm remains a solid weight across my torso. We're in the same position we were in when we fell asleep.

With a flush, I realize that I'm still very undressed and now that Callan's wing is gone and the dark isn't cloaking me…

I slowly raise my arm, but I freeze when Callan murmurs against my ear.

"Don't move, *not*-Lana."

It's the same warning tone he uses when he's in danger of shifting and setting everything alight.

I take another look at his arm, registering his very human appearance. "You're touching me, but you're not shifted."

"This is a first for me." His left hand rests against my right shoulder, his fingertips moving very slowly. "I wasn't expecting to wake up this way."

My heart beats faster. I remind myself that, by design, there's very little to burn in this room except the mattress we're lying on.

"I'm going to move slowly," he says. "I don't want to wake the beast."

"Your dragon is sleeping?"

"Fuck knows," he says. "I don't control him."

My forehead creases. "But I thought shifters were in close contact with their animals. Communicating with them and such."

Callan's quiet laughter rumbles against my neck. "A dragon isn't an *animal*. And dragon shifters can no longer communicate with their beasts. A glimpse of my dragon's shadow is the closest I'll get to knowing who he is. He merely lends me a fraction of his wings' strength and his tough hide to protect my skin."

"And his fire," I whisper, but my brow furrows even further. I remember the way Callan's dragon lowered its head to me in the alley, the way its gaze burned down on me from above. I sensed an immense intelligence, a creature that had no voice but spoke a thousand words in that single accusing glare. Callan calls it a beast, but it's as far from a beast as I've ever seen. It's not mindless, and its impulses aren't random, I'm certain about that.

"I'm not afraid of your beast," I say.

Taking advantage of the fact that Callan won't expect me to move so recklessly, I grab his wrist, lift his arm, and spin, keeping some part of my torso pressed against his for the second it takes me to turn and face him. I hook my upper leg over his hips, press my palms to his chest, and smile up at him. Triumphant. "You're still human."

He's frozen beside me, his upper arm still hovering above me where I pushed it.

"Fuck." He responds so fast that my head spins.

Tugging me closer, he pulls me away from the edge of the

bed and up onto his chest, where I straddle him. My hands slip from his chest to the bed on either side of his torso for the second it takes him to rear up under me, drawing us both into a sitting position—me still straddling him, my knees on either side of his thighs.

I catch my breath after the suddenness of movement, my stomach muscles tensed and ready to propel myself off him if I need to.

Still, he doesn't shift.

His fingers splay across my back, following the line of my spine to my lower back and back up to my shoulder blades, brushing across the spot from which my wings spread. It's a disarming touch, an exploration of my skin from my waist to my neck.

His fingertips graze lightly around my neck to my collarbone and up to my jaw. I close my eyes for the briefest moment before opening them again when he traces the curve of my lower lip.

"It's been years since I touched another person with my own hands," he says.

I swallow against the catch in my breathing. "Not even a human?"

"Not since I came home and killed the old alpha." He gives a shake of his head. "I couldn't risk it after that. Not even with a human."

"But I'm not the first woman to stay with you," I say.

"Some human women prefer a man who treats them well over one who only wants to fuck them." A smile ghosts around his lips. "Although I'd prefer to be able to do both."

His fingers glide through my hair all the way to the ends of the strands before his palms brush across my hips to my bracelet-clad wrists and back up my arms, another slow exploration. His hands cup either side of my lower face before slipping into my hair again.

It's an unhurried caress, and I relax into it, my eyes closing as his palms flex against my lower back. He starts all over again, exploring my arms, my back, my neck, his touch firmer now before he scoops his arm around my backside, drawing me closer.

His touch is… soothing, exhilarating, thigh-clenching… heartbreaking.

I've never experienced anything like it.

Without thinking, I say, "Nobody's ever touched me like this."

His hands pause on my hips.

My eyes fly open, and my cheeks burn. I'm embarrassed and I wish I could take it back. I understand perfectly well that the way he's touching me now has nothing to do with me and everything to do with the fact that he hasn't touched another person with his own hands for a long time.

He isn't touching me for my benefit, but for his.

Maybe. Probably.

The intense heat in his gaze makes me uncertain.

"If you tell me to stop, I will," he says. "No matter what. You're in control."

His lips drop to mine, a soft but somehow bruising contact, before he pulls back.

I quickly draw breath, a sudden heat flushing through me.

I don't stop to question myself.

Darting forward, I press my lips to his. I thought he would taste like fire and ash, but he's earthy and warm, like sunlight heating dewdrops. My arms rise around his torso, my palm to the back of his neck as I explore his lips, the touch and taste of them. The curve of them. The sheer fucking pleasure of kissing them.

With a groan, he lowers me back onto the bed while my legs curl around his hips, keeping his pelvis pressed to mine.

Splashes of pleasure race through my core, building on the tingling sensations in my lips as he continues to kiss me.

Leaving me gasping when he breaks the contact between our mouths, he trails his lips down my neck to the top of my breasts, burning a path across the surface of my bra and down to my stomach. Then lower to the top of my pelvis.

Every inch of skin that he kisses bursts with pleasure and my instinct is to close the gap between us as much as I can, but he's already moving lower, following a path across my hip to the top of my left thigh, nudging my legs apart to taste the soft skin on the inside of my upper leg.

At the same time, he tugs at each side of my underpants. I lift my hips off the bed so that he can slip the material off my legs. As he moves, he keeps one hand firmly pressed to the top of my left thigh, his fingertips brushing back and forth in intoxicating swirls.

As soon as he drops my underpants to the floor, I want to rise up, to push him onto his back and take control, but he stops me, his chest like a barrier above me as his lips return to mine.

"Careful," he murmurs against my mouth, his voice husky, his eyes pure cinnamon. Warm in a way that heats me with a single look. "Stay in contact. I don't know what will make my dragon's instincts reset."

Slipping his arms around my back, he lifts me up off the bed again, reaching for the clasp at the back of my bra and easing it free so that I'm finally naked.

I slip the material from my arms before I reach for the waistband of his shorts, but again, he stops me.

His arm slips around my waist, his other hand presses my shoulder, and with astounding ease, he turns me so that I'm facing away from him. Before I can take another breath, he pulls me back against him so that I'm sitting between his legs.

"Wha...?" My question is soft. Not alarmed. Uncertain.

His lips press to the side of my neck, his arms sweep up

across my naked breasts, coaxing me to relax back into his hard chest.

"This is as close as we get," he murmurs against my cheek before his lips press a path down my neck and the top of my shoulder.

As needy as the ache within me has become, I very much remember the way he told me he'd rather suffer an ant's nest than share his body with me. It seems that touching me without reciprocation is his compromise.

I tell myself I can accept that. Convince myself that I don't need more than the one-sided physical pleasure he's giving me.

My body trembles as his hands stroke my breasts, and my center clenches hard. I grip his thigh when his hand finally slips between my legs, his fingers finding my core. I can't stop the moan escaping my lips as he applies the perfect pressure to intensify the ache between my legs.

The pleasure builds as he strokes me—light strokes that gather the moisture from my center to ease the movement—and I try to process the new sensation.

It's like inhaling spices in the heat of the day, a deep, heady experience. My breathing is erratic, my back arching, an undeniable need rapidly building that is all-consuming and overwhelms me within seconds.

He seamlessly switches from his forefinger to his thumb, and I moan when his middle finger slips inside me, stroking against the most sensitive part of my body. His other arm tightens, anchoring me as I rock against his hand, my body wanting more. Far more than he's prepared to give me.

Only seconds later, the crash ripples through me, the sudden, intense pleasure taking me by surprise. I tremble in his arms, closing my eyes, exhaling all of my tension and allowing the waves to take me with them.

He nudges my earlobe with his lips, making a satisfied sound against my skin, as if he got as much pleasure from my orgasm as I did.

Despite the languid feeling invading my limbs, I'm present enough to sense the moment that Callan's arm loosens, anticipating his next move. He told me that this is as close as we can get, but I'm not prepared to accept that the sex will all be mine. Not without making it clear that I'm willing to go further.

I take advantage of the moment to spin in his arms, hook my legs around his waist, and arch up toward his mouth, running my hands into his hair, coaxing his lips apart to flick my tongue across his.

His arms tighten and his groan is deep when I rock against the hard length of him.

When I draw back, I'm breathing heavily, the high of my orgasm still tingling through every inch of my body, a luxurious feeling that I want more of.

"Callan," I whisper. "When will you get this chance again?"

His hands splay against my back, tangling in the ends of my hair, but he shakes his head, a firm movement.

"Don't tempt me, *not*-Lana."

"Why not?" I ask in a soft whisper.

A darkness enters his expression as he says, "We're still enemies."

It's not anger I feel now, or even self-derision, but sadness. My fist closes around the waistband of his shorts and I speak with all of the vulnerable honesty I can. "I don't want to lose this moment," I say. "My world is filled with enemies. You're not the first and you won't be the last. It isn't realistic for me to hope for any encounter that isn't founded, at least to some degree, in hatred."

I stroke his jaw, pressing another kiss to his softening lips, coaxing away the tense lines. "Enemies can fuck just as easily as friends."

The heat within his eyes intensifies. "But that's not what this would be," he says. "There's more at stake between us." His arms rise around me. "Getting any closer than this will change what we are to each other. Are you fully prepared for that?"

"What will we become that we aren't?" I ask softly, resting my hands on his shoulders. "A dragon and an angel. Two creatures who should never be together. Two enemies who could destroy each other—"

He cuts me off. "A dragon and an angel who feel more for each other than they should."

I freeze as the question in his voice strikes at the heart of me.

He grips my face, but gently. "Tell me I'm wrong, *not*-Lana."

CHAPTER TWENTY-TWO

*C*allan's fingertips stroke my cheeks, and he refuses to release me from his gaze, forcing me to face his question.

I take a shaky breath, my eyes filling as I admit the awful truth. "I can't answer that because I don't know what love is."

He closes his eyes and presses his forehead to mine, but the truth keeps slipping from my mouth.

"I don't know what it feels like," I whisper. "I don't know *how* to feel it. I don't know what it feels like to receive it."

His fingers tangle in my hair as he pulls back far enough to search my eyes. His voice is a low, compelling rumble. "Maybe we'll find out together."

Without releasing my gaze, he shifts so that his hands descend to my wrists, lightly lifting each one. "I want you to take off the bracelets."

I'm sure I've misunderstood him. "What did you say?"

"Take them off. Put them on the bed. You don't have to wear them anymore."

My eyes widen as I stare down at my wrists resting in his upturned palms.

These bracelets are his first line of defense that's keeping me here. They're what he needs to control me. For him to tell me to take them off...

My hands shake as I reach for the bracelet on my left wrist, but I can't undo the clasp one-handed, especially not with trembling fingers. "Will you help me?"

Without hesitation, he slips the clasp free, and I slide the bracelet with the sapphires in it toward the bed. There's an unexplainable moment of resistance, even though it's completely loose, and then it drops to the mattress. Within moments, the bracelet with the ruby charm joins it.

My focus returns to Callan. "Why would you let me do that?"

"Because trust has to start somewhere."

He lifts my now-naked right wrist to his mouth, kissing the skin where the bracelet rested, making me sigh when his tongue swirls against the sensitive inside of my wrist.

Slowly lifting my arm above my head, he tastes my skin all the way down the inside of my arm and across to my breast, drawing my nipple into his mouth.

I gasp and cry out as warmth streaks through me and a burst of *need* spreads through my core. He supports my back with one arm as he switches to my other breast and I tip my head back, my hair falling across his arm and swishing against the bed.

His hands glide down my body, stroking my center before he slides two fingers inside me and I gasp with pleasure, moaning under his touch.

When his mouth returns to mine, I match the demand in his kiss, inhaling his scent and abandoning any remaining shred of doubt. My hands roam across his back and chest, an exploration of his muscles, while his fingers bring me close to another orgasm.

I'm trembling with need by the time he pulls me close and rolls over onto his back so that I'm resting down on top of him, my knees on either side of his waist. Making sure I don't lose contact with his body, he lifts his hips to remove his shorts.

Then he rolls me onto my back, guiding my legs around him before he positions himself over me. There's a moment of anxiety as I sense how tight I am around him, but he distracts me by dropping his mouth to my breast, the rush of pleasure easing my muscles, relaxing me.

"Lana." He lifts his mouth to mine, drawing out the kiss.

I arch up and meet his first thrust, giving in to the explosion of pleasure in my center that seems to fill my entire body. Some of it is aching, all of it is unfamiliar, but more than anything, I focus on the intoxicating heat of it.

He withdraws a little, moving slowly, easing into the movement so that my body has time to adjust and respond to the rhythm. He takes it slow, and I meet his next thrust, moaning as he fills me completely, gasping when his slow withdrawal draws out every second of pleasure, making me cry out when he thrusts again.

My breathing is ragged, and my heart is beating hard as I grip his torso, flexing my palms against his muscles.

The pure pleasure riding my body now feels like flood waters being held in, and I know I have to let go. Abandon my inhibitions.

I match his next thrust and then I demand more, lifting my hips and pushing up, quickening the movement.

"Fuck." He grips the sheet next to my head and I know I've surprised him. "Lana."

I can't help the dark smile that lifts my lips. "I can handle it," I whisper, my mouth crashing against his, demanding more. "Let go."

I sense his restraint falter and then break completely when my hands slide to his hips.

His next thrust is smooth and fast and I'm ready for it, ready for the heady beat of his movements. I brace, one hand on his hip, the other flung above my head to grip the sheet, stretching out beneath him, meeting every thrust until I'm moaning with need and want. My first orgasm when he touched me was quick and easy, but now I'm drowning.

Pleasure. Rhythm. The heat of his body mingling with mine. The knowledge that I might never have the chance to experience this again.

I'm falling into the fire with him, a need that's growing beyond my control, beyond anything I ever imagined, every plunge of his body into mine taking me away from myself until I'm screaming and the crash tears through my world.

He pulls me upward, dragging me against him, his fists forming at my back, golden hues flashing through his irises as a dragon's roar rumbles through his chest.

"Fuck!" He jolts, shudders, crashes, still moving inside me as I tip my head back, the orgasm rippling through me until I think I'm going to lose my mind.

"Asper," he growls, slamming me back onto the bed, both of his fists landing against the mattress.

My eyes fly wide at what he said, but the orgasm that I was sure was abating flares within me again, knocking through me like a wildfire, making me rock against him.

My body wants more. *How can I still want more?*

Callan's gaze burns down at me, his body seeming to respond to my needy gasps. I was sure he came when I did, but he's hard again.

He thrusts into me, a fierce movement, and my body responds with all the wild that I've constrained, my fingernails raking down his sides, my pelvis slamming against his.

He takes hold of my hips, rising up onto his knees, and pulls me against him, lifting my hips off the bed, triggering new sensations until I'm crying out again and I'm not sure how I'm going to survive this heat between us.

The crash builds and then, finally, I experience full release as

I reach a pinnacle I never imagined existed. His groan joins my cry, his stomach muscles tightening, his body shuddering.

I try to catch my breath as I ride the waves, trying to hold on to every sensation I experienced from gentle to rough and all the wild in between while Callan holds me there. The heat in his eyes doesn't fade as he runs both hands along my sides like a brand.

Finally, he lowers me to the bed, eases himself down to me, slips his arms around me, and rolls us onto our sides, keeping me close.

His chest is heaving, his breathing is out of control, but he manages to speak. Quietly this time. "*Asper.*" His gaze is unrelenting. "It means *cruel* in the old language."

I can't breathe. I feel like I'm crashing all over again.

It's been a long time since anyone spoke my real name.

CHAPTER TWENTY-THREE

*C*allan traces my lips with his fingertips and I sense the little puffs of air from my mouth washing across his skin.

"You said I should be able to guess the name you were given at birth," he murmurs.

Not like this. Not now.

"How did you know?" I ask, the tension inside me building.

"Because I want you," he says, tracing my jaw. "If that's not fucking cruel, I don't know what is."

I relax against him, hooking my leg over his upper hip, resting my head against his shoulder, trying to breathe through this moment.

I start to speak and it all tumbles out of me. "I don't know where I came from. I've lived under the Cathedral for as long as I can remember. In the darkness. I have only the scraps of knowledge that the Serene Commander gave me."

About myself. And about the dragons. The more I learn about Callan's people, the more I realize how simplistic my understanding of dragons was.

I trace his chest, following the shape of his muscles while he listens. "She called me 'Asper' until I was fourteen years old… I snuck out of the Cathedral against her orders. My first exposure to the outside world."

My finger stops on his chest. "It was the middle of the night. I ended up outside a nightclub like yours and I stood in the center of the footpath in my ragged clothes, no shoes, staring up at the neon lights, letting the beat of the music wash over me and bring with it all the guilt…"

My hands form fists against his chest, the memory of the fire within me returning in overwhelming waves. "That was the first time I felt rage and it was… overpowering. It was only because the Serene Commander intercepted me that I didn't go in there and turn that place into a bloodbath."

I bite my lip and clear my throat. I force my hands to relax. "She gave me a lashing I'll never forget, and a new name that didn't fit me: *Lana.*"

Callan's brow is furrowed, as if he's trying to remember. "It means…?"

"Yarn," I say wryly. "A simple length of yarn. She told me that my life was hers to weave. She wanted me to remember that without her, I am nothing." My jaw feels tight. "I am worth no more than a piece of string."

Callan strokes my back, running his hands through my hair, down to my hips. "What do you want to be called?"

My shoulders lift in a gentle shrug. "I'm known as 'Lana.' There's no escaping that now. Using a different name will only cause confusion."

"It's never too late to start fresh," he insists.

He makes it sound simple. I don't want to remind him of what I've done in the past that made us enemies. "Isn't it?"

His arms tighten around me as I nestle back into his chest, curling up beside him.

"Will this ever happen again?" I ask him, lacing my fingers with his.

He's quiet. "I don't know."

We lie like that for a long time, drifting in and out of sleep before I finally wake up and find him studying me with a crooked smile. "What do you think are our chances of maintaining contact with each other's bodies for the rest of our lives?"

I break into a smile, my eyes crinkling at the sheer absurdity of it. "Hmm… showering together, feet snuggling under the dinner table… It could get a little tricky when we need to use the bathroom." I cast him a challenging glance. "It's worth a try for a little while."

He gives me a heated smile and scoops me up off the bed.

"Shower first," he says, carrying me across to the open shower at the side of his room, hooking his arm around my waist after he sets me down carefully on the tiles so he can turn the water on.

We take our time, maintaining contact between our bodies—fingers interlaced, an arm around a waist—as we take turns washing each other, a task that turns into a slow exploration. When he trails his lips down my chest, kissing my skin, his hands resting on my hips, I lean back against the tiles and give in to his touch. Before he makes it to my pelvis, my stomach growls.

"I'm starving," I say, smiling down at him. "But I don't care."

He grins up at me, the water running across his head, before he lifts me out of the spray. "I have protein bars somewhere."

Whisking me into the dressing room situated on the left of his bed, he holds my hand as we drip water onto the tiled floor and he rummages through a bag, triumphantly producing two bars. I moan when he breaks the top off one and feeds it to me.

I happily gobble it before he picks me up again and carries me to the bench in the middle of the room. I swallow the last bite just as he props me on the bench, his focus entirely on my body, exploring me with his hands and tongue. Then my moans are for another reason, my hair dripping a puddle onto the floor when I tip my head back while his tongue swirls against my center.

From his dressing room to his bed, the hours are a blur of heated pleasure that I never want to end. By the time we collapse onto his bed, I feel like my backbone is made of molten lava and my body is aching in ways that I always want to remember.

Somehow, we haven't separated for even a second, our fingertips touching even now. I slip closer to him, closing my eyes, and pushing away the inevitable moment when we need to leave this room.

I wake from a deep sleep without knowing I fell into it, finding myself draped over Callan's back, and I let out a breath of relief that he's still in his human form. He's asleep on his stomach, one arm under his head. His chest rises and falls deeply, his features relaxed.

I know I should let him rest, but I can't help myself. I kiss the side of his jaw, inhaling his scent and his warmth as I brush my cheek to his.

I have no idea what time it is and it's hard to care.

He stirs, reaches back, and pulls me to his side as he turns. "Come here." He's still half-asleep, his hair tousled, all of the tension gone from his body. "Stay with me."

"I'm not going anywhere," I whisper, planting kisses along his shoulder, up to his lips.

He makes a satisfied sound and we fall asleep again.

I wake to a hollow in my stomach and Callan's growly voice at my ear. "Food."

I smile against his mouth as he kisses me and pulls me up off the bed. He wraps my legs around him and carries me to the door.

My eyes fly open. "Wait. We're naked."

He pauses. "Good point."

He slides me to the floor, where I can scoop up my bra and underpants while he keeps hold of my left hand. The bracelets are right beside my underpants, so I grab them too, attempting to slip the bracelet with the sapphire stones onto my left wrist while I juggle everything else.

Callan is suddenly frozen. "What are you doing?"

"Hmm?" I glance up at him. "What do you mean?"

He stares at the bracelets, his expression hardening. "I don't want to go back to where we were."

My fingertips press lightly to the bracelet resting across my left wrist as I stare at it, too, replaying the moment when I retrieved it from the floor. "I didn't even think about it…"

The gold is warm against my skin, a surprisingly comfortable sensation.

"If you won't take it off, I will," Callan says, a throaty command as he extends his free hand toward the bracelet.

I catch his hand and whisper, "It feels different."

"How so?"

"Like it belongs where it is." The other bracelet, gripped in my free hand, is also warm, tingling.

Callan's glower changes, his palm turning in the air. He crooks his finger, the same gesture he uses to put his gold on me and take it off again.

Nothing happens.

A look of concentration fills his face—and then he jolts. "Fuck." He removes his hand. "This gold is yours now."

I'm startled. "Mine?"

"Its loyalty has shifted. I can't control it anymore."

My eyes are wide. I don't ask how; that's the same as asking how I survive Callan's fire and why his flames nearly burned their way out of me. There are no answers to those questions. "But I wouldn't know what to do with it."

His expression softens. Plying the other bracelet from my stiff fingers, he moves slowly, maintaining contact between us while he slips the chain with the ruby charm over my wrist and fastens the clasps on both. "Just keep wearing them. When you need them, they will do what you ask."

I'm still shocked. Uncertain. But he whisks me back up into his arms. "Food can wait."

An hour later, we're somewhat dressed—me in my underwear with one of his shirts over the top, him in sweatpants. He surprises me when he heads to the front door, keeping my hand in his, and retrieves a food hamper from outside the door.

"I always arrange for food to be left here after a night at the club because I don't know when I'll wake up," he explains.

Within moments, we're sitting side by side at the table in the sunken lounge, pulling food from the hamper, which has been cleverly packed with ice to keep everything cold: bagels, cream cheese, cinnamon rolls, yogurt, apple slices, and the same green smoothies that Matt prepared the other day.

I try to push away the existence of the world outside, but Callan's mention of the club makes me flash back to my encounter with Beatrix, and then Sophia, in the bathroom.

While we eat, I slowly give Callan all the details of what I've learned: that Beatrix is worried about Byron; that Tyler is sleeping with Tish; and finally telling him about my encounter with Byron.

Callan listens carefully, remaining relaxed the whole time, although I sense it's taking effort not to react to parts of what I'm telling him.

He doesn't ask questions until I finish speaking. "Tell me again what Byron said to you."

"That he's the one who does the dirty work and takes care of the clan's problems."

Callan makes a deep, rumbling sound in the back of his throat. His eyebrows are drawn down as he appears deep in thought. "I've never asked or ordered Byron to do anything that keeps me awake at night."

I speak carefully. "You've never ordered him to kill anyone?"

Callan gives me a sharp look. "In the five years I've led this clan, I've never ordered a death. Not one." He exhales deeply. "I've never had to. Money greases wheels far more easily than violence. And if not straight-out cash, then some other form of enticement. Everyone wants something."

"Then Byron must have killed someone of his own volition," I say, remembering the wash of heavy regret that I sensed within him when he tried to stab me in the SUV. "A death that's eating him up from the inside."

Callan is pensive, asking quietly, although I know he doesn't expect me to know the answer. "What death?" He rubs his forehead. "I have to find out. As well as decide what to do about Tyler and Sophia."

Some of the heaviness seems to lift from his shoulders when he gives me a fleeting smile. "I'm finding it a little hard to believe that Beatrix had a real conversation with you. However short it might have been."

I give him a small shrug. "She's a lot smarter than she makes herself out to be."

"I'm aware," Callan replies. "She's always been perceptive and observant. She has a way of figuring out what people want. If she wasn't so devious, she'd make an excellent beta."

He relaxes even more as he rubs my arms and drops a tantalizing kiss on my cheek. "It's almost sunrise. Would you accept that walk by the river now?"

Slow warmth spreads through me. "I would."

His lips brush my jaw, then my lips, my cheek again, then back to my lips. His expression shifts, the heaviness returning, but it feels different this time.

He takes a deep breath that reminds me of the moment before we collided for the first time and he revealed his fire to me.

"What is it?" I whisper, my mouth suddenly dry. "Callan?"

He speaks carefully, his focus locked on me. "Would it mean more to you if you went to the river on your own?"

A sudden childish hurt rushes through me at the thought that he doesn't want to come with me, but it quickly fades because there's far, *far* more that I think he's trying to tell me.

For me to go on my own means...

My heart is suddenly pounding. "You're letting me go?"

He takes another deep breath. "I am."

CHAPTER TWENTY-FOUR

y thoughts race as I try to discern his motives. "Are you *telling* me to go?"

"Fuck, no," he says. His hands settle around my hips as he pulls me closer. "I want you to come back."

My ears buzz, my heartbeat is going haywire, and I nearly don't hear what he says next.

"I trust you." He rubs my arms, as if he can sense that he has unsettled me. "I want this to be your home."

My home.

It's an impossible dream. The Serene Commander won't let me go. She won't accept that I've chosen not to kill Callen. The angels already hate me. If they perceive that I've switched sides, they won't simply leave me in peace. I'll be a traitor. The Serene Commander may have sworn she wouldn't lose another angel's life in her battle against the dragons, but hunting *me* is a very different proposition.

In fact, a rogue angel might give her the ammunition she needs to convince the Celestial Ascendant to send Sentinels to help her annihilate the dragons.

My hands form fists against Callan's bare chest. I can barely speak, but I have to be honest. "Having a home is not a realistic option for me. If I choose to disobey the Serene Commander, the rules of the game will change. The Sentinels might finally get involved."

He tenses, murmuring, "I know what they are: the strongest angels."

I open my right fist and press my palm across his heart, needing him to hear me. "I've never fought a Sentinel; never even met one. I don't know if I'm strong enough to survive a fight with them. Or if *you* could, especially if a legion of Sentinels comes after us. I can't bring that kind of danger into your life. Not when you need to protect Emika."

The shift in the color of Callan's eyes is so inevitable that I brace for it, expecting to experience the full force of his fury.

Instead, his suddenly juniper-green eyes hold layers and layers of shadows, but they aren't cold, and it's like stepping under a canopy out of the hot sun. Comforting. Safe. So unexpected that my heart hurts.

"I know our situation is dangerous," he says. "I know the other angels won't let you go without a fight. Even with you as their warrior, hunting us, I've wondered if the day would come when the Sentinels would start hunting my people, too. If it becomes known that you're no longer my prisoner, that you're staying with me willingly, the full wrath of your people might finally descend on me. Likewise, I will face my clan's anger for bringing this destruction upon them. We will both be branded as traitors."

"Then you know I can't stay with you," I say. "Not unless we continue this façade."

He traces my jawline, a touch that sends tingles to my toes. "We can only play that game for so long before the truth will become obvious."

"What truth?" I whisper as I soak up his touch. *That I care about him. That I'm connected to him. That the thought of pulling away from him hurts my heart.*

"That we're fighting beside each other, not against each other," he says.

I meet his vehement gaze.

"If you want me in your life, I'll find a way." He pauses. "*We'll* find a way. Even if it means handing my clan over to Zahra so that you and I can disappear."

My lips part in surprise. "That's too much. I would never ask you to do that."

"Why not?" he challenges me. "I was never meant to be their alpha. I fell into that role because of an act of revenge and fury. I govern them through the threat of fire and violence, not love or connection. You've seen my clan. They are not a pack, like other shifters form packs." His voice hardens. "There is no loyalty among dragons."

His speech is bitter and for the first time, I sense the deeply buried frustration he conceals. An even deeper pain that his pack is not like his family.

For the first time, I'm struck by the overwhelming realization that he, like me, is alone.

"You're wrong," I whisper, remembering the way he first spoke about his people when he revealed his true identity to me in the alley. His wrath over the fact that I was hunting dragons. "You do love them. All of them. Even the Grudge and the Scorn."

He's quiet for a moment before he says, "All I ask is that you consider it. Once you know what you want, tell me, and I'll make it happen."

His hand falls from my cheek, but I snatch it and lean forward. I brush my nose to his and then nudge his cheek. I don't know what this gesture means, but it feels right, and it eases the ache in my chest.

"I'll think about it," I whisper.

Seeming satisfied with that, Callan scoops me up, sliding us both off the seat and into the open space beside the table.

He drops a kiss to my lips, diverting my full attention to the contact between our bodies and the lingering promise of more between us before his hands slide away from me and he steps back.

Just like that, we're completely separated, and all I know is that it's too soon.

"I wasn't ready," I say, a bitter burn behind my eyes.

He takes a deep breath. "I would never be ready." His gaze is clear. Compelling. "But I want you to know that you're free."

I force myself not to reach for him, pressing my palms together in front of me.

"What will happen the next time I touch you?" I ask.

He shakes his head. "I have no idea." The corner of his mouth twitches up. "But I look forward to it."

I can't help my smile. I never thought that I would reach a place of peace with Callan Steele, Dread dragon, yet here we are.

I bite my lip. "I guess I'm going for a walk," I say, as if it's the most natural thing in the world for me to stroll out of this building.

"I'd appreciate if you keep your bracelets on," he says. "It's unlikely that my clan will see you, but this way, they can be convinced that I sent you on some sort of errand; setting up a trap for angels perhaps."

Accepting that reasoning, I head to my room to change, soon emerging in a skirt and a comfortable T-shirt. As much as I prefer jeans, my body is aching in all new places. Not bad aches. Just new.

I find Callan in his room, changing his clothes. He left the door open, and I lean against the doorframe, taking in his broad shoulders, sculpted biceps, strong thighs, and everything in between. I fight the temptation to stride across to him and test his dragon's reaction to me right now.

He glances up, even though I'm sure he was aware of my presence from the moment I stepped up to his door. He's quiet as he studies me. His hair is still tousled, his lips relaxed, and his eyes pure, warm cinnamon. He tips his head a little, his focus following my curves to my toes, as if he's remembering the night before, just like I am.

"I'll see you soon," I say, a casual farewell, the only one I can muster because I won't say *goodbye*.

Spinning before I give in to the urge to stay, I head to the door. Even though my footsteps are light, they feel heavy. The act of walking out of his home is not simple and it demands that I decide what I want and where my path will lead.

The elevator stops on the first floor and opens into a brightly lit hallway with a glass wall through which I can see the pool. At the end of the hallway is an opaque door.

As I approach it, my senses tingle.

This building…

Callan seems to rely on modern technology to protect himself, but there's magic in the door in front of me. I only sense it when I'm close to it, and when my hand closes over the door handle, it's a fleeting tingle through my body before it's gone.

It must be some sort of protective spell, although it's nowhere near as sharp and strong as the magic protecting the level of the building above the fifteenth floor. This magic is cloaking the inside of the building in such a way that I can't sense the outside world. I didn't detect this protective barrier when we drove out to the club, but we would have passed through it too quickly.

Pushing open the door, I step into another hallway, this one shorter. As soon as I enter it, I'm aware of the outside world. All of the living souls and the heavy silence of the final hours of night.

There's another opaque door on the left of the hallway and it opens to a short flight of steps that lead down to the walkway beside the street. The streetlights provide dim light, but the brightening haze in the sky tells me the sun is on the verge of coming up.

It's the quietest part of night. The moments between the end of nighttime celebrations and the start of the new day, a small window of time for me to walk the street alone.

Turning to contemplate the building again, I close my eyes briefly and concentrate on sensing the magical shield around it. It's nearly imperceptible. Easy to miss. But very effective. I can't sense a thing about the occupants of this building. From the outside, everything looks completely normal. While we were at the club, Callan mentioned a witch, and I can only assume she put this spell in place for him. It's just another layer of defense that made it difficult to find him.

It drives home to me how connected he is within the supernatural community. The Serene Commander wants me to take him down, but I wonder if she has considered how many other supernaturals might be angered by his death. For that matter, I wonder how many supernaturals consider *me* the enemy.

Shaking off my foreboding, I proceed quietly, my boots barely making a sound on the footpath as I pass cafés, clothing stores, and apartment buildings—all dark and closed—on my way toward the river.

Five blocks later, I reach the walkway beside the river. The walkway is lined with trees and neat gardens and has park benches for people to sit on and watch the water.

The air is crisp and the sound of the water is gentle within my hearing.

A sense of anticipation rises within me.

I've never allowed myself to stop and see the sun rise. Somehow, I couldn't let myself believe that the light of a new day could ever belong to me. Now, I have the chance to perceive my life and my path differently.

Choosing a seat, I fold my hands in my lap and face east, clearing my mind of all my worries as the sky brightens.

A sense of deep peace fills me as I wait. There must be people around in the background, but I don't sense their guilt, don't feel my usual rage or the compulsion toward retribution.

In this moment, I'm freer than I have ever been before.

As the first rays of light brighten the distant skyline, I lean forward, my heart lifting to see the sunrise, preparing to accept that a new path could be mine, and then...

The pure scent of a crisp, winter's day fills my senses.

It hits me like a blow that cracks the stillness of my soul and shatters my hopes.

The quietest footfalls crunch within my hearing, stopping directly behind me.

A delicate hand drops to my shoulder and with it, all of my peace rushes away like the tide pulling out.

A blindfold dangles from her fingertips, falling against my chest.

Please, no. Not now.

CHAPTER TWENTY-FIVE

The Serene Commander's voice is as light as the morning breeze as she continues to press the blindfold to my shoulder. "Put it on."

My shoulders hunch and my lips press together. I stare straight ahead, not seeing the beauty of the river or the imminent sunlight as I say, "I came to see the sun rise. You can't take that away from me."

The Serene Commander's quickly indrawn breath precedes the inevitable change of her scent. It's now a thick haze of anger, a frost that threatens to kill any sprig of new life within its reach.

"You are not meant for the light, Lana." Her voice is hard, cutting through me like a knife. "You know you must cover your eyes in my presence. Put it on."

Still staring straight ahead, I snatch the cloth from her fingertips and tie it tightly around my eyes.

Beyond the blindfold, the air brightens. The first pure rays of a new day begin to shine and, just as she said, they are not for me.

I remain sitting stiffly as she takes a seat beside me, the

bench creaking gently while she settles into a similar position to mine, one leg folded over the other, her hands in her lap. Every move she makes is punctuated within my senses, even more discernible to me because I've been listening to her all of my life.

I sense that her hair is loose. It swishes around her shoulders. I know that she's wearing a dress—it swishes, too—but instead of golden slippers, her feet are covered in boots. They click against the walkway as she taps her toe for a few moments.

"We feared for you, Lana," she says. "I thought we had lost you. Yet here you are, walking around freely and unharmed. Although…" She taps the back of my hand. "It appears you wear chains of dragon's gold."

"I'm not free," I reply, choosing to confirm her assumption that I'm a prisoner even though she won't understand the true bitterness of my speech. As much as I want to believe Callan's assertion that we'll find a way, I know the truth in my heart. I just forgot it for a few hours. "I will never be free."

I sense the smallest movement of the Serene Commander's mouth, her smile as she nods in agreement. "Can I assume that you are on the cusp of succeeding in your task? Will Callan Steele soon be dead?"

For a moment, I consider lying to her. I could tell her, *Yes, I will kill him soon.* But there's an edge to her question, a thickening of the fog of her anger.

"You're testing me," I say. *Testing my resolve. Already questioning my allegiance.*

Her hand closes over mine and squeezes. "Despite your monstrous capabilities, you always struggle to lie. If only the remainder of your soul were that pure." She continues in the next beat. "Aria saw you the other night at the Hollow Rose."

I stiffen before I can stop myself.

Aria is the warrior angel who smells like spring. She must have found a way to see into the balcony. My thoughts churn as

I recall the smoky haze that had hung over the top of the dance floor. It could have concealed service scaffolding on the other side. If she was there, her scent would have alluded me.

"I assume the man you were sitting with is Callan Steele," the Serene Commander says.

If she doesn't yet know which of the dragons is Callan, then I'm not going to make it easy for her. "What was Aria doing in a place like that?"

"Trying to reach a lost soul," she says, her chin tipping up, a pious tone in her voice. "I assume by now, judging by the fact that you're walking out here alone, you've embedded yourself enough in Callan's life that you could break his neck in his sleep."

I sense her gaze on me. It's sharp, biting, and suddenly, her use of the word *embedded* seems like a euphemism.

"After all," she says, leaning toward me, her voice a whisper that slithers around in my hearing, "it's clear to me that you're sleeping with him."

I grit my teeth, my anger rising, but she gives a soft laugh and her fingertips trail across my jaw. "You're transparent to me, Lana," she says. "Your cheeks have never glowed before." Her voice hardens. "You reek of *him*."

All of my rage surfaces and I fight to keep it under control. "What if I no longer want to kill for you?"

"For me?" She gives another cold laugh. "Oh, child. You were never killing for me. You were killing for yourself."

My hands curl into fists in my lap, but I force myself to remain still.

"A snake must strike. A wolf will bite. It's in their nature," she says. "A creature like yourself must kill. I sent a monster to hunt monsters."

"I'm not a monster. I can choose a different way."

Her response is as sharp as a dagger. "Do you think you deserve a different life? Do you think you're worthy of love?

You weren't born to be loved, Lana." She snarls at me. "You weren't born to be wanted. You were born to hunt and kill."

I shake my head. Vehement. Trying to fight off the inevitable. "I don't believe that anymore."

"You think you can change?" She scoffs, her fingertip tapping my jaw. Once. Twice. "For years, you returned to your cell under the Cathedral when you could have walked away. I didn't force you to come back. Yet you did."

My chest feels tight. My breathing is shallow. "You promised me redemption."

"But that wasn't why you returned." The air swishes around her as she shakes her head. "It was because I provided you with the hunt."

She leans into me and snarls a whisper into my ear. "The sooner you face your most basic truth, the sooner you'll find peace, Lana: You're incapable of love."

The constriction within my chest is so tight and painful that I hunch forward, trying not to double over as I grip my stomach. My immediate response is fury, hatred that the Serene Commander would say something like that, but the blood is draining from my face.

In one bitter moment, I'm faced with what could be the heart of my corruption. I always thought it was hate, but now, in a single stroke, the Serene Commander has identified a cruel possibility.

My corruption may not be my hatred or my anger, but my inability to love.

Tears burn behind my eyes, and I don't try to blink them away because she won't see them behind the blindfold anyway.

"Fuck you," I whisper.

Her hand whips out. She backhands me and the impact knocks me to the side. I've always been aware that the Serene Commander is stronger than other angels. Her position requires it. But the last time she used her strength against me was during the lashing when I was fourteen years old. For her to strike me risks my retaliation, and I'm older and stronger now.

I stop my fall, my left hand planted on the seat while I fight the need to react with force. Suddenly, I'm remembering Callan's warning to me days ago.

Hit a dragon and the dragon will hit back.

Perhaps he's rubbing off on me because I want nothing more than to strike back right now.

But I've never hit an angel. Never crossed that line. To strike the Serene Commander would be an unforgivable sin, one I need to be damn sure I want to commit before I do it.

"You have until tonight," she snaps, rising to her feet to stand in front of me, her silhouette lit by the brighter air around us. "Callan Steele must be dead by midnight. Once you've killed him, you will meet me on the back steps of the Cathedral. Then you will resume your life as it was before."

"What if I don't kill him?" I tip my head back, daring to challenge her while I press my fingertips to my stinging cheek. "*You* can't do it. If I choose not to, what will you do?"

She is silent for a moment before she sighs. It's a tense sound and there's no give in her voice at all. "Are you aware that the Celestial Ascendant herself brought you to me?"

My brow furrows. I shake my head, my anxiety building. "You've always refused to answer my questions about where I came from, so how could I have known that?"

"You were barely eight months old," the Serene Commander continues, ignoring my accusation. "She said that you were my burden. It was penance for my failings, you see. She told me I could raise you as I saw fit, but she gave me one condition: I must keep you under control. If I lose control of you, I am to end the threat you would pose to us."

A chill runs through me. "What are you saying?"

"I'm saying that I *will* kill you."

I rip off the blindfold, but the Serene Commander is already moving. Her golden hair flies around her high cheekbones, but I only see the side of her face before she has turned away. Her cornflower-blue dress brings out the gorgeous blond highlights in her hair. She's slender, but her forearms are muscled and so are her calves where they're visible above her ankle-high boots.

"How?" I demand to know, my question scathing. "If you can't kill dragons, how could you possibly kill me?"

She pauses for a fleeting moment with her back to me. "Your assumption that I can't kill dragons is incorrect, Lana. *I*, like *you*, am not an ordinary angel."

Then... what is she?

I try to see her eyes. Need to see her eyes. Need to know her secrets.

"If that's true, why haven't you already killed them?"

She stiffens, stops fully, and her fists clench. "For the simple fact that I don't have permission."

The anger around her is beyond heavy now, a fog that nearly suffocates me.

"You have one day, Lana," she calls back to me as she strides away, "to decide if Callan Steele's life is worth more than yours."

"Asper," I whisper. "Call me what I am."

She doesn't respond. She's already too far away.

The blindfold is a constant reminder of the Serene Commander's threat. I return to Callan's home, gripping the material in my fist, my thoughts churning. I told Callan that a peaceful future wasn't a possibility for me, and now I know it for a fact.

The decision I need to make is whether or not to tell Callan about the Serene Commander's ultimatum. Every instinct within me tells me *no*. If I tell him, he will want to help me. He will want to kill her. But I can't let him do that.

If I fight her, and I win, her death will be on me. Callan will not have been involved, the dragons won't be held responsible, and the Celestial Ascendant will come after me. I will run as far and as fast as I can. Whatever forces she sends after me, I will draw them away from Callan and his people.

If I lose the fight with the Serene Commander, then Callan will not have been complicit in my attempt. He will continue protecting his clan as their alpha, hiding them as he has been doing.

Either way, I have one more day with him.

One precious day.

My footsteps are slow by the time I return to Callan's home and take the elevator to the fifteenth floor. I pause outside the door into his living area, closing my eyes, quieting my thoughts, and preparing myself.

Callan's voice is clear in my hearing from within the room beyond and my heart leaps a little. Just from hearing him.

I'm about to enter the passcode when the tension in his voice makes me pause.

"You found something," he says.

I sink into my senses, expanding my hearing, discerning that he's not alone. He's standing not far from the inside of the door, poised there with one… *two*… other people, judging by the number of heartbeats.

"You asked us to surveil the alley outside the concert hall." It's Brock's voice, and I sense his agitation like a crimson haze in my mind. "I put up concealed surveillance cameras on the building opposite the alley like you asked. At first, the only movement within the service alley was the theater staff. Then we started noticing the same two people returning to the mouth of the alley at different times.

"This woman—every day at midday. And this man at irregular intervals. Both of them kept their faces turned away from the cameras, so we weren't able to get a clear picture of either of them until this morning."

I wonder if the woman is the Serene Commander or one of the angels, but I'm not sure who the man could be.

There's a pause and a swish of paper before Brock continues. "The man finally stepped into the alley before dawn this morning. We got this image of his face when he took the purse."

"*Fuck.*" Callan's response is a sudden snarl that manifests as a swirl of emerald-green anger in my senses.

The crimson haze around Brock intensifies, but Jada's voice sounds next. "You know this man?"

Callan doesn't immediately reply, and Brock sounds increasingly worried. "Callan, we've always respected your privacy, but you need to tell us what's going on. We can't do our jobs if we don't know what we're up against."

Callan gives a snarl that wouldn't alleviate any reasonable person's concern. "I never should have gotten you involved in this. This is for me to worry about."

"Like hell it is," Jada snaps. "First you tell us there's a purse hidden in that alley and then you ask us to watch what happens to it. A fucking *purse*, Callan, like it's a bomb about to go off. And now this man comes and takes it, and the look on your face right now is scaring the shit out of me."

Callan takes a deep breath, as if he's reining in whatever anger he's feeling. The haze around him only intensifies, this time with swirls of cold, white *fear*. "I assume you've tried to identify him."

"We didn't get anywhere," Brock says. "Whoever this guy is, he has no digital footprint. He may as well be a ghost."

"Good." Callan's fear abates. The paper crinkles and I imagine him crushing the photographs in his fist. "Don't try to find him. Don't follow him. I'll handle it from here."

"Callan." Jada's voice carries a warning tone, as if she's reaching the end of her patience. "Who is this man?"

There's silence, a charge in the air that presents to me like splashes of emotional energy, and I picture Callan staring Jada down. "I need you to let this go. Both of you."

She persists. "Why is he a problem?"

"Because he's supposed to be dead."

Callan's statement falls into silence.

For a long moment, nobody says anything while Callan's deep inhalations and exhalations remind me of the deliberate, calming breath he took when he was talking about his fear of killing someone he cares about.

When he speaks, it's quiet. "Do you both understand how dangerous Lana is?"

I picture Jada throwing her head back and glaring at Callan when her response sounds like a challenge. "She disarmed me in one second flat. I know how dangerous she *could be*." Her voice changes. Softer. "She seems more lost than anything and that's something we can all understand."

"Lana has a heart," Callan says. "It's buried under layers of distrust and a complicated life, but she has the capacity for reason and mercy."

The paper crinkles again and I picture Callan raising his fist, within which he's crushed the photographs. "This man does not."

I'm more stunned at his description of me than I am at the threat this mystery man apparently poses. Even if he could be wrong about my heart.

Brock speaks up again. "We hear you, Callan. You're trying to shield us. But if you need help, we're here."

Callan doesn't reply. Again, I sense his movements, his firm nod, and then Brock's and Jada's reluctant footfalls approach the door.

I don't try to hide my presence, but I step to the side so I don't startle them when they emerge.

"Lana." Jada greets me with surprise, her brown eyes wide. She's wearing her shoulder-length brown hair tied back this morning and her eyes appear a little dark-rimmed.

Brock, too, appears tired. He gives me a formal nod.

"Are you okay?" I ask them.

Both of them immediately straighten and clam up, and I have to admire how strictly they adhere to maintaining Callan's privacy. They won't know I heard everything.

"We're fine," Jada says with a small smile. "Have a good morning, Lana."

They leave the door open, and I take my time heading inside. Despite my deliberately calm actions, my thoughts are churning. Of all the people who might show up to retrieve my purse and, presumably, my hair clip, a male person is unexpected.

The angels at the Cathedral are all women. There are charters of male angels in other cities, but not in Philadelphia. An angel from another city could be visiting, but that doesn't take into account that, whoever this man is, Callan thought he was dead.

My mind immediately leaps to the old alpha, but I dismiss it. When Callan spoke about him, it was with anger and contempt, not the fear he exposed just now.

That leaves the possibility that it's another supernatural and my realization this morning returns to me. *How many enemies have I made along the way?*

Callan looks up from the paper scrunched in his fist.

For a moment, he relaxes, his focus diverted to me. He gives me a smile that nearly stops me in my tracks. Genuinely happy. With a full dose of heat. "You're back."

Fuck, it's breaking me.

I try to bring moisture to my mouth as I allow the door to close behind me. Then I approach him, stopping as close as I dare. I don't want to trigger his dragon and burn the photographs before I see them.

"Who is the man in the photograph?" I ask softly. "The one who took my purse?"

A flash of gold flickers through Callan's eyes. "You overheard that?" He takes a step toward me, his bare feet quiet. "How did you hear that conversation? The walls in this room are sound-proof. No sound in, no sound out."

I'm not surprised that this room is soundproof, but like Callan, I'm a little surprised now that I heard what was said.

"I've taught myself to listen to the quiet," I say, answering as best I can. "It helped me pass the time in the Cathedral. It was either that or lose my mind."

I take another step forward and the gap between us becomes dangerously small. I ask again, "Callan, who is he?"

"You tell me," he says, his expression suddenly flinty.

I stiffen as he strides away from me to the table where he spreads the images, attempting to smooth the crinkles out of them.

I follow him slowly before I slip onto the marble seat and peer down at the photographs.

In the first few, I make out the wide alley in which I was captured. A man stands within the shadows at the corner, but in each image, his face is turned away, like Brock said.

The second-to-last image zooms in on the man reaching up to take my purse from the window ledge where Callan left it. His back is still to the camera.

He's wearing a camo-green field jacket and scuffed brown pants. The tips of steel-toed boots are visible beneath the hems. He has pale hair pulled back into a messy ponytail at the nape of his neck. It's difficult to tell the color with certainty, but I'm guessing dark blond. He's tall and broad-shouldered, and he carries himself in a way that makes my instincts flare.

In the final image, the man has finally turned toward the

camera. He appears to be in his forties. The press of his lips, his drawn eyebrows, and the way he crushes my purse in his enormous fist gives me a sense of how intimidating he is.

Callan seemed to think I'd be able to identify him, but my forehead creases. "I don't know him."

Callan studies me as if he doesn't believe me. "You've never seen him before?"

I take another look and shake my head. "What makes you think I have?"

"Because, as far as I knew, you killed him."

CHAPTER TWENTY-SIX

I'm suddenly cold. The only supernaturals Callan would think I've killed are dragons. "What is his name?"

Callan folds his arms across his chest, remaining standing at the end of the table, his expression shuttered. "His name is Solomon Grudge. He's the reason you're hunting us."

A trickle of ice passes down my spine. "Grudge... I was sure I killed them all."

"So were we. But you evidently missed the only one who deserves to die." Callan is stony. "The loss of any dragon life is tragic. But nobody mourned the loss of Solomon Grudge when we thought he was dead."

"What did he do?"

"He started the war between the angels and the dragons by breaking into a Sentinel stronghold, stealing a precious object from them, and killing two Sentinels in the process."

My eyes widen with surprise. "Impossible," I whisper. "Nobody can *find* the Sentinels, let alone get past them. The Sentinels *come out* to kill. Nobody steps into their strongholds."

To guard the objects they protect, the Sentinels live in groups of three within the veil between our world and the heavenly realm. Their strongholds are built within that veil. Doorways into the veil are hidden throughout the United States, but nobody other than the Sentinels know where they are, and nobody can get past the Sentinels' defenses. Only a supernatural with a true right to an object may make a claim on it, and even then, the Sentinels will fight that supernatural to the death rather than relinquish the object.

Three years ago, the Cathedral was in an uproar because of whispers that a priceless artifact had been stolen from Sentinels situated in Portland. I didn't hear what the object was or how it had been taken, but the stories were hard to believe. Apparently, a creature of old magic had claimed an item of magic that was worth more than every jewel the Sentinels guard.

I dismissed the rumors as nonsense. Not only because creatures of old magic are long dead and gone, but because the Sentinels are too clever, too strong, and a single scratch from one of their spears kills within minutes. It's why I'm so worried about them coming after Callan and his clan.

Yet Callan's telling me that this Grudge dragon not only stole from the Sentinels but also killed two of them.

"When did this happen?" I ask.

"Twenty-three years ago," Callan says. "Four years after I was born."

But the same year I was born.

My throat is constricted, but I manage to ask, "Do you know what he stole?"

"I tried to find out. About three years ago, I followed a Grudge dragon one night, hoping he would lead me back to his alpha." Callan's eyes gleam. "He didn't make it home."

"Why not?"

Callan stares at me. "Because an angel more beautiful and

fierce than any I had ever seen snapped his neck with her bare hands."

I meet Callan's eyes, my breathing suddenly rapid. "You saw me."

"I did." He unfolds his arms. "Until that moment, I didn't believe the rumors that an angel was killing Grudge dragons."

If Callan already knew what I looked like, then he must have recognized me from the moment he arrived to the private booth at the concert hall. In fact, he could have tracked me from outside the hall or even from the Cathedral if he was brazen enough.

What really surprises me now is the way he reacted when he found me curled up, panicking, behind the chair in the booth. Despite knowing who and what I was, he'd asked me if I was okay.

"You knew who I was when you came to the concert hall," I whisper.

He takes a deep breath and exhales it quietly. "I struggled to reconcile the killer I knew you were with the woman who was curled up in the shadows. Your knees pulled to your chest." His speech slows; quieter now. "All dressed up in sage-green and surrounded by a cloud of tulle. You looked breakable. I wasn't expecting it."

I raise my eyes to his. "You asked me if I was okay."

He nods. "And you looked surprised. Like nobody had ever asked you that before." He pauses. "I gave you a chance to give up your mission when I encouraged you to leave the booth. I hoped you'd take it."

My hands are suddenly trembling. I remember the way he'd suggested I find a safer place to sit.

Safer from *him*, as it turns out.

Callan's lips tug into a cautious smile. "As difficult as the last week has been, I'm glad you didn't leave that night."

His smile quickly fades as he continues. "For what it's worth, the Grudge dragon I saw you kill was a murderer who was half out of his mind. It's the less common side-effect of our failing power. While some dragons never shift, others lose their ability to reason and they succumb to their beast. You gave him a clean death."

Callan is expressionless, and it's impossible for me to know how he really feels about it. He refocuses on the photographs laid out on the table. "Once the news reached us that Solomon Grudge himself was dead, we thought the angels would be satisfied. That their revenge was complete. We thought they'd stop sending you to kill us. But then the Scorn started dying and we knew it was only a matter of time before you found us. It became clear that the angels want us all dead."

Revenge for a stolen artifact and the deaths of two Sentinels. The object had to be something that was beyond priceless for the Celestial Ascendant to condone the deaths of all dragons and not just the dragon responsible.

I push at the crinkled photographs in front of me, burning the image of Solomon Grudge's face into my mind. "Why did he show up in the alley now?" I look up at Callan. "What possible interest could he have in my purse, of all things?"

"Not your purse. *You.*" Callan towers over me, his features drawn. "You killed his people. He will have heard that you're my prisoner. He may well have been waiting for me to make a move, since I'm one of the few dragons with the strength and the means to capture you. He has an opportunity that he didn't have before. He will see his chance while you're bound in dragon's gold. Make no mistake: He'll come for you."

I consider the tension around Callan's mouth and eyes. I recall the pure fear I sensed in him earlier. Was he afraid... for *me?*

I swallow before I whisper, "I take it I should be worried."

"Solomon Grudge is one of the oldest and most powerful dragons alive today," Callan says. "While I have no reason to believe that he breathes fire like I do, he proved how brutal he is when he killed the Sentinels."

Callan said that Solomon is the one dragon who deserves to die. Yet I didn't kill him. If he evaded me, then I wonder how many more Grudge dragons I didn't find, and whether or not the Serene Commander is aware that I missed him.

More importantly, I wonder if she would change her mind about me killing Callan if I promised her Solomon's head instead.

No other dragon has to die.

I push to my feet. "If I stay here, I'm putting you in danger."

Callan stands directly in my path and I suddenly realize he had already deliberately placed himself there. He knew I'd think through this situation and reach the conclusion that I should leave.

"Step aside, Callan," I whisper. "I won't bring more danger to your door."

"That's not happening." An unexpected smile passes across Callan's lips, so determined that it makes me shiver. "Solomon may be strong, but he won't survive a fight with me. Like I said, I'm one of the few with the strength and means to capture you. I'm also one of the few who could challenge him."

My eyes widen. "You *want* him to come after us."

"If I kill him, and deliver his body to the angels, they will leave us in peace."

I try to breathe. How can I tell him that might not be true? Callan clearly believes that the reason I kept killing dragons is because I was still looking for Solomon Grudge, but I didn't even know Solomon's name, let alone what he'd done. I killed based on my impulses, my need for retribution, and the erroneous belief that all dragons were a source of evil.

Even if the Serene Commander believed Solomon Grudge was dead, she still chose to send me after Callan. And if she knew Solomon was alive, she didn't choose to enlighten me, and, once again, she sent me after Callan.

She wants Callan dead, too.

Her hatred extends to all dragons. Not just one.

I only have one good choice awaiting me at the end of this day, and I already knew it was the path I was going to walk, but now I have no doubts.

I relax. "Okay, then."

A slight crease forms in his forehead as he contemplates me for so long that I ask, "Did you think I would fight you harder on this?"

He narrows his eyes at me. "The fact that you haven't is unsettling."

I twist my hands. "I'm willing to be bait if it brings a dragon to me who deserves to die. You said he won't survive a fight with you, but he won't survive me, either."

My speech is matter-of-fact, but my emotions are in turmoil.

I have one day left with Callan. Only one.

More than anything, I want to slip my arms around him, listen to his heartbeat for a moment, and hold on to the sound for the time I have left with him. "What now, Callan?"

"Now, you stay inside. Solomon won't attack my home. He'll wait until you leave the building. We'll make a plan to lure him to a place of our choosing. In the meantime, I'll summon the Cohort here and ask them to arrive this evening. I'll be back before then."

He turns to leave, but I step into his path. "Wait. Where are you going?"

My final day with him is quickly slipping through my fingertips.

His expression softens. He lifts his hand and runs it through the air beside my cheek, an inch away from touching me. "I have to sort out the problems with my clan."

"You mean Tyler and Sophia? I can help you."

"Tyler, Sophia, *and* Byron." He shakes his head. "What I need to do today can't be done with you by my side. I'll take Jada and Paul with me. Brock and Dermot will watch over my home. You can trust them."

I'm stiff, but I can't think of a way to convince him that I need to go with him—or that he should stay.

My voice lowers to a whisper. "Please stay with me today."

His hand pauses beside my shoulder, his lips pursed. "What's wrong?"

I grapple with an explanation that doesn't involve lies, my mind whirling as I try to find a reason—other than the truth—that doesn't sound shallow or unimportant.

He slowly steps in as close as he can get without touching me. His voice is a low, calming rumble. "Everything will be okay. I promise you. I won't lose you."

I take a deep breath, pulling the warmth of his presence into my chest and into my heart. Maybe I'm incapable of love. Real love. But this feels damn close.

"Okay," I whisper.

I watch him leave, feeling like I'm twisting within the thrall of a new storm, one that won't let me go.

Sinking to the marble seat behind me, I don't see the images on the table, focusing instead on my single goal and fixing it firmly in my mind.

For the rest of the day, I go through the motions. Four hours spent in the gym beating up dummies. Then lunch—which Matt brings me. Another four hours spent meditating and calming my mind. Then dinner. An hour pacing the living room waiting for Callan to return before I give up and head to the shower to prepare for the Cohort's arrival.

Every passing second, each beat of my heart, only reinforces the path I need to walk.

The Serene Commander gave me an ultimatum: Kill Callan or she will kill me. Either way, I'm to meet her at the Cathedral at midnight.

I will meet her.

But, by fuck, I'll bring Solomon Grudge with me.

If I have to kill them both at once, I will.

CHAPTER TWENTY-SEVEN

By the time Callan returns, I'm ready for the meeting.

I greet him at the door, but he hovers within the shadows of the doorway, a hulking silhouette, his shoulders hunched over.

He pauses for long enough that my instincts prickle.

"Callan?" I reach for him before I remember that I shouldn't touch him. "What is it?"

"I took care of a lot of things today," he says. "But I also asked some questions I haven't wanted to ask. I have answers now about Byron that I wish I didn't have." He steps into the light, and I can see how drawn he looks: the tension in his jaw, the tightness around his eyes.

"What's wrong?" I ask. "What did you find out about Byron?"

Instead of answering me, Callan asks, "Will you help me tonight? Will you trust that I know what I'm doing?"

Again, I fight the need to touch him. "Of course."

I mean it. As much as it scares me, I really mean it.

He closes the gap between us, stopping when we're a bare inch apart, his chest close to mine. His arm arcs around the space at my side without touching me. His body heat filters through the air between us, warming me and reminding me of the hours I spent in his bed.

"I really need to hold you, but I can't yet." His lips press together and the hints of juniper green in his eyes drive a feeling of dread deep into my bones.

I search his face again, but his expression is shuttered now.

"I need a shower, then we'll go upstairs," he says, slipping to the side and into his room.

He showers quickly and emerges dressed in jeans and a T-shirt, much less formal than I was expecting, although I won't feel out of place in my jeans and comfortable black shirt now.

Whatever emotions he was dealing with before, he seems to have his feelings completely under control now, but the way he's closed off to me unsettles me more.

"This way," he says. "The Cohort will meet us upstairs."

I'm not sure exactly where 'upstairs' is. When I tried to lift my senses above the fifteenth floor, I was met with a strong magical barrier. We enter the elevator, Callan presses his palm to a panel above the floor numbers, and the elevator rises instead of descending.

"The Cohort can access this level directly from the parking garage," he says. "It avoids awkward interactions with my human friends."

I sense the magical barrier we pass through before the elevator opens into a large and comfortable-looking lounge room, beyond which is a single wooden door painted red. The path to the door from the elevator is clear and wide since the lounge chairs are set up against the walls on either side of the room. There's a small coffee table, too, but otherwise, the room is bare. It feels like a waiting room and makes me wonder what's beyond the red door.

Zahra is already here, and it proves to me just how effective the magical barrier must be since I had no idea of her presence until now. She's sitting on the couch on the right-hand side of the room while Emika sits beside to her, the little girl using the coffee table to draw with crayons.

Zahra jumps up as soon as she sees us. "Callan, what's this about?"

Behind her, Emika rises to her feet, a crayon seemingly forgotten within her fingers as she watches us carefully.

I stay back, keeping my distance, trying to gauge the little girl's fear levels. She focuses on me only for the second it takes Zahra to deliberately step into my line of sight and block her daughter from my view.

Callan holds up his hand to slow Zahra down as she strides toward him. He keeps his voice low. "Emika shouldn't be here. Things could get messy tonight."

Zahra pulls up short. "I couldn't get hold of my babysitter." She spins to her daughter. "Maybe Jada could—"

As she speaks, the elevator doors open behind us and Sophia's voice rings clearly across to us. "I'll watch Emika."

She steps out of the elevator dressed casually, her hair pulled back into a ponytail. I'm surprised to see that she has shaved the lower half of her head on the side where her hair was singed, giving her a tougher appearance than she had before.

Callan steps out of Sophia's path. He doesn't seem surprised to see her, but Zahra glowers at Sophia despite her offer. "This is a Cohort meeting, Sophia. This is not the place for you."

Sophia holds her head high, her large, green eyes wide. "Callan asked me to be here."

Zahra's surprised gaze flashes to Callan. "Is that true?"

"True and necessary," he says. "But it's fine with me if Sophia stays out here with Emika. Provided it's okay with you, Zahra."

His sister presses her lips together, clearly not okay with it. "Okay. Thank you, Sophia." Zahra looks past her. "Where is your husband?"

"Tyler's on his way." Sophia is suddenly stiff, her expression wiped blank. "He wanted to travel separately tonight."

I've remained at the side of the room and neither Zahra nor Sophia seems worried about me, which must mean I put on a good enough show of compliance at the club the other night.

Sophia sweeps past Callan and Zahra, slowing down to take Emika's hand, drawing the little girl back to the table and her drawings.

I'm surprised by how carefully Sophia moves around Emika and how gently she speaks. It's the first time I've seen her behave without guile. "Want to show me what you're drawing, sweetie?"

Emika's eyes brighten, and I'm struck by the way she nestles happily into the crook of Sophia's arm on the couch before she picks up her crayon and leans over the table again. "Sunflowers," she whispers.

I may not have my usual power to discern motivations while Callan is present, but it doesn't take a genius to see that Sophia desperately wants what Zahra has: a child.

I exhale quietly, a small sigh, as I recall that Tyler told me Emika is the only dragon child born to the clan in the last five years.

Moments later, Martha, Davison, and Byron all arrive together. They're also dressed in jeans and T-shirts, but while Martha is impeccably bejeweled with gold bracelets and rings, Byron is disheveled with dark rings under his eyes.

The tension between all three of them as they step out of the elevator is palpable—the kind of friction that follows terse words. It makes me wonder what they might have said to each other in the elevator on the way up.

Callan greets them stiffly, his own tension levels visibly rising.

"Where's Tyler?" Martha snaps as soon as she sees Sophia

sitting with Emika. Unlike Zahra, she doesn't question Sophia's presence.

Sophia gives Martha a helpless look and the silence stretches. I'm reminded that Martha is Sophia's mother when her expression becomes more concerned than annoyed.

"On his way, apparently," Zahra says, her cinnamon eyes betraying a hint of sudden resignation when her focus moves across Sophia.

Beatrix and Felix arrive together only another moment later, both looking sleek in black jeans and black shirts. Beatrix tucks her perfectly straight, short-cut hair behind her ear, her fingers covered in golden rings, her eye makeup only marginally less heavy than it was at the club. Felix is a silent predator behind her as he saunters into the room, both of them surveying the group.

"Well, isn't this a nice turnout," Beatrix croons. "All of our friends are here."

It's even more apparent to me in the full light how tall and lithe she and her cousin are compared to the more bulky and muscular forms of Byron and Davison. And they, in turn, diminish when standing near Callan.

For some reason, the Serene Commander's statements return to me. A snake will strike. A wolf will bite. Each of these dragons combines the nature of both of those animals.

Beatrix catches my eye and gives me a delighted smile, her face lighting up. "Is Night Sky coming in with us?"

"She is," Callan replies, making every other dragon—except Emika—tense. Even Beatrix seems surprised at the answer to her question, her eyes narrowing for a second before she exchanges a glance with Felix.

"Be careful what you ask," she whispers, as if she's admonishing herself.

At the same time, Martha snaps. "What is the meaning of this, Callan?"

"Step inside and I'll tell you," Callan replies smoothly, gesturing toward the wide, red door.

I follow him across the room while Martha grumbles, and I'm hyperaware that she's glaring daggers at my back when Callan leads me into the next room.

It's more brightly lit than I was expecting, with walls that appear to be made out of gray stone. A round table sits in the middle of the room, its surface and the chairs around it also appearing to be made out of stone, while the room is otherwise bare. As soon as I step inside, my heart skips a beat when I realize why it's so bright.

A glass-domed ceiling soars above me, allowing the moonlight to stream inside, lighting up the table and every seat around it.

It's an impossible room to have at the top of a modern building and it can only be imbued with magic—strong enough to have repelled me when I was meditating.

Callan glances back at me with a wry smile before he heads to the seat on the far side of the table.

His dragon's shadow takes my breath away, its golden body filling the space around him, its tail curling along the wall and its wings spreading before they settle against its sides. Its glistening scales are brighter than any dragon's gold and its eyes burn with a fire I may never understand.

I've seen its impact on Callan's life. Its volatile inferno. And now I feel its power even more keenly as it crouches and lowers its head toward the table, its gaze burning me across the distance as it contemplates both me and the dragons following me.

I count the chairs: eight for each member of the Cohort. There is no chair for me, but Callan inclines his head at the space on his right-hand side. "Stand by me, Lana."

I'm struck by how much more he's asking than that I stay

physically close. He asked me if I would help him tonight and I told him I would.

"I will," I say. A promise that I can only keep for another few hours, but I'll make the hours count.

Each Cohort member takes up position at the stone table and each of their dragons is breathtaking.

Zahra takes the seat to Callan's right. When she shifted on the night Callan first revealed his fire to me, her skin became bronze. Her dragon is the same luminous color, a gorgeous amber-bronze. It isn't as large as Callan's dragon, but its form is sleek and muscular, and light shimmers beneath its scales.

Davison's dragon is a dark earthy-brown color; Byron's is gray like ash; Martha's is azure blue; and Beatrix's and Felix's are both a deep wine like the darkest blood. Their dragons are slimmer, more serpentine than the others' and they have sharp barbs on their tails—a cruel beauty like my first impression of the Lamonte cousins. They take seats on Callan's left, although they leave vacant the seat closest on his left and I imagine that's for Tyler, who hasn't arrived yet.

Davison sits to Zahra's right, and Byron slumps in the seat beside him, rubbing his beard. He leans forward, his fingers tapping the table's smooth surface while he scowls across the bright air at me. His dragon swings its ashen head from side to side, pawing at the stone floor before it settles down at his side. Its scales seem to pull at the light around it, a darkness that makes my skin crawl.

The red door into the stone room remains open and in the distance, the elevator finally arrives once more.

Tyler bursts out of it, ignoring Sophia's soft greeting as he storms past her, striding through the lounge and into the stone room with us.

He slams the red door shut behind himself.

The *crack* makes Martha jump. "Tyler! Mind yourself!"

He ignores his mother-in-law, his breathing heavy, his furious eyes finding me across the room.

"*You*," he snarls. "This is your fault."

He strides around the table toward me, shifting at the same time. His black wings tear through his shirt and his skin transforms in a ripple of ebony scales. His dragon shadow rears up above him, its strong neck curved, its powerful legs and sharp claws raking the air as he storms toward me.

Everything else disappears as I focus on this new threat. I have no idea what Tyler thinks I've done. All I know is that he's coming for me and... *freaking hell...* I'm not supposed to hurt him.

His fist smacks my cheek, driving me toward the floor before he grabs my throat, lifts me off the ground, and shoves me against the wall, holding me off my feet.

Behind him, Callan has jumped to his feet with a roar, but unless he wants to fill the stone room with fire, he can't do anything about it.

My hands land on Tyler's shoulders and my legs wrap around his torso. Using my strength, I keep myself from succumbing to the grip around my throat.

While Martha, Davison, and even Zahra seem to have frozen in shock, Beatrix and Felix have both shifted, their deep-red wings beating swiftly as they rise up and fly toward me, landing right behind Tyler.

"Tyler!" Beatrix snaps, raising her fist. "Drop her. Right the fuck now. Or we'll slash you open."

Both she and Felix have clawed hands in their shifted forms, similar to their dragons' spikes, their nails sharp enough to rip Tyler's back apart, even while his skin is hard with scales.

Callan speaks up, but he sounds far calmer than I was expecting. "Back away, Beatrix," he says to her. "Lana can take care of herself."

Ignoring them all, Tyler snarls at me. "You can fucking die, angel." His features are twisted, and I know, without a doubt, that if Callan's presence wasn't dulling my senses, I'd be fueled by rage right now.

Tyler would be dead already.

My eyes meet Callan's, my breathing ragged. I need to ask Callan what he wants me to do, but I can't form sound while Tyler grips my throat.

"Fight back, Lana," Callan says, as if he reads my mind. "You have my permission."

CHAPTER TWENTY-EIGHT

My wings shoot out at my sides and my fist collides with Tyler's cheek. The hit doesn't break through his scales, as he absorbs the blow, but I use my wings to push myself off the wall with a savage thrust, my legs still wrapped around him.

He shouts as I wrench him up into the air and then crash us both down onto the tabletop. Me on top of him. Him thrashing, trying to push me off. My fist knocks against his face, and this time, his scales break. His cheek splits and his head knocks against the table's stone surface.

His cry of pain cuts short and he slumps beneath me, blood dripping down his cheek, his body transforming back to his human shape while his cheek heals.

He regains consciousness a moment later, opening his eyes and blinking up at me, but he doesn't struggle this time.

My neck is sore and my vocal chords are lacerated, but I rasp, "Come at me again, and I will kill you."

His hands drop away from me, palms up, fingers splayed, a gesture of surrender.

I've subdued him, but I sense how precarious my position is

now. Rising off him with a beat of my wings, I return to Callan's side, settling down quietly and folding back my wings before I retreat a step into the shadows behind him.

My knuckles are bloody, and my cheek is burning where Tyler hit me. I don't dare try my voice again—I feel lucky to have formed sound the first time—but it seems I don't need to speak.

Beatrix and Felix return to their seats. Martha is ashen. Davison is stony. Zahra is half-turned away from me, but I sense how wary she is. Callan said that she and I would be evenly matched and he never wanted to see us fight each other again. I suspect Zahra will have observed how I fought and filed away every piece of information she can.

Byron is the only one who continues to lean forward, a light having grown in his eyes. "Is the angel your attack dog now, Callan?"

Martha winces at Byron's description of me, but Callan barely reacts.

"Lana follows me. You should all fucking remember that."

On the table, Tyler groans as he rolls up onto his knees. He's wobbly as he slides off the surface and sinks into his seat on Callan's left, testing his jaw and wincing as he rubs his forehead.

"Would anyone care to explain to me what just happened and why?" Martha snaps, the silvery strands in her dark-brown hair catching the light.

"Fuck you, old lady," Tyler says, sinking further into his chair.

Callan thumps the table, the first sign of fury, and it makes them all jump. He's so strong, I'm surprised the table didn't crack.

"You all know the rules." He doesn't shout, but his voice is so fierce that it has the same impact as a punch to the head. "We don't endanger humans. Not for any reason."

His cold glare lands on Tyler. "Tyler broke that rule. He

risked exposing our entire clan. The human in question has now left town with more money than she ever dreamed about and an iron-clad non-disclosure agreement to go with it. Of course, she thinks you were merely cheating on your wife, Tyler, and that I stepped in to save you from a messy divorce. My reasons didn't seem to matter once she saw the sum I was offering."

Callan reaches into his pocket and spins a gold chain across the table right into Tyler's hand.

"Your gold, brother," Callan says, a hint of juniper green forming in his furious eyes. "I convinced Tish to hand it over to me."

Tyler stares at the bracelet, his brow furrowed. "This is Sophia's. How did Tish get it…?"

His voice trails off into the silence and the blood slowly drains from his face. Callan told me that dragon's gold is poisonous to humans, and it seems Tyler is finally realizing the length to which Sophia was willing to go to protect her marriage. Whatever rebellious feelings he still harbored, they appear to be gone now.

"Fuck," he whispers. "I didn't think Sophia knew."

Beatrix suddenly taps her fingernails on the table. In the seat to her right, her cousin smiles in the way of someone who can't wait to see the fallout. It occurs to me that I've never heard Felix speak, and I'm a little worried about what he might say when he finally does.

"Oh, Tyler, honey," Beatrix says, her dark eyes glinting. "Your wife may be a bitch, but she isn't an idiot."

"Beatrix!" Martha snaps, her face flushed. "Mind how you speak about my daughter."

Beatrix rolls her eyes. "It was a compliment, Martha." She lowers her voice to a mutter. "For fuck's sake."

Zahra is more focused than the others, her voice cutting

across their bickering. "Is this why you called us here, Callan? To tell us about the human?"

Callan doesn't flinch under her steely gaze. "No. There's more." He rises to his feet as they wait in silence. He takes a deep breath. "Solomon Grudge is alive."

Martha gasps, Zahra tenses, and they're all suddenly looking at me. Even Byron reacts with surprise, sitting straighter in his seat.

Zahra is the first to speak, her fingers trembling as she brushes her brown hair back from her face. "But... Lana killed him." It looks like a million thoughts are racing through her head, and she quickly reaches the same conclusion that Callan did, her cinnamon eyes lighting up. "If we kill him, will the angels stop hunting us?"

"It's possible but not certain," Callan replies. "What I know is that he's coming after Lana. No doubt, he's seeking revenge for the deaths of his clan members. He will see his chance now that I have her."

Tyler lurches upright in his seat. "So she's bait," he says with a cold smile. "Right?" He stares at me, as if he can't wait for Solomon Grudge to beat me into a pulp. "Something finally makes fucking sense."

Martha leans forward, the rings on her fingers seeming to twist of their own accord as she levels an accusation at Callan. "Did you know Solomon was alive? You told us your plan was to use Lana to lure the angels to you, but did you intend to lure Solomon all along?"

"I didn't know he was alive," Callan says, his back stiff. "But it's our best course of action."

Beatrix's straight hair falls across one side of her face as she contemplates me. "What does our beautiful Night Sky think of all this?"

Everyone turns to me again. I consider for a moment

whether or not our façade requires Callan to speak for me, but he indicates that he wants me to answer. "Lana?"

My cheek is bleeding, and I swipe my bloody knuckles across it. My voice is still raspy, but stronger now. "If Solomon Grudge deserves to die, I will kill him."

Beatrix leans back, folding her arms across her chest. Her lips settle into a solemn line. "Well done, Callan," she says quietly, all cunning vanishing from her features. "We all witnessed Lana's strength when Tyler pulled his little stunt just now. We know she can kill dragons and now we've had a glimpse of her fury. Yet here she is, promising to kill *for* us."

"Your point, Beatrix?" Callan asks, but not as roughly as I was expecting.

Beatrix's gaze flashes to me again, as if she's going to ask me a question, and I glimpse, for a moment, a deep concern in her eyes. She takes a quick breath before she appears to reconsider what she was going to say, but it only leaves me with a growing feeling of dread.

"To play with an angel's fate is dangerous," she finally says, her dark eyes boring into me. "We all knew it when we agreed to capture Lana. But this is different. This involves the death of a dragon. We don't know where this will lead."

Zahra speaks up, but she's equally pensive. "We tied Lana's fate to ours when Callan captured her. There's no stepping off this path now."

Callan is tense, and I catch the flash of his cinnamon eyes as they quickly transform to juniper green, a color change that doesn't seem to be lost on his clan. They all consider him warily, even Zahra, whom I know he would never hurt.

"I will find an abandoned warehouse and Lana will lead Solomon there," Callan says. "He may not come alone. If he's alive, then other Grudge dragons could be, too. I expect each of you to be prepared to fight any dragons he brings with him."

Beatrix's expression is drawn and worried. "So we'll start a war with whomever remains of the Grudge clan, for the purpose of ending the war with the angels. Callan, is this really the way?"

"It is." Callan's voice cracks through the room. He scans each member of the Cohort, his eyebrows drawn down and his lips set into a firm line. He plants his fists on the table. His shoulders hunch and his voice lowers. "With our low numbers, we all feel the loss of any dragon life keenly. But sometimes, there's no other choice."

For a moment, Callan's focus falls on Byron, who slowly leans back in his chair as if he wishes to retreat into shadows, but there are none in this bright room.

"We all knew for years that the Grudge clan was deteriorating," Callan continues. "Succumbing to their beasts. None of us wants to admit that, for years, Lana saved us from facing our inevitable duty. There's no way to save a dragon whose beast dominates them. They are a danger to everyone around them."

Callan pauses for a beat, as if he's giving the Cohort the chance to disagree, but nobody speaks up this time.

With a nod, he says, "You will wait for my instructions. For now, this meeting is over."

He stands and strides to the red door, and I fall in close behind him.

Beatrix watches me pass, concern flickering in her eyes, while across the distance, Tyler's lips are twisted, but it's Byron who unsettles me the most. His stare is dark and his hands are twitching where they rest on the table.

Callan pauses beside him. "Byron. You will stay after the others leave. I need to speak with you."

"Whatever you say, Callan." Byron's response is nonchalant, but his fists clench. He rises to his feet as soon as I pass him and I think he's going to grab me, but he steps in right behind me instead.

I watch him from the corner of my eye as Callan opens the red door and strides into the lounge room.

Ten paces ahead of us on the left, Sophia has remained with Emika, sitting on the couch. They look up when we appear and Emika lifts her drawing as if she's preparing to show Callan. It's a bright sunflower that takes up the entire page, so large that it's visible across the space between us. Sophia appears more relaxed than she did before and it's such a sweet image of them sitting together that for a moment, my tension fades. Sophia and I might have our issues, but there's no doubt she adores Emika.

I sense Callan relax beside me also.

There's hope in his eyes when he looks at his niece.

She is the future he's trying to protect.

Beatrix skirts around behind us, slipping past Byron, who has remained on my heels. She appears to be heading for Emika, while Byron is practically breathing down my neck.

He's far too close now, and my instincts scream a warning as his hand darts out toward me.

"You will know my pain," Byron snarls as his hand wraps— not around my arm—but around Callan's.

Callan's head shoots up and his eyes fly wide.

"No!" My shocked scream breaks the silence before Callan bursts into flames.

His shift is more brutal than ever before, his golden scales forming in a rush, his chest expanding, and his wings cutting through the air. They knock Byron onto the floor, where he tumbles and crouches, lifting his face to growl up at us. A wild beast.

A few steps ahead of us, Beatrix whirls as the flames rush toward her, lighting up her face. She gives a cry of alarm, her muscles bunching as she spins toward Emika.

Behind us, Zahra is screaming and crying as she shoots through the red door into the lounge. *"Emika! Not my baby!"*

Emika's wings are clipped.

She can't use them to protect herself.

In the distance, she holds up her sunflower drawing, not yet realizing the danger.

The blood drains from her face as the heat billows toward her. The piece of paper floats from her hand a second before Sophia grabs her and dives to the floor.

Sophia turns her own body into a shield, but she has no wings to protect either of them.

CHAPTER TWENTY-NINE

My heart thuds within my chest.

I spin to Callan and step directly into the path of his fire, cutting off the first plume and taking the brunt of the explosion.

My wings spread wide, ripping through my black shirt. With all of my might, I throw myself against him, my arms slipping around his chest, my legs wrapping around his hips.

My mouth crashes against his, swallowing his flames.

I wrench us both into the air and drive us back toward the stone meeting room.

His wings nearly catch on the doorframe as we pass through it, and so do mine before we retract them just in time. As soon as we're through, he spreads his wings again and with the next beat, he helps me push us back through the room, flying over the top of the table and to the far stone wall—as far from Emika as possible.

Behind me, I'm aware of Martha, Felix, and Tyler, the last ones to leave the stone meeting room, throwing themselves through the red door and slamming it closed behind them.

Not that the wooden door could hold Callan's fire for long.

But his flames are no longer hurtling around us.

Instead, they fill my mouth, pouring into my lungs, burning my insides until I need to scream. Still, I hold on, taking it all in until I'm whimpering against his lips.

I can't... can't take much more...

I'm burning, my skin is scorching, my chest filling so full that I need to exhale or I won't survive.

Callan's hands rise to the back of my head, his wings close around me, and I know he's trying to speak as we collapse to the floor, wrapped up in the cocoon of his wings, but I can't afford to let him go. Not until I know it's safe.

"Asper," he murmurs, and it feels right that he calls me that right now.

I cough against his lips, breathing out a little of his fire, my eyes squeezed shut, tears leaking from them.

"It's okay." Callan strokes my back and my hair, the glow around us dimming with every passing second. Far faster than his fire has been subdued before. "It's okay. You saved her. I could see past you. I could see Emika when you pulled me in here. She's okay, Lana. She's okay because of you."

I slump against his chest, my fists clenched, trying to breathe, unable to keep all of the fire inside.

I'm a well, and the well is overflowing.

"Lana?" Callan's voice becomes more urgent.

"I can't..." I choke. Try to breathe. Cough another plume of fire. Somehow, the flames have soothed my lacerated vocal cords, and the worst of the pain is within my heart. "I can't..." Tears stream down my cheeks as I swallow the words I want to say. *I can't stay with you.*

He grips my shoulders, then brushes his nose to mine before he nudges my cheek, trying to get me to look at him. "Lana? *Not*-Lana. Look at me!"

"I'm okay," I whisper, finally able to raise my eyes to his.

"I need you, Lana," he says, his expression hard, determined, but his face is pale. "I have a murderer to kill."

I press my cheek to his, my tears slipping between us. "*I* will end Solomon. You don't have to kill a dragon. I will do it for you."

"I'm not talking about Solomon."

My head snaps up.

Callan's jaw tenses. His hands press to my back. "I'm talking about Byron."

I pull back, my eyes wide. "But you said that Emika's okay." I jolt out of his arms, suddenly desperate to see for myself that the little girl is unharmed.

Callan doesn't let me go, gripping me. "Emika's safe. There are six other dragons out there right now who will fight Byron to the death to ensure he doesn't attempt to hurt her again. She's okay." A snarl forms on Callan's lips. "But Jada's sister isn't."

I stare at him. My breathing increases and my heart starts to pound again. A deep anger like I haven't felt for days rises within me and even Callan's presence can't quell it. My voice is icy as I say, "Tell me what you know."

"I asked questions today that I didn't want to ask. I called in favors with contacts and I've put the pieces together," Callan says. "I know now that Byron was dating Jada's sister. He met her through Jada. His housekeeper saw him come home that night covered in blood and she said he burned his clothing after. I know it wasn't a hit and run."

"Dragon fists." All the fire in the world couldn't warm me now. "Why did he do it?"

"That's the only question that remains unanswered." Callan rises to his feet, lifting me with him, holding me close, his cheek pressed to my forehead. "He's my responsibility. I have to kill him. But to kill a dragon—"

"Is a tragedy," I whisper. No wonder Callan had looked hard

at Byron when he spoke of ending those who are a danger to everyone around them. And then he'd asked Byron to stay behind tonight. "Let me do it. I can keep your hands clean. This is what I was built for." My hands tighten on his shoulders when he shakes his head. "This is my purpose, Callan—"

I cough again, a small plume of fire, conscious of Callan's focus on the stream of flame.

Oh, no.

"I took your flames," I whisper.

"He wouldn't have known you could do that. But he must have guessed his time was up when I asked him to stay back. If he triggered my dragon, the worst of my fire would be spent before I could use it on him. I can't burn out his heart now."

"But for him to endanger Emika and Sophia…"

"To lose Emika would have killed me," Callan says. "More than physically weakening me, I think that was his purpose."

You will know my pain.

"We have to get back out there." I tug away from Callan and pull off the loose pieces of my shirt that hang around my torso after my wings tore through them.

Spinning away from Callan, I pause when he catches my hand.

"This is my fight, Lana." He pulls me close and drops a kiss to my burning lips. "Stand by me."

I give him a firm nod.

He lurches toward the red door, tucking his wings to his sides. The door is blackened on this side and it comes off its hinges when he opens it and flings it to the side of the stone room.

His head is down, his shoulders hunched. He has to bend to get through the doorway in his shifted form.

A moment later, I can see the chaos in the waiting room.

Sophia is kneeling, hunched over on the floor near the elevator, as if she crawled there trying to get away. Her shirt and the top of her jeans are burned off her back, her skin is red and raw, and she's shaking violently.

Tyler crouches opposite her, but when he reaches for her, her scream cracks across the room. "Don't touch me! Don't ever touch me again!"

Closer to us on the right-hand side of the room, Davison supports Martha, where she slumps on one of the couches. She looks barely conscious, she's bleeding from a cut across her forehead that she didn't have before, and she's nursing her arm —also burned, but nowhere near as badly as Sophia's back. It looks like both of Martha's wounds are already healing.

On the left-hand side of the room, on the floor in front of the couch, Beatrix is huddled with her wing curved around Emika. Felix stands beside them, his blood-red wings spread and curved like a second shield. His hands are raised, as if he's prepared to fight off anyone who comes near them.

Emika is pressed to Beatrix's chest, and Beatrix has covered the little girl's eyes with her hand, but Emika is struggling against her hold.

She's screaming, "Mama! Mama!"

In the open space in the center of the room, Zahra is fighting Byron, the hard thuds they exchange making me wince. They're both shifted, scales glistening across their faces and arms— Zahra's bronzed and Byron's ash-gray.

Byron is a brutal fighter, keeping his wings close to his sides and favoring his fists. Zahra evades his punches while delivering blows of her own, using her wings to her advantage. She's like a reed bending in the wind, elegant and fluid, but Byron's hits are so fast and vicious that she can't avoid them all.

Just as we step into the room, Byron's fist collides with Zahra's chin and the impact is so intense that she gains air, tucking her wings before she hits the floor, where she rolls back up into a crouch, preparing to leap back into the fight.

Byron sees us and pauses, his chest heaving. He snarls at us while Zahra also hesitates, her face raised to Callan.

The look in her eyes...

It freezes me.

She hates Byron, spits blood at him, but her expression changes rapidly when she focuses on Callan, her lips beginning to tremble.

"You could have killed her, Callan," she whispers.

Callan is frozen a step ahead of me. I can't see his face, but my senses are going haywire, my chest aching with his pain. I reach out, press my palm to the middle of his back, lean in, close my eyes, and breathe warmth across his broad shoulders.

His tension eases. His muscles relax. He exhales and, as I draw away from him, he steps forward again, his wings tucked close to his sides.

"Beatrix," he says. "Get Emika out of here. She shouldn't see this."

The dark-haired shifter doesn't hesitate, holding Emika close and rushing toward the elevator with Felix close behind.

Within seconds, they're gone, and Callan moves fast.

So fast that I wince.

His fist collides with Byron's jaw before the other man can step out of the way, hurtling Byron halfway across the room. The bearded man hits the floor with a thud, shakes his head, jumps to his feet, straightens his wings, and strides back to meet Callan.

His fists land on Callan's chest, his shoulder, his stomach, knocking Callan to the side, but Callan's face is visible to me now and his eyes are pure gold, pure fury. With a roar, he lifts Byron off his feet and slams him onto the floor again, dropping to his knees beside him, both fists crunching down onto Byron's chest.

The *crack* of his ribs is a horrible sound.

Callan grips Byron's head between both of his hands while

the other man tries to catch his breath, the air wheezing from his mouth.

"Why?" Callan roars down at Byron, his hands gripping so hard that Byron's jaw pops and he roars with pain.

Callan doesn't relent. "Why Jada's sister?"

Byron's response is soft, wheezed. "I loved her. She was everything… to me."

Callan's brow furrows with surprise. And then loathing. "Then how could you kill her?"

"She saw my shadow. She panicked." Byron is pale. "I had no choice. Better my fists than yours."

Callan freezes. His hands loosen on Byron's face. "I wouldn't have killed her. We could have worked something out."

Byron's eyes widen. "No."

He struggles vehemently against Callan's hold, punching his side over and over, but Callan's scales appear to protect him. He doesn't even flinch.

"You don't get to tell me that now!" Byron roars. "Don't fucking tell me there was another way. Don't fucking lie to me. There was no other way!"

He lurches upward, a fury of punches aimed at Callan's face and chest, but once again, Callan moves fast, his big hands twisting.

There's a *crack*.

Byron's roar cuts off sharply.

His body goes limp before Callan lowers him to the floor and hunches over him, one hand pressed to Byron's chest.

Silence fills the room.

My legs wobble, but I have nothing to lean against. I've remained standing a few steps from the red door while Zahra is the closest to me, kneeling only a few paces away, her expression drained. Watching Callan end Byron was like looking into a mirror of the many times I've killed a dragon and it's… brutal and unwanted and feels like a dagger slicing close to my bones.

Callan speaks into the quiet, his golden eyes fixated on a point above his sister's head. "Zahra's right. Until I can control my dragon, I'm a danger to all of you."

Zahra's chest continues to rise and fall rapidly, her lips trembling. "Callan?"

"I'll take care of Solomon Grudge," Callan says, impossibly calm despite the death in front of him. "Then I'll leave the city. I'm handing leadership of this clan over to you, Zahra. Effective immediately."

He rises to his feet, folds his wings tightly to his sides, and turns to Davison, who has remained with Martha. The older woman has buried her face in Davison's shoulder, her hand over her mouth as if she stifled her scream.

"You know what to do," Callan says to Davison.

Davison nods. "I'll take care of the body."

Then Callan holds out his hand for me.

I take a step toward him, but Zahra lurches upward and catches my hand.

Tensing, I prepare for a fight, but her expression is clear. "Thank you for saving my daughter." Her voice lowers as she continues. "Please look after my brother."

It surprises me that she assumes I'm going with him, but she gives me a wry smile, as if I'm somehow transparent to her.

I give her a small nod, unable to speak.

As soon as I join Callan, he heads straight for Sophia. She's shaking, curled up against the wall beside the elevator, her face pale and her breathing shallow. Up close, the extent of her burns become horribly apparent.

Tyler crouches nearby, but Callan ignores him as he crouches beside her. "You need medical attention. Will you let me help you?"

She appears to nod her head, although her trembling makes it hard to tell.

Before Callan can scoop her up, Tyler steps in, reaching for Sophia. "My wife doesn't need your help."

My hand whips out to catch Tyler's arm, but I'm shocked when Sophia is faster. She bats him away with a scream. "Get away from me!"

He stumbles, rights himself, and glares down at her. "You're out of your mind, Sophia."

She stares up at him, her eyes wide. Bloodshot. She bares her teeth at him. "You hurt me, Tyler. You hurt my heart. I may not be as strong as you, but I'm done needing you."

Tyler's lips twist, his expression filled with contempt. "You can't survive without me."

Her expression changes, shifting from pain and fear to stony cold. For the briefest moment, her skin glimmers, a luminescent shade of cerulean blue.

A quick glance at Callan tells me he saw it, too.

"Watch me." Sophia reaches up and punches the down button for the elevator before she slumps against the wall again.

This time, Callan catches her, slipping his hands beneath her stomach so he doesn't mess with her burns. His wings carefully form a sling to support her while she curls up against his chest.

He steps into the elevator and turns to the room, briefly meeting his sister's gaze before he says, "You all know the way out."

The elevator doors close and I can breathe again, but my thoughts are a mess and it's difficult to process everything that happened. Byron's death, Tyler's rage, Sophia's injuries, the danger to Emika, and the flames I swallowed.

Callan speaks quickly. "I'll call Jada for help. We need to get Sophia to the fifteenth floor. Her dragon is finally surfacing. My living area is the safest place for her."

I hear what he's not saying: in case Sophia can breathe fire like he can.

Half an hour later, Sophia is sleeping peacefully on a

makeshift medical bed in the middle of Callan's marbled living room. All sorts of medical apparatuses are attached to her while Jada monitors her closely.

Callan resumed his human form as soon as he laid Sophia safely down on the floor and now he sits in the metal chair he pulled from his bedroom. It's pushed up against the wall. His arms are folded across his chest. I lean against the wall near to him, having retrieved a fresh shirt and pulled it on.

Now that Sophia's sleeping, Callan's focus is far away.

Jada throws him concerned glances, but he doesn't explain what happened, and I hope that Jada's loyalty to him will continue to override her curiosity.

I wonder if Callan will ever tell Jada about her sister.

I can't see how it's possible without exposing the supernatural community—the very threat that cost her sister her life. But the further Callan's shoulders slump, the more I sense that the weight of what he knows is pressing down on him.

Jada finally approaches quietly. "Sophia is stable and sleeping for now. I need coffee. Can I get you one, too?"

"Yeah, thank you," Callan says, but I shake my head.

"None for me."

After Jada closes the door behind her, Callan finally rises from his seat to hover beside Sophia, one hand resting on the edge of the medical bed. He rubs his forehead. "I only asked her come to the meeting tonight because I wasn't sure what Tyler would do. I wanted to make sure Sophia would be safe when everything blew up." His hand tightens on the railing at the side of the bed. "Fuck."

"You did the right thing."

He shakes his head. "Only time will tell." He rubs his eyes again. "I need to keep watch over her. You should get some sleep. We can talk about Solomon Grudge tomorrow."

It's difficult to monitor the time in here, but I judge I have no more than an hour until midnight. I try to slow my heartbeats, wishing that time might stand still for me. Just for a few minutes.

Stepping up to his side, I place my hand on the edge of the medical bed right beside his. Not touching.

I close my eyes and inhale his warmth. The fire I swallowed has settled now. The last time I consumed his flames, it was a day before I faced the consequences.

But right now, I have to go.

I clear my throat quietly. "You know… I think I do want that coffee after all."

I catch his murmured 'okay' before I force myself to walk to the door, where I pause.

I whisper, "I'll be back soon."

Somehow, I make it to the elevator. Hit the button for the first floor. Wait for the doors to close.

My hope is that Callan won't realize I've left until Jada gets back with coffee and I don't return with her. He used to be able to track me with the bracelets, but they belong to me now. I'm determined that by the time I get back, Solomon Grudge and the Serene Commander will no longer be threats to him or me.

The farther away from Callan I go, the clearer my senses become, the cold reality of my situation creeping in and, with it, my anger. The rage that he dulls.

By the time I pass through the magical barrier and leave the building, heading toward the concert hall, I have only one goal in mind: Survive the night and return to him.

CHAPTER THIRTY

The alley outside the concert hall is quiet and still. Patrons of the mid-week performances will still be inside while the staff will have finished delivering pre-performance drinks. But soon the walkway will flood with patrons leaving the hall.

I have no guarantees that Solomon Grudge is surveilling this area, but I stand directly beneath the streetlamp, my head held high, my features visible to anyone who is looking. The bracelets catch the light as I tuck my hair behind my ear, the dragon's gold tingling against my skin.

Lucky for me, there's a public clock high on the corner of the arched building opposite the concert hall. I've stood here for ten minutes, and I have twenty-five minutes until midnight.

I wait a little longer, but my hopes of drawing out Solomon Grudge are quickly fading.

Never mind. I knew it was a slim possibility that he'd see me.

I wanted to fight both Solomon and the Serene Commander —ideally, have them fight each other—but I'll face the Serene Commander either way.

Turning away from the alley, I pick up my pace as I head toward the Cathedral, only pausing when I sense movement in the shadows behind me.

Glancing casually over my shoulder, I discern the silhouette of a man standing at the corner ten paces away. He could be anyone. A mere passerby. I'll only know he's a dragon if he steps into the moonlight.

It's a clear night. Moonlight poured into the Cohort's meeting room and it doesn't look like the clouds are going to gather anytime soon.

The night is on my side for once.

A perfect night for doing what I do best.

I've prowled these streets and alleys often enough to know exactly where I'm going when I pick up my pace again, staying within the light, taking a circuitous route to the Cathedral, the path with just enough shadows to lure someone after me who doesn't want to be exposed to moonlight.

The closer I get to the Cathedral, the more my follower hesitates. Of course, if he's smart, he won't set foot near it. That would be like kicking a hornets' nest. But the question is how desperately he wants me dead and what he'll risk to achieve that goal.

When I'm only three blocks away from the Cathedral, I cross the street, my boots clacking on the pavement. The other side of the street is empty. This close to midnight, there are few humans who are going about their business openly. What happens in the shadows is another matter.

I stop on the other side of the street, making my movements clear as I finally step away from the light and into the dark opening of the alleyway there.

Scanning the walkway on the side of the street I left behind, I find my pursuer paused, the hulking figure hesitating in the last patch of dark available to him.

The only way to follow me now is to cross through the light —unless he wants to risk losing his chance to catch me before I reach the Cathedral.

I tip my chin and allow a smile to touch my lips before I whisper, "You want me. Come and get me."

Too late, I sense a presence darting up behind me.

I spin. My fist flies out. I connect with flesh, a hard hit to my new assailant's ribs, but his arms are already closing around me, wrenching me off my feet and back into the alley.

I inhale the scent of the forest and it freezes me momentarily as it transports my mind. It's as if I'm suddenly sailing between branches toward the oldest tree with the darkest bark and landing beneath its canopy, where the raindrops drip from its leaves and slide down my arms onto the moss beneath my feet... The scent is earthy. Ancient. *Powerful.*

I know it. In my deepest memories, I know this scent. But... *how?*

I don't yet fight back, don't even dig in my heels, as my attacker drags me into the darkest part of the alley, where he stops.

He doesn't let go of me, crushing me so hard that I struggle to breathe while he towers over me like Callan does. He's wearing the same field jacket he was in the photographs—or one just like it—and his hair is pulled back in a ponytail. His features, as far as I can see them in the shadows, are rugged and uncompromising, his lips drawn into an unforgiving line.

"You're... Solomon Grudge," I say, my chest constricting the tighter he squeezes me.

His voice is a low growl. "Give me one good reason why I shouldn't crack your ribs."

"I don't... have any... reasons," I gasp. "I'm just here... to kill you..."

He throws his head back with a gusty laugh before he stares

down at me again, his arms never loosening. "If ever there was a sin I didn't think you'd commit, Cruel One, it would be an act of hubris."

I manage to string more than a couple of words together this time. "It's not pride if it's true." I wheeze another breath before I point out, "I didn't say... I'd succeed..."

His eyes gleam.

Shock runs through me when his pupils constrict into vertical slits with jagged edges, the hazel color brightening like the rising sun.

Callan's eyes have glistened gold, flickered even, but *this*...

I manage to draw a deep enough breath to gasp. "You can partially shift!'

"I can do a great many things," Solomon says. "Crush your chest. Rip off your head. Claw out your stomach."

As he speaks, sharp objects cut through my shirt, pricking my sides, and I realize with another shock that he has extended his claws. *He has claws!*

Solomon scoffs at me, his arms loosening, as if he doesn't believe I'll escape him anyway. "Didn't your Serene Commander warn you about me?"

"She didn't tell me anything about you. Until this morning, I didn't even know your name."

Solomon jolts. His reptilian eyes widen a second before he shoves me away from him as if I'm poison. I keep my balance, crouching for a second, looking up at him as he begins a slow prowl around me. "If she didn't tell you, then why have you come to kill me?"

"Because your death will free me," I say. "And stop the bloodshed."

"My death will free nobody," he says.

"You doomed dragons to a life of being hunted!"

Solomon's expression is as hard as stone. "Hunted by *you*. So from whom would I free you except yourself?"

My jaw clenches, but my voice lowers. "I'm an instrument in the hands of a vengeful master. She won't stop until you're dead."

He turns a little in the shadows, eyeing me from his intimidating height. "My death will not bring peace, Cruel One."

"Why do you call me that?" I ask, my hand pressing against the dirty pavement. The sides of the alley are littered with trash, but all I need are my wings and my hands. The dirty ground will coat my palms with the grit I'll need to give me grip.

"Because it was the name the Celestial Ascendant chose to give you." He spits. "Only angels are capable of such fuckery."

I narrow my eyes at him. "How do you know about my name?"

He paces back and forth, every step quiet, the toes of his steel-capped boots glinting in the dark, but his eyes gleam brighter.

"How did you escape from the Dread?" he asks, taking his eyes off me for long enough to pass a rapid glance around the alley, as if he's suddenly unsure that I'm alone. "Callan Steele's home is a fortress. I never expected you to emerge from it."

His focus flicks to the bracelets around my wrists, but he makes no comment about them.

I draw my lips back over my teeth. "Are we exchanging questions without answers now?"

"It seems so."

I exhale slowly as I rise to my feet. "Then why don't we cut to the fight already and see which one of us survives?"

He snarls at me. "If you wish to play with death, I won't deprive you."

My shirt is torn anyway. It's the second one that I've ripped tonight. I pull it off and spread my wings, comforted by the steady weight of the feathers that I trust to lift me when I need to lift, move me when I need to move.

He slowly removes his jacket and then his shirt, revealing the frightening breadth of his chest and shoulders before he folds up his clothing and rests the items on top of a trashcan.

He stretches his thick neck from side to side.

His fist darts out, but I sidestep the blow.

"Hmm," he says, narrowing his eyes at me.

Again, he comes after me. Two hits toward my chest, one at my head, and then he attempts to kick my feet out from under me. I twist to avoid the blows to my chest, duck to evade the one to my head, and jump into the air to avoid the kick.

My wings spread while I'm airborne, my lips set in a determined line, and I dart toward him, landing a hit against his broad chest, darting back to avoid his retaliatory blow, spinning in the air to kick his stomach.

When he leaps out of reach of my foot, I drop my wing to the ground, grating it across the pavement and curving it so that I sail around him, pushing back up with my wing and kicking his face with both feet.

Thump!

He stumbles beneath the blow, dropping his hand to the ground to steady himself so he doesn't fall.

With a snarl, he launches himself at me, but I'm already beating my wings and rising above him, aiming another kick at his head as I soar over him.

C'mon, Solomon. Follow me into the air.

He watches me with his reptilian eyes, and I know I've made him angry.

With a *thud*, his wings spread wide. They're the color of the deepest, darkest tree trunk and they glisten as if rain has made them glossy. The tip of each wing has curved spikes like claws.

Callan's wings are breathtaking, but Solomon's are frightening.

I land on the edge of the roof at the top of the alley, my wings curved around my body, my feathers brushing my nearly-naked back when the breeze blows them.

Solomon is silent as he lifts off the ground and flies after me.

I hurry to backpedal across the rooftop, checking that I'm far enough back from the street now that humans won't see us. I already took a risk lingering at the edge of the roof for a few seconds.

I brace for Solomon to emerge into the light, holding my breath in anticipation of finally seeing his dragon's shadow in the moonlight.

My heart beats twice, waiting, and then he rushes up into the light, his wings spread, his skin covered in glistening scales.

I look wildly left and right, searching, but...

He doesn't have a shadow.

My heart is suddenly hammering within my chest. Callan can breathe fire and Solomon can not only partially shift, but he doesn't cast a shadow. It's the final fissure that cracks apart everything I believed about dragon shifters.

I know... *nothing* about them. Not really.

My chest heaves as Solomon looms over me, frustration building within my chest. "You don't have a shadow," I say, wanting to scream into the void of my knowledge.

He drops to the edge of the rooftop, his wings curved around himself, his claws retracting. But he gives me a smile that chills me. "Your leader really should have told you about me."

A snarl builds within my chest.

It doesn't matter. It doesn't change what I have to do.

It's nearly midnight and I'm painfully conscious of the passing minutes.

Rising into the air with a beat of my wings, I fly at him. He lifts off the rooftop and meets me midair, his fist colliding with my chest at the same time mine hits his jaw. We both soar backward, correct our trajectories, and fly at each other again.

He's strong, but so am I.

Our fists are a blur and our wings beat hard as we trade

blows that crunch against our bodies. Every hit hurts. *Damn, they hurt.* But I swallow my pain and persist.

With every move, I draw us farther and farther backward, closer to the other side of the rooftop, allowing one of his punches to land so that he propels me in that direction and plows after me.

I launch myself across the street—an empty lane—and onto the next rooftop, fully aware that the Cathedral is only one more block away. I just need to keep Solomon focused on me and not where we're going. Even if it means allowing him to land another three blows, each one driving me farther backward.

Then I fight back, kicking his chest, his stomach, punching so hard that the scales across his shoulder *crack*. It's a deliberately antagonizing blow, intended to make him mad enough to follow me.

He winces, stunned, pulling back to check his shoulder while I back away and teeter at the edge of the final rooftop.

That's when he looks around and sees where we are.

"The Cathedral," he says. "This is what you wanted."

Daring him to follow me, I beat my wings and lift into the air, flying slowly backward and landing lightly on the Cathedral's gently sloped roof.

Solomon squares his shoulders. His wings curve around his body. He doesn't take his eyes off me, his irises piercing in their brightness.

I have no guarantees that he'll follow me, but I'm out of time.

I step carefully backward, balancing on the tiled roof as I ascend to the peak. The streets around the Cathedral are deserted—other supernaturals don't come to this building, let alone at night, and there are few humans in the vicinity—but I need to get off the roof as soon as I can.

Behind me is the side alley with the concealed door that I've used as an exit many times over the years and the back steps where the Serene Commander wants to meet me. Unlike the lane where Solomon grabbed me, this one is wide, pristinely clean, and bright with moonlight.

I sense the Commander's presence down there already, the scent of a winter's day chilling me to the bone.

Tipping my chin at Solomon, I step off the ledge and drop out of his sight, plummeting to the cobblestone surface.

It's up to him if he follows me now.

I land facing the door and the hook beside it where a blindfold hangs.

For a long moment, I stare at the strip of material before I reach for it and then stop.

My hand drops.

The Serene Commander's presence is overwhelming as she approaches from behind me, but she stops in her tracks when I say, "If we're going to fight, then I'll do it with every weapon at my disposal."

She inhales sharply. "You didn't kill Callan Steele."

"He won't die by my hand." I whirl toward her, my eyes uncovered.

For the first time in my life, I get to see her face.

She's beautiful. As unearthly as the first fall of snow. Her skin is pale, her eyes are the color of cornflowers, and her blonde hair is like spun gold pulled up into a ponytail and secured with a decorative pin.

It's her armor and makeup that really give me pause. She's wearing a flowing, white dress with a mahogany leather breastplate and high mahogany boots. A band of flat gold about half an inch wide rests across her forehead. The skin around her eyes and temples is painted with mahogany wings.

When I look into her eyes, she doesn't wince, and I'm surprised—and a little dismayed. My first thought is that she lied to me all of these years like she did about so many things, but then she taps her temple.

"I thought you might refuse the blindfold," she says, pointing to the wings across her eyes, the mahogany substance glistening like magic. "So I came with my own shield."

"You're a Sentinel," I say.

A trickle of fear chills my heart. She wasn't lying when she said she could kill me.

CHAPTER THIRTY-ONE

"*I* was a Sentinel," the Serene Commander corrects me. "Before I watched my sisters die at the hands of Solomon Grudge."

My lips part in surprise. The Sentinels guard their artifacts in threes. She must be the one who survived. "Solomon Grudge killed your sisters and stole from you."

Her lips twist. "He paid the price for his crimes when I sent you to kill his clan. A poetic justice when you ended them without mercy, just as he ripped out my sisters' hearts without a thought."

My own heart is heavy within my chest, but her declaration doesn't surprise me. "You used me for personal revenge."

"No, child," she whispers, her hair glinting in the light. "I gave you the outlet you needed."

She begins to circle me. "Do you remember the night you stole away from the Cathedral when you were a teenager?"

I nod. I'll never forget it.

"That evening, you were reminded of all the guilt in the world. Until then, I had done my utmost to shield you from it.

But after that, there was no stopping you. Much like Callan Steele's dragon bursts into flames at the slightest provocation, you could not be suppressed. All I could do was channel you in the right direction."

"You knew about Callan's fire," I say, an accusation. "You raised me to believe that all dragon shifters are heinous imposters, that none can breathe fire. You told me that they are not brave or honorable like the dragons of old because their power isn't pure anymore. But Callan..." My voice chokes. "Callan is more honorable than any angel I've ever met."

The Serene Commander's arm flies up as if she's going to backhand me, but she stills herself. She drops her arm with a sneer. "Of course I knew he could breathe fire. But I needed you to believe that dragons are not worthy of life. I needed to control you. To steer your rage in their direction, like a river that must flow somewhere lest it drown us all."

I take a deep breath and square my shoulders. "You don't control me anymore."

"I was afraid you'd say that," she whispers. "I'll give you one more chance, Lana. Come inside. Return to your cell. Resume your shackled life. You must know that if you refuse, you will become an enemy to all angels. You have no idea what the Celestial Ascendant will do if you're a threat to us. Think carefully and choose wisely."

She waits for my answer, and I take a moment to consider it.

All I want is to walk away. I just want her to let me leave. I want to put the Serene Commander and the angels and my past behind me. Start a new life...

But they'll never let that happen.

I grit my teeth. "If my freedom starts with killing you, then that's what I'll do."

Her eyes widen—she appears genuinely surprised—and I'm sure she thought she had enough sway over me to convince me to stay.

Her expression hardens. "Very well."

Continuing to circle me, she reaches up to her hair and plucks the pin from her ponytail.

What I thought was a decorative piece elongates within her palm, golden light bursting around her hand as the pin extends and morphs into a golden spear like the ones I saw illustrated in the books in Callan's library.

A single cut from a Sentinel's spear can kill.

Suddenly, my game plan is forced to change. A long, drawn-out fight between us—the kind of fight that might draw Solomon Grudge into the fray—is not an option anymore. The longer the Commander and I fight, the more chances she'll have to end me.

I need to finish her quickly.

I take a deep breath, calm my mind, and close my eyes, harnessing all of my senses. I remind myself that I've fought in dirty sewers and back alleys. I've killed dragons quickly and efficiently.

This is no different.

The air *whooshes* as she moves her feet, her scent becomes heavy, and the fog of her anger fills my chest. Golden light cuts the air as she swings the blade toward me, a cut that would surely slit my throat.

My wings spread and beat once, pulling me backward. My foot kicks upward at the same time and connects with her wrist. It's a brutal hit that knocks her off-balance. At the same time, my right wing drops to the ground, allowing me to balance on it and control my body's arc beneath the blade.

My left hand closes around the weapon and I push with my wing, launching myself up again, somersaulting over her, both of my hands now closing around the spear.

I rip the weapon right out of her hands.

Her wide eyes are like bright-blue pools as she follows my landing—a smooth touchdown on the other side of her.

Her golden ponytail flicks against her cheek as she leaps backward, her own wings spreading, beautiful feathers glistening in the moonlight. I'm already rebounding, launching myself forward, the spear held aloft in my right hand while my left fist collides with her cheek.

She hits the ground on her side, and I land on her—*hard*—my knee knocking against her ribs and pinning her.

The spear stops right above her throat.

She stares up at me, the color draining from her cheeks. "How did you do that?"

"You forget what I've been fighting all these years," I snarl. "While you've lived in comfort, I've killed wild things in the dark."

She struggles beneath me but stops when the blade whispers across her neck, her own movement nearly breaking her skin.

"I raised you," she whispers. "I'm the closest to a mother you will ever have. You can't kill me."

"Why would I care?" I ask. "I'm not capable of love, remember?"

Despite telling me that her painted wings are a shield, she won't look me in the eye and, for the first time, I wonder if it has nothing to do with my nature and everything to do with facing her own guilt.

I risk losing control of the spear when I lift my left hand from its hilt and drag my fingers across the mahogany wings painted across her eyes. The magic makes my skin tingle, biting, close to a burn, but I scrape my fingernails hard enough to draw her blood.

I sense when the shield breaks because she jolts as she stares up at me. Tears fill her wide eyes and she screams, but I grab her chin and force her to look at me.

"You caged me. Hurt me. Kept me in darkness and fed me lies about the dragons." My hand shakes around her face. My palm is slick with sweat where I grip her spear. I told her I didn't care about her, but her death will be harder than any other. "Look at me! Look at what you did!"

"If you kill me, there's no coming back from that," she says.

My rage is beyond my control. "I don't want to come back!"

With a scream, I drive the spear downward.

My cry turns to shock when the spear veers off course, lurching to the side of its own accord, and rams into the pavement beside the Serene Commander's neck. It twangs and sticks, vibrating so hard that I'm forced to let it go.

Freed from my hold, she rolls up into a crouch a few paces away from me and gives me a cold smile. "My spear won't obey you, Lana. It's made from angel's gold. Gifted only to the Sentinels. You're lucky you could even hold it."

Fuck, no. I should have realized there was more to it when she seemed so shocked that I held it to her throat. I was never going to be able to kill her with it.

The bracelets around my wrists suddenly tingle, reminding me that I made them mine, but it took days, and I don't know how I did it. I won't be able to control her spear.

Cold fear fills me. My only option now is to keep the Serene Commander away from her weapon long enough to kill her.

My heart is in my throat as I fly toward her, my fists outstretched, but she's just as fast, reaching the spear before I can block her path.

With a roar, she swings the blade up from the ground, tearing up through my feathers toward my wing bone.

My own momentum is against me.

Black feathers rip from my wing, filling the air around me. A sickening burning scent joins them, and a single heartbeat suddenly feels like forever.

Desperately, I attempt to adjust my trajectory, trying to rise up before the blade connects with my bone and shatters my wing.

Not my wing!

My arms fly wide, but I don't have a chance.

Panic rushes through me and I scream as the blade connects.

There's a *clang*.

Light blasts between us.

The explosion throws me back so far that I hit the stone wall on the far side of the alley and fall to the ground, stunned and unable to work out what happened.

The blade should have sliced right through my bone. Instead, it stopped and hit something equally hard.

I'm groggy, but I try to see my wing, confused by the glint of gold wrapped around the exposed bone and the fact that the bracelet with the sapphires on it no longer rests around my left wrist.

I have only seconds to replay what happened in my mind. My arms flew wide. The bracelet slipped from my wrist and wrapped around my bone like armor. My wing is disheveled, many feathers are missing. I won't be able to fly, but the bracelet saved me.

The Serene Commander plows toward me through the cloud of black feathers, plucking one of them from the air and pushing it to the side with a snarl. "This is not the way I wanted you to die, Lana."

The feather floats to the ground, the light catching the new golden hues in it as I take a deep breath.

I don't bother to tell her that I'm not done yet, that I'm remaining right here, not because I'm finished, but because she's so focused on me that she's lost awareness of her surroundings—

The air rushes around us as leathery wings fill my field of view and Solomon Grudge tears across the space above the Serene Commander, ripping her from her feet and hurling her against the wall at the end of the alley.

She crashes against it so hard that it makes me wince. The air leaves her chest in an audible *whoosh*, her spine crunches against the bricks, and she slumps, dazed, to the ground. Her spear slips beside her, making a delicate clatter across the cobblestone surface in the sudden silence.

It rolls all the way to Solomon Grudge's feet, where it stops.

I freeze against the wall, my hands splayed against it, my wings tucked close.

"Fucking angel's gold," he says, flicking his hand through the air.

The spear shoots up off the ground and flies into the side of the Cathedral, right through the bricks as if they're made of butter, until its length is half-embedded.

He tucks his wings and half-turns to me, his reptilian eyes pinning me to the spot. "You want me to kill her."

"Or her to kill you," I say, remaining crouched.

His eyebrows rise. "Your honesty is refreshing. But your wish will not be granted today. As much as your Serene Commander and I have history, to kill an angel on Cathedral grounds will bring the full might of the angels crashing down on me. I'm not that foolish."

My shoulders slump as he crouches so that he's eye level with me but far enough away that I would have to leap forward to attack him.

"Your hatred of your leader intrigues me," he says. "But curiosity is not enough to save your life. Instrument or not, you killed my people, and for that, I have no choice but to end you."

"What happened to not killing angels on Cathedral grounds?"

He sighs. "Somehow, I don't think that protection applies to you any longer."

As he rises to his feet and steps toward the opposite side of the alley, he flicks his hand again, and I'm not sure what he's doing until multiple bands of metal glint in the air, dropping from the rooftop above us.

At the same time, five men appear at the edge of the rooftop.

Each man is broad-shouldered and muscular and wears similar clothing to Solomon's.

None of them casts a dragon's shadow, but I have no doubt that they're dragon shifters when they leap down into the alley. Their hands are outstretched, as if they're each controlling one of the bands. From that height and without wings, the men land hard, cracking the cobblestone, but without apparent injury to themselves.

All I care about is avoiding the golden chains they're throwing at me.

Immediately retracting my wings, I duck and roll, darting away from the wall as the chains hurtle after me, two of them smashing into the bricks in the space I left behind.

Diving across the alley beneath another metal band, I race toward the nearest man on my left, launching myself at him and making it as far up his body as his shoulders. His head is in my hands when—

Smack!

A golden band wraps around my neck from behind and yanks me up off the man and into the air.

No!

I claw at the metal, terrified that it will rip my head from my shoulders—or strangle me like a noose. It's wrapped around my neck completely and twisted at the back, the long end stretching up into the air.

Managing to get my fingers under it to create enough slack to breathe, I release my wings again, desperate to keep myself aloft. But my damaged wing can't achieve traction. The air *whooshes* through the gaps in my feathers and I tip to the side, whirling dangerously. Sickeningly.

Solomon's footfalls are hard thuds before his hands close around my waist, stopping my spin and easing me toward the ground—but only low enough that I can support myself with my pointed toes while my good wing continues to beat, slower now, as I try to maintain my balance.

My eyes water with pain and my vision starts to blur when the noose does its work around my neck.

Four of the men circle around me, controlling the remaining golden bands that twist and twine in the air, ready to use against me. The fifth man is crouched closer to the open end of the alley, his hands upraised, maintaining the band's tightness around my neck from afar. None of the men speak and I struggle to focus on their features.

At the back end of the alley, the Serene Commander remains unconscious where she's slumped against the wall, but I'm aware of the presence of many more angels approaching now. Slowly and cautiously.

Aria appears at the lip of the roof above the Commander's position. Even though I've never seen her face, the heavy floral scent of spring precedes her, a cloying aroma.

A row of angels appears on each side of her, their wings tucked to their sides, no weapons in sight, although they're all wearing golden armor. At a gesture from Aria, two of them drop to the ground on either side of the Serene Commander, spreading their wings briefly to slow their fall. Quickly checking her, they nod up at Aria. I guess they're telling her that the Commander is alive.

Solomon's dark glare rakes across their number and the other men have tensed, positioning themselves for an attack, but Aria speaks up quickly.

"We will not interfere," she calls without looking at me. "Lana Harlowe's death has now been sanctioned by righteous decree from the Celestial Ascendant. If you do not kill her, we will have to try."

Her choice of words doesn't seem lost on Solomon. He *harrumphs* quietly. "Try, you might."

As he returns his focus to me, Solomon's eyes shift back to their human shape, a deep hazel in the moonlight, his expression solemn.

"I take no joy in your death," he says to me. "Particularly as your own people watch on and do nothing to save you." The corners of his mouth turn down as he shakes his head. "Only angels would partake in such duplicity."

He squares his shoulders again. "But it falls to me to do what Callan Steele couldn't. There was never a way to save my people but to kill you."

I don't have breath to speak or scream. My arms are straining, my fingers slipping around the band. I'm already in danger of passing out when Solomon inclines his head at a man on his left—an older man, judging by the speckles of gray in his hair.

"Clip her wings," Solomon says. "Break her neck. If her death isn't quick, I will finish her."

Fear and adrenaline shoot through me. The moment my wings are clipped, I don't have a hope of staying aloft.

My neck will snap under my own weight.

"No!" I gasp, a single protest before I give in to the fury I've been containing and my gasp morphs into a roar.

My scream rages through my gritted teeth. A useless fury and a hopeless scream that will get me nowhere, but it's all I have left as I try to balance on my toes and stay aloft with only one good wing.

The older man opens his palm and a golden spiderweb of chains floats up from his fist. The clip glides toward me, a gorgeous, sparkling thing that's about to kill me.

As my scream dies, a cruel laugh follows it as I face what fate has given me tonight.

It's a fate I recklessly welcomed, and I'm forced to acknowledge that I never really believed I'd live to see tomorrow. Sometimes, it's true that surviving means taking a risk. But sometimes, the risk is too great.

I was told that others would fear me, and they did. I was told my strength was corrupted, and I believed that, too. I learned never to trust anyone and never to ask for help, and now my brokenness has brought me here alone. To an alley bathed in moonlight where I will take my final breaths under the watchful eye of angels.

I knew I might not walk away from this.

I just hoped I'd take my enemies with me.

But now... it seems I'll die alone and without any of the answers I crave.

The bracelet with the ruby heart glimmers at the corner of my vision, a final reminder of all the could-have-beens. A life with Callan; a peaceful heart that doesn't rage; the freedom to make my own choices. The belief that I'm worthy of all of it.

Somehow, I was born the way I am, but I didn't start the war between the angels and dragons.

Solomon did.

With a groan of effort, I pull at the band around my throat, aware of the seconds I have left before the clip adheres to my back. It may not be the question I need to ask. I have so many. But it's the one that matters most in this moment.

"What... did you steal?"

He freezes opposite me, his shoulders hunching, his jaw clenching, and for the first time since he appeared to me tonight, I sense the heaviness in his heartbeat. True remorse.

"I took one of the angels' most valuable prizes," he says, his voice a deep rumble that washes over me. "One of the first Avenging Angels born in centuries. A newborn baby with a heart already filled with the purest rage and a need for justice. Destined to be their greatest warrior. Until I took her, and by so doing, I doomed her."

The clip descends to my back, the metal is cold against my shoulder blades, and with my last gasped breath, I ask, "You stole... a child?"

"You," he whispers. "I stole you."

He reaches for my neck, preparing to end me as he says, "My deepest regret is giving you back."

Find out what happens next in Lana and Callan's story in Chase the Shadows (Supernatural Legacy 2).

CHASE THE SHADOWS
(SUPERNATURAL LEGACY #2)

The dragons only let me out to hunt.
But this time, I'm hunting angels.

My need for vengeance drove me into danger. I sought redemption for my past, determined to put an end to the conflict between the angels and dragons.

Instead, I ignited a spark.

Now, the angels are summoning their strongest warriors, and the dragons are preparing for war.

A wildfire burns around me that could destroy the fragile seed of hope that Callan Steele planted in my heart. Even the flame he kindles within me can't light the path I must walk.

All the while, my most dangerous enemy is hiding in the shadows. A dragon of such power that he threatens to destroy my life and the life of the man I love.

Unless I join him.

Some angels fall, but I won't shatter and break.

Content information: Chase the Shadows is a dark paranormal romance, the second in the Supernatural Legacy series. Recommended reading age is 17+ for sex scenes, mature themes, violence, and language. Ends on a cliffhanger.

ALSO BY EVERLY FROST

SUPERNATURAL LEGACY - COMPLETE

(Angels and Dragon Shifters)

1. Hunt the Night

2. Chase the Shadows

3. Slay the Dawn

4. Claim the Light

DARK MAGIC SHIFTERS

(Dark Urban Fantasy Romance)

1. Wolf of Ashes

2. Bond of Flames

3. Crown of Fate

KINGDOM OF BETRAYAL

(Fantasy Romance)

1. A Sky Like Blood

2. A Sin Like Fire

3. A Storm Like Iron

4. A Soul Like Glass

BRIGHT WICKED - COMPLETE

(Fantasy Romance)

1. Bright Wicked

2. Radiant Fierce

3. Infernal Dark

STORM PRINCESS - COMPLETE

(Fantasy Romance)

1. Book 1

2. Book 2

3. Book 3

ASSASSIN'S MAGIC - COMPLETE

(Dark Urban Fantasy Romance)

1. Assassin's Magic

2. Assassin's Mask

3. Assassin's Menace

4. Assassin's Maze

5. Rebels

6. Revenge

7. Rogue

8. Assassin's Match

SOUL BITTEN SHIFTER - COMPLETE

(Dark Urban Fantasy Romance)

1. This Dark Wolf

2. This Broken Wolf

3. This Caged Wolf

4. This Cruel Blood

DEMON PACK - COMPLETE

(Dark Paranormal Romance)

1. Demon Pack

2. Demon Pack: Elimination

3. Demon Pack: Eternal

MORTALITY - COMPLETE

(Science-Fantasy Romance)

Mortality Complete Set: Books 1 to 4

1. Beyond the Ever Reach

2. Beneath the Guarding Stars

3. By the Icy Wild

4. Before the Raging Lion

<u>Stand-alone fiction - dark romance</u>

Corrupt Me: Immortal Vices and Virtues

ABOUT THE AUTHOR

Everly Frost is the USA Today Bestselling author of fantasy romance, urban fantasy and paranormal romance novels. She spent her childhood dreaming of other worlds and scribbling stories on the leftover blank pages at the back of school notebooks. She lives in Brisbane, Australia with her husband and two children.

amazon.com/author/everlyfrost

facebook.com/everlyfrost

instagram.com/everlyfrost

bookbub.com/authors/everly-frost

goodreads.com/everlyfrost